About the Author

Rob has co-written two full-length musicals and written two plays, all of which have been staged. Rob wrote a book about his English Channel swim in 2012 called *From Starr to Starrfish*, which was published in 2013. Rob lives in Brighton with his wife Sharon and their three children, Asher, Mia and Jesse. Rob's passion is open water swimming and he swims every morning at 6:30am throughout the year from the Palace Pier in Brighton. This is Rob's third novel.

Also by Rob Starr

Fiction:
What the Tide Brings Back
The First Widow (Kiara Fox Book 1)

Non-fiction:
From Starr to Starrfish

ROB STARR

BLACK GOLD

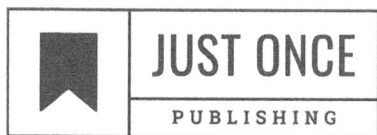

First published in 2025 by Just Once Publishing Ltd
Copyright © Rob Starr 2025

Rob Starr has asserted his right to be identified as the author of this Work in accordance with the Copyright, Designs and Patents Act 1988.

ISBN: 978-1-7394101-2-4

Editing and design by Fuzzy Flamingo
www.fuzzyflamingo.co.uk

A catalogue for this book is available from the British Library.

For my UK Starr family Sharon, Asher, Mia & Jesse
and my South African Waterston family Tyrone, Troy and Mattie.
Love you all.

PROLOGUE

Kiara crouched down as the flames took hold of the top deck and the smoke became so thick that the only way she could breathe without choking was to stay low to the ground.

She had no idea how long an oil platform could last under this intensity of heat as the explosion must have already weakened the structure and left it vulnerable to the elements. It felt as if the ocean was now shaking the entire rig back and forth like a fairground ride. She could imagine the sea waiting impatiently, it's hunger building, desperate for that final moment when it could swallow them all up and drag them hundreds of metres down into its bowels.

She needed to get moving before they caught her again, but the smoke was making her eyes water so much that she could hardly see which way to go. She shook her head, trying to clear her senses, but the first explosion had been so close that her eardrums had taken a battering, and the noise around was strangely muted, as if she were in an aeroplane as it suddenly dropped thousands of feet in a few seconds. She wiped her eyes once more to clear the tears and forced herself to look through the thick haze. She could just about make out shapes darting around trying to find a way down to the lower levels and the life support boats.

She assumed that everyone had the same thought she had, that being in the sea would protect them from the raging fires. Her brain was going into natural fight or flight mode: there was fire and there was water, so head for the water.

But something was holding her back and making her wait. Despite her brain screaming at her to get up and run, her instincts were telling her to stay put and come up with a better plan. No matter where she found herself or how precarious her position, Kiara always ignored the doubts that flooded her head and did what her instincts told her to do. Over the years, they had saved her more times than she could remember and, right now, they were about to save her life again.

Somewhere in the back of her mind, she recalled reading that a sinking boat could end up dragging you down as the force of the suction pulled you with it. *Or was it a film?* she thought to herself. She closed her eyes and visualised Jack screaming at Rose as the Titanic was plunging into the icy water to swim as far away as she could to stop being dragged under. *But maybe that was just the movies and for dramatic effect.* But it seemed right to her; even amongst the madness around her, it seemed logical that that would be the case.

And she had seen enough disaster movies in her life to know that burning oil could even turn the sea into a floating furnace.

She shook her head again to try to clear her mind.

Think, Kiara, think, she said to herself as the lack of oxygen was making her mind drift away.

There had to be a way of surviving this by staying up on the top platform, she just didn't know what the hell it could be.

Another explosion rocked the rig, sending Kiara to her knees and shooting a burning oil barrel high into the sky and over the edge, propelling it a hundred metres out into the sea, leaving a trail of black smoke in its wake. She watched in horror as a helicopter that had recently landed slid sideways over the edge as the pilot tried to take off again, sending him and his bird plunging down into the waves.

She tried to control the panic that was building inside her, as the smoke from the burning oil continued to fill her lungs and the heat from the fires threatened to set her hair alight. She stayed down on her knees, as low as she could, to try to grab some breathable oxygen and give herself some extra seconds to make a plan.

Through her blurred vision, she could see another helicopter hovering above them, the noise of its blades tearing through her damaged eardrums. She watched with fascination as it somehow landed almost perfectly on the H where the previous one had also touched down. The blades continued turning as it tried to find balance. She could imagine the pilot fighting with the controls to keep it from sliding down the deck. She had no idea why the pilot had taken the decision to land there, considering the flames were spurting up randomly from below and could set his machine alight at any given moment, but whatever his reason, it gave her a hope of escape. If she could make it over there, it could be her chance of getting off this thing alive.

She reached behind her and grabbed the railing, yanking herself to standing, trying as hard as she could not to take in a lungful of acrid smoke. She pulled her hands away with a scream as the metal railing had already heated up to such an extent that the skin on her fingers instantly blistered up.

Looking around through the billowing clouds of smoke, she tried to find a safe path to the landing pad. By now, the platform was awash with burning oil and the scarred bodies of men who had been caught out by the second explosion and flung into the fiery puddles. Their screams, mixed with the noise of the dying rig, added to the chaos around her.

"Boss, she's not there."

Kiara stopped moving and held her breath. Despite her ears still making everything sound dull, she recognised the three voices that were standing close to her.

"What did you say, boy?"

"I went back down to kill her as you told me to, but the room was empty."

Kiara could hear that they were standing close, but because of the smoke, she didn't know how close. If she made a run for it now, she might just crash straight into them. She tried to stay still despite the movement of the rig beneath her.

"She was gone, boss," the second man said.

"Then find her, before I rip your faces off," the other voice screamed back.

"But, boss, we need to get off this thing now, before we all die."

"Just get her!" he screamed back at the men. "She must have run down to the lower platforms where the escape ships are. Get down there, and do not let her board any of them, or the fires will be the least of your problems, you understand?!"

Kiara moved slightly to her right and caught sight of the tall man with the long dreadlocks talking to his two juniors. Even though they were clearly scared of dying in this place, they seemed to spring into action the moment he raised his voice to them. They knew that if they didn't kill her then they were dead either way, by the sinking rig, or by his hands.

Standing next to him, she felt like a small child next to a giant. He was huge, at least seven foot, and built like a brick wall. She couldn't let him see her. She crept further to the left, hoping that the smoke would keep her hidden.

She waited until she saw the two men rush back off, before reaching down and picking up a large copper pipe that had found its way to where she had been crouching. Stepping out, she raised the pipe over her head to take a swing at him, just as he turned. He raised his hand and grabbed the pipe from her before she could hit him with it, sending her backwards once again into the hot railing. She screamed as it burnt through her top and scorched her back.

He swung the pipe so violently it looked as if he hoped to take her head off in one go. At the exact same second, the platform reared upwards from yet another explosion, throwing them both off balance, Kiara back onto her knees and him onto his back, stunning him as his head hit the metal floor. Before he had a chance to recover, Kiara was up again and had jumped over him. She sprinted towards the helicopter that had not only somehow survived the next explosion intact, but was now readying itself for take-off.

The big man had managed to pull himself off the floor and was running after her to the landing pad when yet another explosion rocked the platform, sending them both once again to their knees. Kiara looked up as the helicopter managed to lift itself off the floor, avoiding the movement that had sent the last one over the edge. Her heart sank as the only means of survival lifted further into the air.

Her thoughts immediately turned to her twin daughters back at home and how they would cope with losing their mum so soon after the loss of their dad.

"No!" she said out loud. "I will not do that to them, I will not die today!"

CHAPTER 1

One Month Earlier

The call from Tyrone had left Kiara in a pickle. On the one hand, she desperately wanted a case that would not only challenge her mentally, but also would fill up the coffers a little, as the new house was starting to take a toll on her bank balance. On the other hand, the widows had left her so emotionally and physically drained that a case this big could easily be the straw that broke the camel's back.

It had been only six months since The Lady had vanished and yet Kiara still found herself constantly looking over her shoulder, expecting to hear the roar of a speeding car coming around the corner, heading directly at her, or the sound of a gun as it spat a bullet from its chamber. Every time she was walking down the narrow lane between her house and Hurstpierpoint High Street, she felt her life and the life of her daughters might still be in danger. The Lady had said that as long as Kiara 'walked away and stopped looking for her', she would never hear from her again, and of course, Kiara would never break that promise, but once your life has been threatened by an assassin, you never quite feel a hundred percent safe again.

Every night, after Mia and Jasmin were fast asleep, she would lie in her own bed, always on the left-hand side, and replay the moment Asher crashed down in front of them at the airfield, the parachute still folded into the bag on his instructor's back and both their bodies lying broken and still. Sleep would eventually come, but it never lasted more than three or four hours and it always ended with her waking up crying. She never expected to get over the loss of Asher, she wasn't sure she ever actually wanted to, but she did hope that, somewhere down the road, the tears could stop and the dreams would get easier.

She also prayed that her girls would find some peace. Ever since losing their father, they seemed to cling to her as if afraid she was going to leave them as well. She needed to find a way of putting a little distance between them all, but not too much to make them feel abandoned, so that they could start standing more on their own feet like they used to do before it happened. At nearly seventeen, they really couldn't be following her around every single second of the day, they desperately needed to start college, and she needed to be able to properly get back to work.

That prayer was answered much sooner than she'd expected.

It came about on the morning Tyrone had called.

Kiara had just returned from a long run around Hurstpierpoint, which included a slope of over two hundred feet up Wolstonbury Hill. She had set off on her run at four in the morning, just before the sun was up. Before losing Asher, when they still lived just off Brighton seafront, she would be up and out of the house by six o'clock, Monday to Friday, every week throughout the year, no matter the weather or the conditions. She would run the five kilometres from her house along the flat seafront all the way to the Palace Pier and her swimming club.

Brighton Sea Swimming Club, the oldest sea swimming club in the country, had its changing rooms just east of the Palace Pier in one of the council-owned arches. It was a small facility, but a perfect place to safely leave her running clothes before her swim, and somewhere she could dry off afterwards before the five-kilometre run back home afterwards. As an early morning swimmer, the arch was always quiet when she arrived, especially during the winter months, when there were perhaps no more than five or six other people there. But a small group meant close friendships were formed, especially when the activity was as dangerous and exciting as sea swimming was. Before Asher's death, she only missed her morning swim when she was on a family holiday or had an unusually early morning meeting in London, otherwise she'd be there every day, as if it were a religious observance that she was unable to break. But since his death, she hadn't been down to the arch even once. Her friends of course knew what had happened, it had been all over the press, and every one of them had tried to contact her, but she simply couldn't face the normality of life anymore. Going back to the arch and swimming around the pier every morning, even though it was something she knew would be good for her, reminded her too much of her old life, of what she had lost, and she just wasn't ready for that yet.

After a brief stay with her in-laws, she had rented out the family home and bought the house in Hurstpierpoint. She had hoped a change of scenery, being closer to the girls' school and tucked away in the countryside, would allow them all to start the healing process. But of course, you can't run away from your pain, it just clings to you like a sad song. The three of them settled into the new home quickly enough, though, but she knew it could never reset what they had all lost.

Whilst she was no longer swimming in the mornings, she at least had Wolstonbury Hill on her doorstep, as well as the fields around her house to keep her occupied. From a physical perspective, she was probably fitter and stronger now than she had ever been. Every morning since moving there, whilst the rest of the village was still snuggled up in bed, she would either run for ninety minutes up and down the hillsides or she would get on her mountain bike and ride the country lanes. Apart from her lack of swimming, she was ready to face the triathlon season again, with the knowledge that she was possibly even fit enough to beat all her previous PBs. Getting back to triathlons would perhaps be the first step in recovering some of her old self.

The other benefit of hitting the roads so early was that it meant that her exercises never had an impact on her morning routine with the twins, nor her time at work. Usually, after her run, she would have time for a quick shower and a cup of coffee before the girls stirred, looking for their breakfast.

This particular morning, she really needed to be back on time. Today was the first day they would be back to school, starting their first year as sixth formers. It was a huge day for them all. The girls had been filled with anxiety about leaving Kiara and facing all the questions that they knew would come, but equally, they were desperate to get back to their friends and some kind of structured routines that only a school day could provide. The tension in the house had been building steadily for the last couple of weeks in anticipation and was starting to reach boiling point.

So, her private mobile phone ringing at just six in the morning, almost as soon as she had stepped into her garden office had startled her.

"Hello?" she said into the handset with trepidation, expecting it was her in-laws, *as who else would call at that time of the morning?* Her stomach turned as she waited for the bad news that one of them was unwell and was being shipped off to the hospital again. The stress of losing their son had taken a heavy toll on both of their health, and they had aged a lot since his murder.

She was relieved when the voice on the other end was neither of them.

"Is that Fox Investigations?"

"Yes, it is," she replied, "do you realise how early it is, and that you've called my private number not my work number?" she asked the caller, surprised that anyone would think this was a good time to make a work call.

She heard the annoyance in her own voice coming through clearly enough for him to pick up. It was a reminder to herself that she really needed to get back to the beach and calm herself down as soon as possible before she started to alienate people.

"I believe it is just after six o'clock in the morning in the UK. Which means it's eight o'clock here in Johannesburg, so my day began an hour or so ago. I was told you often get back from a run around about now, and I wanted to catch you before your workday actually started."

It had not been long since Kiara had been hunted by the assassin who took the life of her husband and had almost taken hers. So, getting a call from a stranger before the sun had even risen, especially one who seemed to know too much about her routine, put her fully on alert. She opened the WhatsApp application on her laptop and started to type an SOS to the local security company, who, thanks to the help of her friend Nick Taylor, now kept a close eye on her and her family.

"How did you get this number?" she asked sternly down the phone, trying to keep the fear from her voice.

"Mrs Fox, please forgive me," the caller said, aware that he may have overstepped the mark calling so early. "My name is Tyrone Waterstone. I'm CEO of a company called Worldwide Marine Insurance, based in South Africa. We share a good friend, my London lawyer Nick Taylor. He told me you wouldn't mind me phoning you."

"Why would Nick give you my private number?" she asked, still not totally convinced of who he was.

"He and I go back years; we are more like brothers than friends. He knows it is urgent for me to get hold of you, so he must have thought this was the best number to try. He said that you are the best fraud investigator in the business and are someone who does not let go of a case until it is solved. And that is a virtue I desperately need if my business is to survive the next few months.

If you want, you can call Nick before we talk further, he's usually at his office by nine-ish, and I am sure we could arrange a Zoom call for us all after that."

Kiara let out a long breath that she didn't even realise she had been holding in. It was a genuine business call, after all, and it had come as a recommendation from one of the only people left in her life whom she felt totally able to trust.

She deleted the SOS message before it sent.

"I'm so sorry for my reaction, Mr Waterstone. You caught me off guard, that's all. I will speak with Nick later anyway, but I'm okay to talk now, if you like."

"That's great, and sorry again for calling so early, but it's the only time I could reach out to you today as I am backed up with meetings."

"It's fine. I shouldn't have overreacted. How can I help you?"

"I own a South African insurance company. We specialise in cargo insurance, covering goods being shipped from one country to another. One side of our business, the most profitable, is insuring the movement of oil across the major oceans. We cover any financial losses our clients suffer, if, for instance, an oil tanker is hijacked, or maybe goes down in a storm. We also cover things like contaminated oil or environmental damage caused, such as oil leaking into the ocean. It's a very specialised field and I like to think we are one of the most experienced insurers in this market. Specifically, I wanted to talk to you about a large client of ours called Adesco Oil. They are one of the largest producers of oil headquartered in this part of the world, owning a number of oil rigs in some of the world's biggest oceans, with their own ships carrying oil all around the globe. We've been insuring their ships for around ten years now, and they've been claim free throughout. But suddenly, just in the last eighteen months, we have had to pay out several claims to them recently, some rather large ones. Then, one month ago, another claim was reported, and this one was very sizeable, around twenty million dollars. It's the first one that my team have brought to my attention as I have to sign off claims over ten million myself. We haven't paid it yet as we've been investigating the loss, but I think we will probably have to settle soon, and now I am worried even more will follow."

"Twenty million? Wow."

"As I say, quite sizeable."

"But surely, in your particular business, losses of that size are all part and parcel of what you are covering? When they happen, they happen big. You must expect that?"

"Of course we do, and as you say, that in itself is part of the business we run. But to go from no claims for years to a regular number, all in the space of a few months is odd. And for them to double in value each time is not something we've ever experienced before."

"And you haven't paid this last one yet, you say?"

"No, not yet. And that also bothers me, of course. We pride ourselves on the speed of our claims handling. But, when you see a pattern form, you have to ask yourself why."

"Of course you do. But if you have paid the others and they are all very similar then I assume you've completed your investigations and found them to be genuine," Kiara asked.

"Well, that has been slightly problematic. Our client has certainly been very open and has let us send my head of claims to their offices and to the ports. But he found nothing to suggest that they are involved in the losses themselves. I do trust them, I really do, they have a strong reputation in the industry, and of course, I trust my own guys as much as I would trust my own family."

Kiara knew she should end the call now, as this was way out of her usual type of work. But her curiosity was piqued, and she found herself needing to know more.

"So, how are the losses occurring?"

"Well, this is the thing, it's always the same type of claim, but we can't figure out why or how it keeps happening. Basically, the claims are for loss of oil. Each time the oil has been offloaded at its destination port, it has been found to be in good order, no water contamination or anything like that, which is something we often see with shipments like this. However, each time, it has arrived at a different weight to when it first left port. This means, somewhere along the journey, oil has been lost. But we have found nothing in the ship's logs to suggest any other vessels close enough to them for any thefts to have occurred. And there has been no visible leakage from the tankers into the sea. The first claim showed that at the loading port the weight of oil was fifty thousand tonnes, but at the final destination, it was only forty-five thousand tonnes. The loss to us of the five thousand tonnes was around three million dollars."

"And you paid that?"

"Of course. And then another one followed, but this time it was an almost six million loss. So far, in the last year alone, we have paid out over fifteen million dollars in claims to them. We have looked at all the loading and unloading procedures and nothing seems out of place. We have checked all the CCTV on the ships themselves, both in and around the ports, and we are at a complete loss as to how it's been happening."

"You've already paid out fifteen million dollars?" Kiara was staggered at the amounts he was talking about.

"Last year, the global theft of oil was in excess of a hundred billion dollars. Mostly from piracy. So, our losses are small in comparison, but for a company our size, they are, of course, significant and could really affect the support we get from our re-insurers; without them, we can't continue to write this type of cover. There is something else, our client also owns a number of their own oil rigs. So far, we have not been involved in insuring those, we've only insured their tankers and stock. But they have now asked me to quote for their entire operation, which includes all their existing offshore rigs, plus a brand-new rig that they are calling Neptune. It's the largest oil rig that has ever been built, anywhere in the world. It's an incredible opportunity for me. If I picked up their entire business, including Neptune, it would overnight double my business. Up until now, my re-insurers have been fully supportive, and it looks like we have them on board to cover Neptune. But if I now submit another claim so soon after the last one, especially a twenty-million-dollar claim, they will pull back from supporting the expansion. Equally, if I don't pay Adesco this claim, which could well be genuine, then they are likely to pull my account in full, so I will not only lose their new rig, but also their existing business. Either way, I lose. If I pay the claim, I lose my re-insurers, but if I refuse the claim, I lose the client. So, as you can see, I am in a very difficult position, caught between a rock and a hard place."

"Forgive me, Mr Waterstone, I am not entirely sure what you think I can do for you. I've never worked in the oil business and have never handled claims anywhere near this size. I honestly don't think I'm the right person for you."

"It's Tyrone, not Mr Waterstone, please."

"Okay, Tyrone. I don't know what Nick has told you, but I've never worked large corporate fraud cases before, all my work has been based around family fraud. I honestly would have no idea where to begin."

"Nick told me you are the most tenacious person he knows. Perhaps to the point of being OCD about your work."

"That's certainly true," she said with a sigh, knowing where that had led her in the past.

"And that is why you are the perfect person for the job. I need someone who is not willing to just give up at the first hurdle. I also need someone who will have no choice but to ask the dumb questions. It's those questions that are not being asked at the moment and are leading us to lose millions of dollars, and this massive opportunity."

Kiara paused and tried to work out if she could really do this, if she even had the emotional strength to take on such a big project at the moment.

Tyrone, sensing he was losing her, continued with his pitch. "Nick said you were desperate for a case that you could get your teeth stuck into. So, what could be better than this? If you help me find out what is going on, then you would save me tens of millions of dollars in claims and possibly the biggest piece of business I will ever be offered. Quite frankly, if I can't prove to the insurers that this claim is genuine and then try to help Adesco avoid further claims like this, then it could ruin me, which right now is a real possibility. I need you, Kiara, I really do."

That feeling of excitement as the adrenalin started to surge around her body was starting to become intense. The thought of taking on such an exciting project was like a drug to her, something that she needed just to survive, but it was then tempered by thoughts of getting herself drawn into something new, and the amount of time it could take her away from the girls.

Despite the butterflies now flittering away in her stomach, she knew that the reality of her life, as it now was, meant taking on a job this big just wasn't feasible.

Her mind was made up.

"I'm sorry, Tyrone, as much as this might have tempted me a year ago, I have more than just myself to think about now," she replied. "This job could mean several trips for me, as I would have to be on site part of the time, so I would have to get help with my girls now they are just about to start college, which means drop off and pickups, plus the sports clubs, dinners; there's a lot I would have to arrange. And I can't just up and leave them considering what they've gone through recently."

"I'd make it worthwhile, I assure you."

"I'm sorry, I really can't. It's just too soon."

"It pays six figures."

Kiara was taken aback. That was crazy money to her for just a few weeks' work. She thought about what she could do with that sort of cash behind her. It would not only help her with the costs of the new house, but it would also be a massive bonus with the girls' college fees.

"If I'm right about this being fraud, then I have a real chance of helping my client, and growing the business, as well as keeping my re-insurers on the books," Tyrone said, knowing that the number he had thrown at her was going to be too much for her to turn down. "And your girls can take some of the trips with you if you need to come over a few times, if that helps. It could be an adventure for you all."

"I just don't see how I can," she said, the reluctance coming out in her voice.

"I understand your concerns, I really do. So, maybe after just one visit, you can do the rest remotely, that's a real possibility."

"Okay, well that might work for me, but no promises; let me talk to the girls tonight and see how they feel about me leaving them so soon after…" she couldn't finish the sentence *losing their dad*, it was too painful even to think about, let alone to say out loud to a stranger. "Can you give me a few weeks to think it over?" she asked him.

"Unfortunately, I can't, this needs to be looked at now or else I have to just pay the claim, and then it could be game over for me. I can give you a couple of days, but no more. And then I will need to find someone else. But it's you I want."

"It's just not enough time for me to decide. I'm sorry, but I can't," she said, coming to the conclusion she knew would be the right one. "I'll be wasting your time if I lead you on. As I said, a few months ago then possibly it would have been a nervous yes, I might even have bitten your hand off, but not now, it has to be a 'no' with things the way they currently are."

"How about you let me email you the claim files. Just so you can have a look. Would that be okay?" he asked hopefully.

She took a second to think.

"Kiara?" he prompted her.

"I'm sorry, Tyrone, but honestly, I can't, I'd just be wasting your time, and it doesn't sound like you have a lot of that left to waste."

"Okay. I get it. But I'm sorry as well, I really am. I think you could really have helped save me."

With that, he ended the call.

Kiara looked up at the clock on her wall; it was 6am already and the girls would be waking up any time soon. She just had time for a quick shower before the day truly began.

She tried to push the phone call from her head. *But God, it would have been exciting*, she thought. She pulled off her trainers, stepped out of her running clothes and jumped into the shower.

As the hot water poured over her, removing the mud from her ankles gathered on the run up Wolstonbury Hill, she stood there and tried to calm her mind. The problem was that she was desperate to say yes to Tyrone. Not just because of the money, which would certainly make things easier for her and the girls, but also because she needed to stretch her mind again. She was sick of just sitting around all day and thinking about what could have been.

To fill her time and earn some money since moving into the new house, she had been taking on some small, insignificant jobs for the motor and household insurance companies in the area. But she really was getting to the point where she couldn't face another case from someone claiming to have lost a gold watch on holiday or a family who pretended to have damaged their TV by dropping a vase full of water over it. It was mind-numbing nonsense and pointless work that she thought she had left behind years ago. She needed more than that, she needed something that would get her adrenalin pumping again. But what the hell would she say to Mia and Jasmin? How could she tell them that she would be jumping on a plane to the other side of the world to take on a case that she knew she could not solve?

I know you'd tell me to take it, she said to Asher.

But the empty room said nothing back for the hundredth time since she'd lost him.

CHAPTER 2

The rest of the week had gone fairly smoothly considering all the angst in the house. The girls had started college, just for a few hours a day for the first couple of days, before going back full time near the end of the week. They were now in the sixth form rather than the main school and the change of pace, as well as the extra freedoms they got as sixth formers, seemed to show in their attitude right away. In just a few days, they seemed to have gone from sixteen-year-old schoolkids to almost seventeen-year-old adults.

Maybe I do need to give them some more freedom now? Kiara thought to herself as she stood in the transition field, racking her bike and setting up her race box. *Maybe I should call Tyrone back and see if it's not too late to take the job, after all.*

She pushed that thought from her mind. It was too late, anyway, she'd missed that opportunity. She'd said no to him almost a week ago and he must have appointed someone else by now.

She went back to focusing on her race set up and tried to clear her head of all work issues; today was about what she loved to do and nothing else. This was her first triathlon since the widows had thrown a hand grenade into her life and her nerves were all over the place. The drive from her home in Hurstpierpoint to the seafront near Beachy Head in Eastbourne for the annual Tri-Bourne Olympic-Distance Triathlon had given her just enough time to fully wake up. She had almost turned around and driven back home about half a dozen times during the journey, finding

14

the thought of competing again frightening. Usually, she would have been full of excitement rather than trepidation, but the recent events in her life had left her a changed person. This particular triathlon had been one of her favourites in the calendar and one where the girls and Asher had always made the effort to come along and cheer her on. It had a fantastic mix of a swim around the pier, then hilly climbs and fast descents on the bike, up and over Beachy Head twice during the forty-kilometre route, and then lastly a fast, almost flat sprint along the seafront for the ten-kilometre running route. The sea section, which was a fifteen-hundred-metre swim to start the event, was usually her strongest discipline, but having not been in the sea for many months, the butterflies were really kicking in. It also made her sad to think that this was the first time her husband would not be at the exit to the swim waving the Fox flag and cheering her on.

"Olympic competitors, those with the green swim caps, please make your way down to the beach for the briefing. Again, just those with the green hats, please make your way down to the beach for your briefing," the announcer called out through the Tannoy.

Kiara, now dressed in her wetsuit, with goggles and green hat in hand, gave her bike a quick pat for good luck and then headed down to the beach along with the other hundred and fifty or so competitors in her age group.

As soon as the hooter went off, signalling the start of the race, the sea became its usual melee, full of arms and feet kicking out in every direction, causing mayhem and bringing on feelings of claustrophobia, especially to anyone who had not experienced it before. The swim route was a simple one compared to other races she did. At most open-water triathlons, the swim was set up as a 500m loop that the Olympic competitors had to do three times. But this one was just one 1500m swim, 750m along the coastline to the pier and the same back to the beach. As she always did, she stood to the side to let the less experienced competitors run into the sea as fast as they could. As usual for a mass swim start, the sea looked as if there were a pod of seals fighting to pick up the first shoal of mackerels of the season. It was pure and unadulterated chaos. Within the first thirty seconds, a dozen swimmers had their goggles kicked from their face and had to put up their hands for the support canoes to take them out to safety, whilst another two dozen found themselves pushed backwards with the eastern tide far away from the first buoy.

Kiara watched all this happen before she slowly walked forward and entered the sea as calmly as her nerves would allow. She swam wide to get away from the splashers and then headed diagonally back to the first buoy. Even though she hadn't swum in months, the feel of the water on her body instantly put at her at ease. It was like she was at home once again, back in her comfort zone. She lowered her head and shoulders into the sea, which naturally drew her lower body up, giving her that smooth and aerodynamic position that let her glide through the water. She slowed her breathing right down, making sure she never hyperventilated and then she carefully blew out each breath into the sea as she turned her head from left to right. She breathed in just before her face went down into the water, turned her head to the side, breathing out the air as her head was straight down and then drawing in a new breath as her head turned and her face came out the other side, then she repeated on every third stroke. Her arm movements were also fluid, reaching out front as far as she could with one arm, whilst pulling back hard under the water with the other arm, the arm out of the water being relaxed so not to waste energy on the movement out of the water, whilst the other arm, the one in the water, pulling hard to propel herself forward. And repeat. As someone who was used to swimming in the sea every day, she was very experienced at spotting. Where pool swimmers were used to following a line on the pool floor and unable to spot the buoys high up in the sea, Kiara could take one look up, see the buoy ahead and then let her muscle memory find its way there. In no time, she had overtaken most of the pack and was now in the front ten percent, only the professional triathletes able to stay ahead of her; she knew that, come the end of her swim, she would be right on their tails.

She turned from the first buoy and headed in a straight line towards Eastbourne Pier, where she would then head out into deeper water up the side of the pier to the turning buoy, heading west to start the swim back to the finish. The whole swim usually took her around thirty-six minutes to complete, but this time she got to the exit as the first amateur competitor in her age group in just thirty-four minutes and twelve seconds, her first swim PB in years.

She left the sea, pulling her wetsuit down to her waist and taking off her hat and goggles before jogging barefoot to the transition area. Being amongst the first swimmers back meant that transition was almost empty of people but still full of bikes. She followed the number lines and found her spot. Quickly stripping off her wetsuit, she stood dripping in her one-piece suit. She grabbed her bike helmet and put it over her wet hair, before slipping into her cycle shoes, popping on her race number and sunglasses and then she finally pulled her bike from the rack. She ran, pushing the bike next to her, to the exit of transition and then, as instructed by the volunteers, jumped on her bike as she crossed the start line.

The bike course was a total of forty kilometres, and started with a steep 5% climb to the top of Beachy Head, before a long and fast descent down to the Birling Gap, some ten kilometres away, before turning around and retracing the road all the way back up to Beachy Head once again, followed by a fast and scary descent down to the seafront to the starting point near the big wheel on the promenade. It was a total of twenty kilometres, exactly half the ride. Once she was back at the starting point, it was a case of simply repeating exactly what she had just done, back up the 5% gradient to the top of Beachy Head, followed by the fast descent, which saw her hitting the sharp corners at a mind-boggling sixty kilometres per hour, before turning back for a final climb up to the top of the head again and then shooting down to the finish line and into transition, ready for the last discipline.

On returning to transition, Kiara racked her bike, remembering to only take her helmet off once the bike was set. Taking off the helmet first would have meant a time penalty or, even worse, a disqualification, which had happened to her a few times during her first events around fifteen years before and which she swore to herself would never happen again.

With the bike and helmet safely set aside, she swapped her cycling shoes for running shoes and turned her race number from the back of her suit to the front. The whole time in transition from racking her bike to running out of the area took her under two minutes.

For both the swim and the bike legs, she could do nothing more than concentrate on being in the moment; anything other than that would have meant drowning in the sea or crashing at stupid speeds and ending up in hospital with broken bones. But the final part of the event, the run section, was her time to really think about Tyrone's offer and wonder about the lost opportunity.

She hit the flat run route at a super-fast pace of under four and a half minutes a kilometre, much faster than her usual pace of five minutes. She was on course to beat her fastest ever time, and to prove to herself that she could not only survive in this world as a single mother, but she could also be a stronger athlete than ever before. She no longer had a husband looking out for her and the twins, now it was all down to her. Whatever they did from this day on was on her, and she was not going to let Asher or the twins down.

Tyrone's offer had certainly come at the right time in her

life. For the last few months, since Asher's death, she had slowly got back to work as a means of not only bringing in some much needed cash, but also as a way to ease herself back to some form of normality, although she still had no idea what her new reality would look like. The jobs she had been taking had certainly paid the bills, but they by no means stretched her ability or tested her brains. They had all been small, almost insignificant cases, which she could almost do in her sleep. This contract from Tyrone, though, was the diametric opposite. It would push her into the world of corporate fraud rather than individual fraud, which was something she found deeply exciting, and it was an area of work that she had never tackled before, as well as being in a country she had always wanted to visit. But was it still too soon to throw herself into a job that would inevitably bring with it huge amounts of stress? Could she really step up to the plate with that big a challenge so soon after everything? And what about the girls, how would they feel about her leaving them and travelling to the other side of the world when they have just moved home and then started college? But just thinking about the contract, and all the work it would entail, gave her shivers of excitement. It was this type of job that she had spent years being trained for. It was the exact type of case she had always been looking for. And let's not forget the pay day, it would be the highest paid contract she had ever taken on, which was not a small thing.

She knew that she had to take it, even before she reached the end of the run.

The conversation with the girls would be difficult, though. Telling them she was going away to the other side of the world without them, even for only for a few days, would be hard to justify to teenagers. But they did need the money, as without Asher's income, things would soon start to bite. And if they wanted her to stay sane and not lose her mind to the loneliness of a single person, then they had to let her sink her teeth into something solid.

Her mind was made up, she had to say yes. She just hoped, now having come to the decision, that she could convince Tyrone to give her a second chance.

She completed the run in an impressive forty-four minutes. She stopped her Garmin watch as she crossed the finish line and collected her finisher medal and race T-shirt. The entire triathlon had taken two hours and thirty-six minutes. It was a massive ten percent faster than she had done before. Even though she had gone there on her own and competed as an independent athlete and not part of a club or group, she still basked in the congratulations of all the competitors around her. That was one of the things Kiara loved about triathlons; whilst it was a lone sport, you against you, it still had a thriving community that encouraged you to share your accomplishments with your fellow athletes.

CHAPTER 3

The meeting had not started well. Tyrone sat in the small claims office, surrounded by his key managers, all of them waiting for him to calm down. They were not used to him losing his temper like that and it had created a dark atmosphere in the small room. He had called them together to talk about the recent claims on their marine book, expecting to be given an update on where they were with their investigations, but instead he was handed a spreadsheet simply detailing all the claims paid in the last twelve months, as well as confirmation of the ones they were about to settle.

He took a deep breath in and tried to remove the anger from his voice before he spoke again. "So, explain to me again why you thought it was acceptable to pay out a series of claims without coming to me first?"

"On our marine book you gave Jan authorisation to pay claims up to a quarter of a million dollars without referring to you…"

"For one client, not per claim," he said, turning his anger on Mufuka, his chief financial officer.

"That's not how I remember it," Jan said.

"To be fair, that wasn't how it was written," Mufuka agreed with Jan, their head of claims.

"Oh, come on, surely you knew it was my intention to give Jan a level of control up to a point, but for me to still keep some level of control over the numbers. I mean, you've had claim payment authorisation now for what, eighteen months? And from this spreadsheet it looks as if you've been paying claims almost every month since then," he said, looking straight at Jan.

The other man couldn't look Tyrone in the eyes.

"I know how it looks, Tye," he said, trying to keep the embarrassment from his voice. "If I had known all these claims would start pouring in, I never would have asked you to give me the pen to pay them myself. But, up until recently, we were having no more than maybe a dozen claims a month across our entire book, so it seemed like a normal extension of my job to do that for you. It's standard practice at most insurance companies that the head of claims makes the settlements."

"The larger insurers, maybe, but we are still a small team with a relatively small book of clients in comparison. I trust you to use some common sense, though. Surely you'd know I would want to be kept up to date on what was happening with our largest client."

"So, you don't trust me anymore," Jan replied sadly, at last looking up at Tyrone.

"You know I didn't mean that," Tyrone said, backing down a little. "You have been with me almost from the start of the company. All of you have," he said, looking around the room. "I trust you like I would trust my own family. In fact, I treat you all like family, don't I? It's not about trust, it's about common sense. Surely if our largest client is suddenly suffering multiple claims then not only should we talk to them to see if we can help, but we have to make sure we are not leaving ourselves low on capital."

"I get it. And I agree I should have brought this to your attention. But I honestly thought my new position meant I could pay single claims up to a quarter of a million and that you didn't want me to draw you into those. And, until this latest one, all of the others have been significantly under that."

"I get it, Jan, I do. That was my fault for not making my intention clearer. But surely you understand that I would want to talk to the client to find out why they'd suddenly go from almost zero claims to one a month?"

"Actually, I have to take the bullet for that one," Bea said.

Where Jan was head of claims and Mufuka was head of finance, Bea was the one who handled the client relationships.

"I have built up a strong relationship with the finance team at Adesco, especially their head of finance. She's the one who handles claims their side and who, ultimately, we send the money to. I have spoken to her each time a claim comes through, and on the last one, the biggest yet, I met her on site at the port with our assessors. We did a thorough investigation on them all and just can't find out where the losses are coming from. She was totally open book with me and has even paid half of the loss assessor's fees, matching us dollar for dollar, as she needs this to stop as well before her CEO gets wind of it."

"You mean Gavin doesn't even know about the claims either?" Tyrone said in surprise.

"He's left the entire claims handling process to her, just like you have done with Jan and me. He's been too tied up for the last couple of years with the launch of their new oil platform to get involved in the day-to-day running of their business. Even I don't have access to him anymore."

"Why the hell didn't you tell me that?! I could have called him myself."

"If I remember, the last time you two met you almost ended up losing the whole account," Bea reminded him.

"That's true," Tyrone had to agree. "He's a difficult bugger."

"That was why you left me to handle the relationship, up until he started on his new platform, we used to meet monthly, but since then, my only contact has been Karly, and if I am being honest, she is much easier to deal with than him, and she really does know her stuff, so I never pushed back."

Tyrone let out a deep sigh and leant back in his chair.

"This is not really getting us anywhere, is it?" he said, far more softly than he had been speaking. "We need to get a handle on what's going on. I accept that you have been thorough in your investigations…" he said to Bea "… but the claim files are really poor…" he said to Jan. "One of you, or both of you, need to sort that out. I need chapter and verse on every claim, especially if I am going to have to hand them over to a specialist."

He picked up on the fact that all three of them around the table looked at him in surprise, which had been his intention. He carried on speaking.

"It's not a matter of trust, I trust all three of you implicitly. But I cannot keep haemorrhaging money like this. Someone is stealing a lot of oil from Adesco and we need to help them find out who it is, and so far, you guys have not got a clue how to do that. Even your independent loss assessors have come up blank. So, I have reached out to someone, a fraud specialist. She comes highly recommended and works in the Lloyds of London market, representing some of the largest underwriters. She hasn't accepted the job yet, but I am hoping she will. I want her to be shown everything that has happened so far. And not just the big claim we are now facing, but all the claims on Adesco's marine account since Jan started handling them."

"Oh, for Christ's sake," Jan said, "I thought this wasn't personal."

"It's not," Tyrone responded to her. "It's business, nothing more. And I am not pointing the finger at you, or at Bea, but one, or both of you have taken your eye off the ball and it's in danger of taking us down."

Both Jan and Bea looked at each other to see if one of them would take the fall if needed, and then both turned their attention back to Tyrone.

"You think we've taken our eyes of the ball? That's pretty unfair, considering you had no idea these were even happening, and you're CEO," Bea said. "Surely you should know everything that goes on here, even before we do?"

Tyrone knew Bea was outspoken but even he didn't expect such a rebut from her. His initial thought was to bring her down a peg or two for talking to him like that. But she was right, of course. He should have known what was happening. It was hard to argue on that basis.

"Fair enough, I've taken my eye off the ball as well. I've been so busy chasing new business that I haven't really been watching what's happening right under my nose. So, I'll take that, this time. But it'll never happen again, I can promise you that."

Bea breathed a sigh of relief when she realised she wasn't about to be shouted out for being so honest with him.

"So, how are the numbers looking?" Tyrone asked, turning to Mufuka.

"Not great. We are still within our legal boundaries, but if we were to pay this last claim it would take us down to around 90% of our allowable capitalisation."

"And you only tell me this now?" he replied, shaking his head.

"I would have told you if it had got to that, but we are expecting some big premiums in, especially if Adesco agree to letting us insure the new platform when it launches in a week or two."

"Okay, but it's still very tight and I don't like that. Let me know immediately if we hit the 90% and I'll have to visit our bank and make some provisions to recapitalise. Meanwhile, Bea, I want you to try to reach out to Gavin as I think he needs to know what is happening. And Jan, get those fucking claim files in order. I want them ready for when she gets here."

"The investigator?" Jan asked him.

"Of course the bloody investigator!" he replied.

CHAPTER 4

Whens his team left him, Tyrone picked up the phone to his PA.

"Lesseti, did you pick up the boys?"

"Yes, sir, they are in your office."

"Okay, tell them I'm on my way."

"Yes, sir," she said, ending the call.

He left the first-floor office and walked up the glass staircase to the top floor, where his own office was. He walked in and found his twin boys sitting on the coach watching the seventy-five-inch TV that took up most of the end wall. The TV was usually used for looking at detailed presentations, but right now the boys were watching a live football match between Liverpool, Tyrone's team, and Brighton & Hove Albion, their favourite team. Tyrone was dismayed to see the score sitting at one nil to Brighton, despite it being over twenty minutes into the game.

"Hey, Dad," Troy and Mattie said to him as he sat down next to them on the couch.

"Looks like my boys need to up their game," Tyrone said to his sons.

"We've got you beaten, already," Troy said, getting a giggle and agreement from his brother.

"Not a chance, you rascals!" Tyrone said, pulling them both in for a huge bear hug.

"Daaad!" the boys screamed in delight.

"Ha!" Tyrone said, letting the boys go and leaning forwards to see Brighton concede a penalty. "That'll even it up. Right, chaps, you guys stay here while I finish up some work and then I'm treating us to a burger at your favourite place."

"Yey… oh no!" the boys said in unison at the good news about dinner and then the bad news as Liverpool took the penalty and evened up the score.

Tyrone logged onto his computer and rattled off two quick emails. The first was to his bank in Cape Town, putting them on notice that he may need to organise a transfer of funds from his personal holdings to his business account. The second was to the UK, to Kiara, trying to get her to agree to come to his rescue.

CHAPTER 5

"South Africa?" Mia said, clearly not happy at the prospect of her mum going so far away from them.

"How long for?" Jasmin said with equal concern.

"He hasn't said yes, yet, so it's not definitely happening, but if I do go, then it'll be a short trip, I promise, just a few days."

"But Mum, I don't understand why you have to go at all. You said you have been getting some jobs recently and that it would be enough for us."

"Is it about the money? Didn't Dad leave us enough? Are we going to have to have to move house again? I love it here," Jasmin cut in.

"It's not just about the money and we are not moving house, I promise you. I mean, it would be great to have some more money, wouldn't it? But Dad left us enough to cover the school fees and the new house, and we still have the rent from our old home. So, we'll be fine if I take the job or not."

"Then why take the job at all?" Jasmin asked again.

"It's hard to explain."

"Give it a go," Mia said, trying to be pushy enough to draw her mum into an argument as she felt that was the only way they could convince her not to go.

"There's no need to be rude, Mia. You know I was always busy at work, even before…"

Each time she thought of the 'before', it seemed to take her breath away.

"… but it wasn't just because of the money I made. I needed to be busy. Busy is just what I do. It's why I do my triathlons. You know how much I hate just sitting around. You two are exactly the same as me in that, aren't you? You probably won't remember what I was like before I took a full-time job. You were too young to really get it, but once, when I had about three months free in between contracts, I drove your dad nuts. I was still up at stupid o'clock every morning, even when I had no reason to be. I was like a lady possessed!"

"Actually, we do remember, don't we, Mia?" Jasmin said, looking at her sister and giving her some raised eyebrows.

"Oh my God, you were a nightmare, Mum," Mia said. "How many times did you phone Dad at work? And do you remember how early you would come to school to pick us up?! I definitely don't want that Mum back again!"

"And you remember, we even had to stop you trying to do our homework for us!" Jasmin said, starting to laugh at the memories.

"Exactly. And that is about to happen again, but only ten times worse if I don't do something about it," Kiara replied to her daughters. "None of us can live like this, me just taking one or two small jobs every couple of weeks and you two going to college and then coming home and being glued to me every spare minute you have."

"We don't do that," Mia said.

"Er, yes we do," Jasmin said to her sister.

"We all need to get back to a solid routine or we'll never be able to move forward," Kiara said.

"But South Africa is so far away!"

"And isn't it dangerous there?" Jamin said, agreeing with her sister. "You know we've read about it at school, they have guns and crime, and it's really poor and…"

Kiara cut her off mid-flow.

"Don't believe everything you hear. Sure, there are some areas you wouldn't go to, but that applies everywhere, even in Brighton. I'll be going to Johannesburg, and I'll make sure I stay in a really good hotel. I'll probably just have a few meetings and then I'll come home. I've just got to meet the guy who phoned me, who came from Nick, by the way, so he must be okay, and then I'll come home and can do everything else for him from here. So, it'll only be for a few days, I promise."

"And where will we stay when you're gone?" Mia asked.

"I'll have your grandparents move in here. They'll love it. And it'll do them good to have something positive to focus on."

The girls looked at each other and shared the 'twins' look that they had perfected.

"I'll take that as a yes, then," Kiara said, giving them both a hug. "And let's not forget he hasn't even given me the job yet."

CHAPTER 6

The main board members of Adesco Oil sat around the table, with the two brothers facing each other from each end. Gavin, as CEO, had dominated the meeting, whilst Tony, as his second-in-command had sat back and said nothing up until this point.

Staying silent had always been hard for Tony, although it was something he was used to doing when they were in a sales environment as he accepted his brother was a far better salesman than he was. However, when it came to the subject of green energy, Gavin would always over-egg the subject, eventually sounding like a preacher. And no one liked to be preached to, especially capitalists like his fellow board members. So for once Tony was more than happy to sit back and let his brother dig his own grave.

"... And the oil will eventually run out, we all know that. And then what happens to your families, to our families? Sure, for now, you have it all, and your kids, they will be fine. But what about their kids, and their kids, the future generations? What happens to them when the money has stopped pouring in? And what about the planet we have left for them, the mess that global warming has caused to their home? You've seen the billions invested into solar and wind by the governments around the world, and you've seen how unstable they are. The solar farms, even when at full capacity, can only gather energy for seven or eight hours a day. And then that is only used to power our vehicles and heat our homes in the dead of night. And as for the wind farms, does anyone know now

31

much diesel and oil is needed to just get them turning? And like the solar farms, they are only active for a fraction of the day. So, why has no one invested much in the one element that covers the majority of the planet's surface? And it is also the one element that moves constantly, that is not subject to weather conditions or the sun for it to generate energy. It is the element that we at Adesco, and the entire industry, is already plugged into, the sea, it is where we are based. It is where our platforms are plugged into. So, who better to lead this new revolution for green energy than us? Just imagine the energy each of our platforms could generate if we fitted each one with turbines deep under the surface. Each of our platforms could generate enough energy to run them almost cost free. You work out the saving that we will be making. And then what if we can somehow store that energy to be used on our tankers, our helicopters and our trucks? And then what if we can even take it further, and we sell that energy on to the cities around the world? And, alongside this, whilst we are saving billions of dollars for ourselves and providing green energy to the world, think of the benefit to the planet. Ladies and gentlemen, think about the new future you could create for your families."

Gavin stopped talking and took a breath, almost the first one since he had started his sermon. He looked around the table at his board of directors, most of them family members, cousins, uncles, aunties, and he could see the fire he had lit in their eyes. Then he turned to his brother, Tony. He knew that he was never going to win him over. Tony was an oil man through and through, and nothing would ever change that.

"How much more are you asking for?"

Gavin turned to his uncle, his late father's youngest brother and the last remaining board member who had been there when his father had taken over the business from his own father fifty years earlier. He had been waiting for that question since the meeting had started and he knew it would have been his uncle or his brother who would have been the ones to ask.

"I would rather you framed the question as, 'how much shall we invest in our future'," Gavin replied to him.

"I would rather you focused on the question, young Gavin. How much more over and above the one point two billion dollars you have already invested will you now be asking us for?" His uncle asked him in such a way that it was clear to the entire board that he disapproved of his older nephew's plans.

"Firstly, let's be clear. The one point two billion was mostly for the build of the new platform. And let's also be clear that this is not only the largest platform in our fleet, but it is the largest in the entire world. Even without the investment into our green turbines and our energy university programmes, we would be spending around a billion dollars."

"So, you have spent over two hundred million of our money on your underwater engines?"

"I have given us a way of eventually reducing our running costs by over eighty percent. And helping to repair the damage our own business has been doing to the environment."

"And I'll ask again, how much more do you want us to agree to?"

Tony sat back, happy to let his brother deliver the news.

"We need another two hundred and fifty million to fit out the turbines and another twenty million to complete the university on site."

"Outrageous ask!" his uncle said.

"Hear, hear!" came the chorus around the table.

"Just look at the numbers!" Gavin shouted them down. "Look at how much we will save in the coming years; it dwarfs this investment."

"But we will make twice as much as that by just using the new platform for what it is intended, bringing oil to the surface."

"And what about the damage to the planet? What about the

future of our company and the future of our families?"

"Yes, what about the future of our company?" Tony said, getting to his feet, ready now to add his voice to the conversation. "Surely what we should be focusing on now is not the cost of bringing the oil to the surface – we know those costs, we've been doing this for over a hundred years. We need to be putting our efforts into ensuring the world knows that our product is used in almost everything we touch. Whilst my brother is trying to convince the world that we don't need oil anymore, that it is somehow destroying our planet, what he is failing to tell them is that without it we will not be walking around with these shoes on our feet, or wearing the clothes on our backs. And not one of us will have a mobile phone in our hands or computers running our businesses. We won't have the fridges and freezers to store our food, and we won't even have the choice of food we have got so used to ordering. Our oil touches all of these things, and more. Without our oil, the world will end far sooner than even my brother can predict. Our product, our black gold, touches every part of human life. It enables climate activists like our CEO to enjoy the freedoms that being the dominant species on our planet gives us. So, my friends, let's not now invest our hard-earned profits into stopping what we are doing, let's do the exact opposite, let's invest our profits into more oil, more of what the world needs. Let's educate the world into what we are doing for them. And for God's sake, let's keep the value of our barrels of oil between the eighty and hundred dollars it needs to be if we are to keep Adesco as one of the most profitable in the world."

With that, Tony sat back down.

The board members were stuck between the devil and the deep blue sea.

"Caroline will send you all the agreements to sign," Gavin said, addressing the table. "Thank you," he said, signalling that the board meeting was over.

After the room had emptied, he looked over at his brother who had not yet taken the hint to leave.

"They'll all sign it," Gavin said to him.

"Not all of them will."

"Maybe not all, but enough." He leant his arms on the table and fixed his brother with a stare. "When Dad left us the company, he did it so we could create a long-lasting legacy…"

"He did it so we could keep building his dream."

"And what was his dream then, Tony? Was it to see us add to climate change, and destroy the future for our children? Or was it to give back, to help the world, to not just focus on profit in the bank, but maybe to focus on the world around us? To give back to the planet rather than rape it…"

"Keep your sermons to yourself and the other fools around the table, Gav. I'll not let you ruin us in pursuit of some unnecessary and unproven dream to be the next messiah. I'll find a way to stop you, one way or another."

With that, Tony got up from the table and headed to the door.

"Next week is the AGM," Gavin reminded him. "I expect your support in front of the shareholders."

"You have my word," Tony said with a smile, pulling the door shut behind him.

Gavin sat back in his chair, ran his hands through his hair and let out a huge sigh. He pressed the button on the intercom set into the boardroom table and waited for Caroline, his executive PA to answer.

"Is the meeting finished?" she asked.

"Yes. Can you come in, please?"

Less than a minute later, Caroline was standing in front of him.

"I need you to send the amendment forms out to the entire board, including my brother, and tell them I expect them signed in agreement and returned to you within twenty-four hours."

"Did they all agree to it?" she asked.

"They will; maybe not Tony, or Uncle, but the rest will, if they know what's good for them." Even though the room was empty, and the door was closed, he lowered his voice to a whisper. "Is my other project still happening?"

"Yes," she said.

"And no one suspects anything, not even the man himself?"

"All he knows is that the money is getting to him, he doesn't know that you know anything."

"And our auditors?"

"Our little lady in the accounts department is actually doing a great job hiding it. If we hadn't set the whole thing in motion ourselves, there is no way we would have been able to spot it."

"Good," he said, relaxing back into his chair, "and let's keep it that way until he's ready, or we are ready first."

With that, Caroline left the room.

Gavin got up and walked over to the window, looking out over his beautiful South Africa.

"Not long now," he said to no one, "not long now."

CHAPTER 7

The annual general meeting of Adesco Oil was being held at the Wits Linder Auditorium in Parktown, Johannesburg, and all one thousand and sixty seats were occupied. Amos looked around the room at all the other shareholders, knowing that he was, in all likelihood, the only one there who owned no more than a single share in the company. In terms of value, it was almost irrelevant to him; however, it was enough to get him a seat in the room and be included on their regular annual shareholder emails, which was all he needed.

The board of directors filed in from behind the stage and took their places at the long table that had been set, with all the seats facing outwards towards their shareholders. The board was made up of twenty-one individuals, of which sixteen came from the founding family – aunties, uncles, cousins – who between them held overall control over the company. This meant that the remaining shareholders, even if they clubbed together, could not sway the vote if the family did not want to be swayed. That was not to say that they did not have a voice in how the company was run, as the head of the family wanted to ensure that everyone was listened to. Even the smallest of shareholders had the opportunity to present their views on company business. It was why at every AGM the entire board would be seated facing into the room whilst the CEO, Gavin Adriaanse, now the eldest of the family, would address all the minor shareholders as if they were equally as important as his main board. Directly next to Gavin, on his right-hand side, sat his brother Tony, younger by just eighteen months and his COO, the second-in-command.

The meeting started as always, dead on 6pm.

"Ladies and gentlemen, welcome to the seventy-fifth AGM of Adesco Oil."

Gavin got up from his chair and walked around to the front of the table, so that the audience didn't feel that there was a barrier between him and them.

The audience applauded him, as they always did.

When the room was once again quiet, he continued.

"Our grandfather…" he continued, turning around briefly to acknowledge Tony and his other family members, "came over from the Netherlands nearly a hundred years ago and started Adesco Oil with very little money, two younger brothers in toe and a helluva big dream. I cannot begin to imagine what he would think of the fact that his once small oil exploration business is now considered to be one of the largest, and certainly most profitable oil companies in Africa. Today, we not only own all of our own platforms and tankers, but we are drilling in almost every ocean on the planet. Our own fleet of tankers never stop moving, allowing us to distribute oil to every corner of the globe."

He paused to give the audience time to take in what he was saying.

"And now, in our seventy-fifth year, with the full support of my family, and you, my shareholders, we are about to deliver our greatest project yet, and what will undoubtably be the most dramatic shift in our business since the day my grandfather launched our first ever oil rig in the North Sea…"

He again paused for effect.

He looked around the room and could feel every eye on him.

"In one month from today, our newest, and the largest oil platform ever built in the entire world, Neptune, will be fully functional. But Neptune is far greater than just its size. It is the first ever oil platform that will be run entirely from the power generated in the ocean where it is anchored. Underneath the main platform, twenty feet below the surface, its turbines will be collecting the power from the movement of the sea, transferring it to Neptune's generators, providing us with one hundred percent free energy, running every part of the floating community that Neptune will house.

"With over five hundred personnel eventually living on site, our turbines will provide enough energy to power every part of their working and living life. And we will go further than that. All our transport boats, and even our helicopters, will be powered by the same free energy. And housed within Neptune, we will have the first ever energy university. Its purpose will be to educate and innovate on the power of the ocean. One day, perhaps even in my own lifetime, we will see Adesco no longer be the oil company that we are today. We know we have to change, we know that the planet needs us to stop producing fossil fuels, we have to find a way of repairing the damage we have done to our planet. We must move away from coal, gas and oil to free energy. Around 71% of the world is made up of water and our oceans hold around 96.5% of that. Can you imagine the energy that this creates? And who is better placed to solve this problem than us oil companies, the very people who have up until now been guilty of ignoring the power of the sea and have been a major cause of the effects of global warming. But we no longer have to be the cause of this devastation. We will use Neptune, and the Neptune Universities, which we will expand across all our platforms, to study the ocean's power and to one day be the provider of free energy for the world."

The audience responded with a thunderclap of applause.

Gavin struggled to raise his voice above the noise. He had to use his hands to direct the audience to quieten down.

"Were it not for the amount of investment our family make each year back into the exploration of sustainable energy, we would likely be the most profitable oil producer of them all. But with your continued blessing, and the support of my entire board, we will continue to reinvest our profits into solving the problem being forced onto future generations. No other company within our space hopes to one day be able to reduce fossil fuels to the bare minimum and replace it with free, clean energy for the world. No other company invests in the one area that could ultimately decimate their own industry, but we do it gladly and we do it with a clear conscience, and why do we do it? That is the question the financial markets ask of us almost on a daily basis. Why would we invest in the one thing that threatens our own income? And why do our own shareholders, and our investors, encourage us to do that? In fact, not only encourage us, but demand it of us? It is because, ladies and gentlemen, we believe the health of our planet is of greater importance than the health of our bank balance. The Adesco Oil company will one day achieve a carbon-free energy source, and we will deliver it free to the world. And we will bring our competitors with us, even if it means dragging them across the coals to do it."

The roar of approval rang around the theatre.

With a smile on his face, Gavin turned around to face his board, challenging them to stay seated if they dared. One by one, they reluctantly stood up and joined in the applause, encouraging the audience to join them on their feet.

The last person still seated at the table was his brother Tony.

Unlike Gavin, whose main mission was to ensure that the family business moved into the green space as soon as possible, Tony's plan was to continue drilling for oil and making Adesco the most profitable oil company in the region. In his mind, the planet would survive no matter what they extracted from it. Tony held the opposite opinion to his brother. He would argue relentlessly that the only reason oil deposits had even built up over the millennia was to be used to protect humans from the ravages of mother nature. Tony never bought into the fact that humans had created climate damage and he never would; as far as he was concerned, climate change was the planet's natural cycle and it was something that they could, and should benefit from.

Gavin turned back to the table and dared Tony to stay seated. The exchange between the brothers was clear to anyone who looked closely enough, but no one ever did. Tony slowly pulled himself up from his seat and joined in the applause, in the most unenthusiastic way he could, his eyes never leaving those of his brother.

As the clapping died down and people retook their seats, one man stayed standing. He spoke into a portable microphone that was attached to his lapel and had been missed by security when he was checked in. The software that connected the microphone to his mobile phone had been written by himself and was designed to automatically locate the speakers around the room, attaching itself to their signal and allowing him to talk to the entire room from where he stood.

"Mr Chairman." Amos walked forward as he spoke. "On behalf of all the people in the world, I want to thank you for trying to repair the damage caused by your industry."

"Who the fuck is that?" Tony said, walking around the table to Gavin. "Security!" He spoke into the microphone at the front of the stage. But Amos's software had blocked all the other units, giving him sole access to the speakers.

Amos continued talking as he neared the front of the stage. He could sense the security guards moving, so he needed to be quick.

"What you're doing with Neptune, attaching your turbines underneath it, is incredible, but you won't need even a fraction of the power you'll be storing. Think about this, what if you can transfer it immediately to portable batteries, batteries so small that you can transport them on your own tankers, each one capable of powering a small neighbourhood for a month."

When he reached the front of the stage, he placed his mobile phone down and started its projector application. Immediately, it sent a beam of light directly up onto the ceiling of the stage. Everyone, including Gavin and Tony, instinctively looked upwards.

"What is that?" Tony said to his brother.

"It's Neptune," Gavin replied, "from underneath the water. They are our turbos at the bottom."

The security guards reached Amos and grabbed his arms.

"Leave him!" Gavin called down to them.

"What the hell!" Tony said to his brother.

"Let him go," Gavin repeated. The security team took a step backwards.

"I call it Rising Tide," Amos continued speaking, as the adrenalin coursed through his body. He pressed another button on the phone, adding another layer to the bottom of the picture. "This is the missing piece of your puzzle," he said proudly. "My batteries, attached to the underside of your platform, running directly from your own turbines, storing all the energy that you will waste in my own battery packs, which once full can then be removed and replaced with new ones. You can then send these batteries around the world on your tanker. It's exactly why you are setting up your universities, to find a way to keep and share the energy, but I've already done it for you; this is the answer you have been looking for…"

Before Amos could say anything more, Tony marched to the front of the stage and stamped on the phone so hard that he smashed the cameras and ended the show.

"Security!" Tony bellowed to the men surrounding Amos. "Get him out of here."

Before Amos could react, his hands were fastened with zip ties, and he was being dragged out of the hall.

"I'm what you've been searching for!" he screamed at Gavin, but with his phone smashed, his voice no longer could be heard above the noise. By now, the shareholders had found their voices again and the noise in the room grew to such a crescendo that even Gavin couldn't break through to them.

As Amos was dragged back out of the hall, Gavin's head of security tried to bring order and calm back to the room.

"Was that stunt organised by you?" Tony said into his brother's ear aggressively.

"What?" Gavin replied, surprised by Tony's sudden anger.

"If you think I'm going to let you hijack our company AGM like that, you're fucking nuts!"

"Not in here, boys," Caroline, Gavin's PA, said to the brothers as she walked onto the stage from behind, "everyone is staring at you."

She signalled to the family to leave the stage and take Gavin and Tony with them, before taking the microphone herself.

"Ladies and gentlemen, our apologies for the disruption. Please take your seats and our board will be with you again shortly."

With that, she left the stage.

Backstage, she found Gavin and Tony shouting at each other whilst the rest of the family looked on. She went straight up to them to pull them apart.

"I'm Chairman and CEO of this company, not you, and I've got the shareholder approval I need…"

"Not for long, you haven't," Tony shot back at his brother.

"They want me to do this," Gavin continued shouting at his brother. "It's why they've invested in Adesco. It's what makes us stand out. They want us to find a better, cleaner source of energy. It's why they've backed me all this time, it's why they keep investing in me."

"Investing in us, not in you!" Tony shouted back. "Investing in a profitable oil company, not in the madness of its CEO, but not for much longer, money talks, brother. So, tell me, when was the last time we paid a dividend? What was it, three years ago?"

"I've shown you the numbers, they work. And we can be

so much more than just money," Gavin said, trying to calm the situation down. "Yes, our profits are taking a hit right now, I get that, but we have to do something. We are killing our planet, there'll be nothing left if we carry on like this."

"Too right there will be nothing left. Nothing left of the business our family has built up for years. You're going to tear it all down with your absurd project, and I for one will not just sit here and let you do it."

With that, Tony pushed Gavin back into the wall and stormed out.

Caroline stepped forward, taking his place.

"You've got to get back out there," she said, as her team started to move the other board members back onto the stage.

"I'm still CEO and I still have the majority vote," he said to her. "Tony can say whatever he wants, but he'll not remove me from this job. Deep down, the family and the shareholders know I'm right, even if that arsehole doesn't believe it."

"I'm not sure the family are all behind you," she said to her boss, hoping she was not overstepping her position.

"What do you mean?" he asked her.

"It's just that, well, I've heard talk that Tony has been speaking to them all, separately. He's been showing them what you've been spending on this."

"They know I'm doing it for the good of the planet, and for the reputation of our company."

"I know, and I get it," she said, trying to keep him calm. "But the talk about dividends not being paid for another year is starting to spread."

"Fuck them all!" he replied. "This is my company, not theirs. And I'll run it however I fucking want," he said to her as he marched around the curtain.

"Do you want me to contact him?" Caroline asked, following him onto the stage

"What the hell was he thinking doing that here?" Gavin said angrily, desperate to shout at Amos, but knowing he had to keep his own position in the matter secret.

"He still doesn't know it's you, does he? So, he's still trying to get your attention."

"Well, he's now got Tony's attention as well."

"What do you want me to do?"

"I think it's time I had his plans for myself."

"I'm on it," she replied.

CHAPTER 8

Today was the twins first set of tests since they'd started sixth form. The tests themselves were not overly important, as they were really just to see if the sixth formers were ready to step up to the next level of learning, but Kiara had still been nervous for them as they had been away from education for longer than all their friends and they had found it hard getting back into the routine of school.

She was not entirely sure that they had been ready to get back and see everyone, but this was the start of their A levels, the most important time they had ever faced in education and what they had been working towards for the last eleven years. Any more time off would have meant them being put back a year, which she would have hated for them. Also, it would have meant an extra year of college fees for her to find, which would be a struggle that she could do without.

As usual, both Mia and Jasmin met the challenge head on. They walked through the college entrance as if they had not even had a day off, let alone a number of months, and she watched as their friends surrounded them once again. She was so proud of them. *Asher would have cried seeing how strong they are,* she thought to herself as she drove away.

Once she got home, she went straight to her office and turned on the computer, desperate to do something that would take her mind off the empty house. She was relieved, and slightly nervous, to see an email from Tyrone waiting in her email inbox. When she had told him she couldn't take the job, she'd thought that would have been the end of it.

The email was short but included a number of attachments. It read:

Kiara, if you really can't come over, I will understand, but in the hope that you may have a last-minute change of heart, I have booked you some flights. I've also attached some of the claim files, just to see if I can pique your interest. Sorry to be pushy, but I really hope you will change your mind. Tyrone

She opened the first attachment and was greeted with tickets for return flights to South Africa. He had bought her business-class flights with British Airways from London Heathrow to O'Tambo Airport in Johannesburg, along with confirmation of a suite at the Saxon Hotel near Rose Bank; the best hotel in the area. She opened a link to the hotel and saw that it boasted to being the hotel where the late Nelson Mandela stayed when he was visiting the city.

He was certainly doing his best to get her to take the job on.

She looked at the dates on the tickets; they were for three days' time. She sat back and wondered if she really could do this. She knew her in-laws would support her, they always did. And the girls might moan, but they would get over it quickly enough. But just three days from now would mean she'd have a lot to do in a very short time, from clearing the jobs she was already working on to getting a list together for her in-laws, so that they knew where Mia and Jasmin needed to be every day. Both girls had extra sport and art as part of their college days, and it was a job in itself working out the pickups and drop offs. *The day the girls get their driving licences will be a game changer for everyone,* she thought.

Her in-laws wouldn't bat an eyelid, of course, but since Asher's death, they really had aged so much and she worried this would be a bit too much for them.

Maybe I'm the problem and not them, she thought to herself. *Perhaps it's me who has aged more than anyone.* She decided she'd see what the claim files Tyrone had sent her looked like before she called them up, just so she could be sure that she really wanted to take him up on his offer. There was no point getting them to agree to move in before she even knew she would be going.

She closed down the file with the flight tickets and clicked on the first claim. Her mobile phone rang before she'd had a chance to read anything.

"Hey Nick," she said.

Nick was one of Kiara's oldest friends and had been her biggest support since she lost Asher. They had met about twenty years ago at university where both of them were studying law before she moved into the insurance industry. They had stayed close friends ever since.

"Did Tyrone call you yet?" Nick asked.

"Yes. He called me yesterday."

"And?"

"Well, the money he offered me was insane for a few days' work, but I'm not sure I can take it, to be honest. I really want to, but it means leaving the girls, which I'm not sure I can do. So, I told him I couldn't do it."

"The girls will be fine. You underestimate them, they are tougher than you think they are, especially Mia, she's a mini you. In fact, I would suggest that perhaps it's you clinging to them now more than they are to you. You need to give them a bit of space to get used to being just three of you now instead of four, and it was only last week you told me you couldn't face working on any more of those little claims you keep being sent. You said you needed something you could get your teeth stuck into, and I promise you, Tyrone's work will definitely keep you occupied for a few days."

"You could be right," she conceded. "And it's certainly the sort of challenge I was looking for."

As usual, Nick had read the situation perfectly.

"Will you reconsider TR's offer?"

"Well, he's making it rather difficult for me to say no. He's already sent me some claim files to look over, and he's already booked me flights and a hotel!"

"Really? It's not like TR to be so bold, usually he's much more subtle than that, he must really need you if he's done that."

"How long have you known him?"

"Since school."

"But you've never lived in South Africa, have you?"

"No, I haven't, and in fact, I've never even been over there, though I keep meaning to visit him. We met over here in primary school. His mum's English and she married a South African guy, so Tye was born here, and we went to school together. I was the youngest in the year and always the small kid, and he kind of became my unofficial bouncer. I was really mouthy back then, I bet that's hard to imagine," he said with a laugh, "… and without him I probably would have taken a pasting every day. Why he stuck by me, I have no idea, but he did. Then, when we were about sixteen, his parents moved back to Africa, and he went with them. He ended up working with his dad in the insurance business before taking it over in his thirties. It's a decent sized business, makes a lot of money, so I was surprised when he called me a few weeks ago and told me he was in trouble."

"So, you told him to call me?"

"Too right I did. It all sounded a bit off to me. He's been so caught up in building the business that he took his eye off the ball on what was happening internally. Classic, really, the dad starts the business, and the son spends so much time building it that he loses it. I hope you can help him stop that happening."

"Do you have any feel on who's doing this to him?"

"I think it could be someone in his company. I tried to tell him, but he wouldn't listen. So, I said he needed to take a bit of a step back and let you take a look for him. I've never heard him this worried before, he usually has a handle on everything, but this time I think he's in over his head. He really could do with your brain on this. You'd be doing me a favour if you took the job. I wouldn't ask you if I didn't think you'd be able to help him."

"But what do I know about the oil industry?"

"Fair point, but you do know about insurance, don't you? And you certainly know about fraud. What does it matter whether it's life insurance, car insurance or marine insurance? Fraud is fraud, isn't it?"

Kiara thought about what he was saying. Of course, he was absolutely right. She might not understand the product, but she certainly recognised a criminal when she came across one. She'd met enough of them over the years and, whilst they came in all shapes and sizes, they had one thing in common, they all eventually got cocky and made mistakes.

"I guess you're right," she admitted.

"Of course I am. Take the job. You'll love working with him. I mean, he's going to drive you crazy and not let up until you solve the problem, but you'll earn a good wage, you'll get to use your brain again, and it might just open you up to a whole new market."

"I guess so. But I do still need to check the files he sent me first."

"Well, I wouldn't take too long to decide. He needs someone now and currently you're the only one he's talking to. If you do go to see him then Jen and I don't mind the girls moving in with us for a few days."

"Thanks, that's amazing, but, as you say, I need to stop treating them like kids, they are almost seventeen, so they can take themselves to college each day. I think I'll ask my in-laws to move in, though, as the girls would love to have them around and I think it'll do Peter and Judy good to be here with something to keep them occupied for a few days."

"How are they doing?"

"Not so great. They'll be okay, though, we all will, I guess."

"Asher would be super proud at how you're coping."

"Thanks."

"You know where I am if you need me," he said before hanging up.

"Thanks," she said back, already knowing what she was going to do next.

When the call ended, she pulled up Tyrone's email again. With barely a hesitation, she hit reply, thanked him for the tickets and told him she'd take the job and would see him in a few days' time.

I probably should have read the files first before sending that, she thought to herself.

But Nick was right. Whatever or whoever was doing this, it was just another criminal, and the rest was just detail to her, and she really could do with a big payday right about now as the life insurance she'd received a few months back had all but gone on buying the new house; what was left wasn't going to last that much longer.

CHAPTER 9

Hamilton stood alone on the sandy beach and looked up at the house, pondering on how the universe chose who got to live where. Whilst he languished each night in the slums of a South African township, Amos was surrounded by the beauty of both the ocean and the mountains. Whilst he had to sleep amongst the poor and the forgotten with no electricity, barely any running water and with one eye always open, Amos got to sleep in silk sheets with the sound of the waves sending him into a slumber with the protection of Table Mountain over his shoulder.

If life was a lottery, then he had drawn an unwinning set of numbers.

He looked around the beach at the people now spreading out their rugs and picnic blankets and envied them their simple lives. He never wanted to be the devil he had turned into, but he had had no choice, survival had demanded it of him.

He had been born the youngest of nine children, all boys, and all of them left to fend for themselves from an early age. Their mother, the only person who had cared for them, had been killed in a fire that had ravaged the illegal township that they lived in. Their father had run away that very same night, leaving them all to die with her, unable to care for himself, let alone look after a family. Hamilton had only been three at the time of the fire and had to rely on his brothers to survive. The boys managed to carve out a small corner for themselves in the township that sprung up next to the fire ravaged one that had been their home. The new area drew people in quickly and, over the next five years, it grew to become the largest illegal township in Cape Town. It covered over eighteen square miles and housed over a million people, every one of them living day to day without clean water or reliable electricity. The locals named it New Home, but to Hamilton it could never be a home. Whilst his brothers seemed content to live hand to mouth, he kept his own eyes firmly to the southeast, to the forty kilometres that separated them from the city of Cape Town, to the better life that could be his if he was brave enough to take it.

As soon as he was old enough, he forged a name for himself with the various gangs who ruled the area. His regular trips to the city of Cape Town, especially to the tourist trap that was the Waterfront, became the stuff of legend in the township. He would often return after a three or four-day absence in a stolen bakkie filled with enough food and medicines to care for hundreds of people. But he would only share his spoils with the gang leaders, the people who he knew could one day help him leave that place. Leaving the township and enjoying life in Cape Town was his one and only focus in life.

"We need to go," Zara said, walking up to him and bringing him back from his dark thoughts.

"Hi, guys," Karly said, joining them both on the beach, along with Dan.

"Look at this place," Hamilton sneered to the three of them.

"It's beautiful, isn't it?" Karly replied, gazing up at the majestic Table Mountain behind them. "We must be living in the most beautiful country in the entire world."

"It's disgusting!" Hamilton said with anger in his voice.

"What is?" Karly said, turning to him, surprised.

"All this," he said, gesturing to the houses around them and the scores of people descending on the beach. "I have to sleep in a metal tent each night, whilst these people get to live in palaces."

"I'll treat you to an ice cream if that will cheer you up," Zara replied with a laugh.

He turned on her quickly, all but ready to put his hands around her skinny neck.

"Hamilton," Dan spoke to the bigger man. "Not with all these people around."

"If you disrespect me again…" he growled at Zara.

"Ooh, I do love it when you get all masculine," Zara said, with a seductive look, edging one step closer to him.

"Stop it, Zara," Dan said, moving between them. "She doesn't mean it. She just gets a kick out of seeing how far she can push you." He threw Zara a look to make it clear that this was not the time to wind the man up. Zara responded to Dan with a smile and a shrug.

"She should be careful what she says to me."

"What the fuck's going on?" Rene interrupted them, having just come down to the beach to join them.

By now, the beach was starting to get busy with the morning swimmers. Today was also the annual 'swim and picnic in the bay' put on by the Polar Bear swimming club and crowds of people were suddenly streaming down the narrow path from the main road, filling up every available area of the small bay.

"It's Zara," Dan said to him privately, whilst giving her a sideways look. "We need Hamilton and his men more than we need her; she needs to understand that."

"I was only playing with him," Zara said, having heard what he said. She walked around to Rene and linked her arm into his as Hamilton stomped off down to the water's edge. "I'll be nice from now on, I promise," she said back to Dan, flashing him one of her beautiful smiles.

"I've no time for this shit today," Rene responded to Zara, pulling his arm out of hers. "We've work to do."

"You shouldn't say those things," Karly said, walking up to

Zara. "Hamilton wasn't born into a rich family like you were."

"Oh, the poor love," Zara shot back.

"You've never even been to the townships before, you have no idea what it's like living there."

"Oh please…" Zara said, turning her back on the other lady.

"Enough, all of you!" Rene shouted at them, drawing the attention of the swimming club who had started to lay their beach blankets in big circles to claim the public space as their own.

He turned to Zara and gave her a look that told her to stop causing trouble. She returned his look with a simple shrug.

He walked up to Dan, taking his arm and drawing him away from the others.

"I don't like this," Rene said to Dan. "You said you had Hamilton under control. It doesn't look that way to me."

""You can never full control a man like that, all you can do is try to limit any damage. But he needs our money if he's ever going to break away from the township. So, he will do whatever he has to do to help us."

"How reliable are his men?"

"They'll do what he tells them to do. He controls all the gangs in the area. He can bring us as many men as we need. But if Zara keeps pushing him like that, he's likely to snap her neck in two and I'm not sure any amount of money would stop him."

"I'll speak to her."

"She's a bloody sociopath," Dan said, whilst looking over to her as she started to walk amongst the swimming club members, making a nuisance of herself. "And she doesn't give a damn about our cause."

"She's the best computer hacker there is in the whole of Cape Town," Rene shot back at him. "Without her, we can't access the servers of either Worldwide Insurance or Adesco Oil, and we'll have no way of moving our money around. So, right now, she's as important to us as he and his men are."

With that, they turned and walked back to the two girls, just as Hamilton had rejoined them.

"So, what's the plan?" Zara asked him.

"It's time to let Amos in on the bigger picture. He needs to know what we are actually planning if we are going to get this to the next step. The next payment we've arranged is bigger than he will ever have seen, and we need to know he'll not try to keep it."

"He's not going to be happy when he realises that we've been using his little charity for our own purposes," Zara said, laughing. "This is going to be a fun meeting, I can already feel it."

"What if he threatens to go to the police?" Dan asked Rene.

"He won't," Hamilton replied threateningly.

"He won't tell anyone," Dan said, agreeing with Hamilton. "We'll let him believe that we're still supporting his plans as well, so all sides win, and he'll have no reason to turn against us."

"And I'll make sure he understands that he is in too deep with us now, so he's got no choice but to keep quiet, or else he'll be going to prison for the rest of his life, and that is only if Hamilton hasn't got to him first," Rene said.

"But what if he really doesn't want to go along with us?" Karly asked nervously. "You know he's against any form of violence, I just don't see him agreeing to this."

Rene turned on her. "We don't need his agreement, we just need access to his charity, and his bank account."

"You promised you wouldn't hurt him," Karly replied, having heard the malice in Rene's voice.

"You knew from the start what we needed from him and what the consequences would be if he tried to stop us."

"He's a good man, Rene, and he's trying to do the same thing we are, just make the world a better place."

"And he thinks he can make a change just by talking."

"He's not just talking, though, is he. His invention will work if we just give it a chance."

"Don't be so naïve, Karly. His invention, just like his words, will change nothing. Thousands before him thought they could make the difference by doing good deeds, but at the end of the day, it's just words and platitudes."

"And you really believe that our way will be different?"

"The only way long-lasting change has ever come about is through direct action, and revolution. This whole country only changed because we had individuals who were prepared to put their lives on the line to make it happen. The planet is dying and all we are doing is watching it happen and hoping people like Amos will one day save us. All anyone does these days is talk about it, no one is prepared to take real action. Do you really think big businesses are going to stop throwing shit into the atmosphere just because we tell them to? Do you think the oil producers will stop drilling in our oceans? The only way to stop them is to take them down, to bring the bastards to their knees. And that is what we are going to do. And don't forget, that is exactly why you joined us, and you are now as much a part of this revolution as the rest of us."

CHAPTER 10

The bell rang through the house at almost exactly the moment Amos had been told to expect them. He went to the door, ready to welcome just the three of them and was surprised to see two other men standing there as well. Both were huge compared to him, they stood well over six feet tall, and both looked as solid as the walls that held up his house.

Rene pushed past him and walked into the hallway, with the two men and Zara following closely behind him. Only Karly stood back for a moment and waited until Amos stood to the side and nodded, welcoming her into his home.

"Who are they?" he whispered to Karly, keeping an eye on the two strangers as they went up the stairs heading to his office.

She knew he would find out soon enough, so she decided there was no harm in preparing him. "The white guy is Dan, he's Rene's partner in all this; he's the muscle where Rene is the brains."

"And the other one?"

"That's Hamilton," she said with no further explanation.

Like most native South Africans, Amos had heard stories about a gang leader from the township by that name.

"Is he the same one…"

"Yes," said Karly before Amos could finish the question.

Amos went pale.

"Are you joining us?" Rene shouted down the stairs, making it clear this was not merely a suggestion.

Karly led the way up the short flight of stairs to the small office above Amos's garage.

With all of them there, the office looked tiny and, whilst Karly waited in the open doorway, Amos had to squeeze past the two big men to reach his chair.

He tried to keep his eyes from meeting those of the gang leader; instead, they fell on Rene's girlfriend, Zara, who returned his stare with a look that radiated both malice and humour. Despite her being a fraction of the mass that Hamilton was, she was still as intimidating as him, perhaps even more so. There was something so unpredictable about her that Amos felt unable to hold her gaze for more than a couple of seconds. He turned his head a final time, stopping on Karly.

She was another matter altogether. To him, she was like an angel in a room full of devils.

He gave her a nervous smile as the meeting began.

"I know you called this meeting," Amos said, addressing Rene. "But, before you start, I have something to tell you first. It really feels like it has moved our plans on."

Rene nodded, letting the other man continue.

"Since you started working for me, things have really pushed forward. I don't know how you've been able to raise so much money so quickly, but it's been amazing."

"And you've never thought to ask us how we've done that?" Zara cut in. "We've brought in millions of rand for a project that no one cares about. And you don't think that's odd?"

"Zara," Rene said to her sternly.

"What?" she shot back. "Is he really that stupid?"

"Carry on, Amos, tell us your news," Rene continued.

Amos looked over at Karly for support. She smiled and gently nodded, giving him the encouragement to carry on.

"As I told you, my focus over the last few years, apart from my invention, of course, has been to get a meeting with the board of

Adesco Oil, to get them onboard with my plans. Being the only oil company in the world who are finally doing something about the damage their industry is causing to the planet, they are the perfect partner for me. But up until now, I have found it impossible to talk to them at any senior level."

He turned to face Rene.

"Because of your help, I have now been able to complete and test my first battery, and because of you, I am able to now demonstrate to them exactly what we can do. I have no words to thank you for your belief in me."

Rene looked back at him with the same bored expression that he had had when he invited him to start talking.

Amos looked around the room, trying to catch everyone else's eyes, making sure he was getting their attention.

"I went to their AGM at the weekend to show them what I've been building and how it can fit into their new oil platform. I took along my own wi-fi breaker, something I had designed specifically to pick up the frequency of their own sound system and was able to take control of the entire meeting. I put on a show that they will not forget in a hurry," he said proudly.

"And that's your big news? Well done you," Rene said sarcastically.

"I don't think you understand the significance of this. They not only saw me, but they actually had no choice but to listen to me. I was able to show them how my batteries fit in with their new plans and how together we can start to really collect and share the energy from the sea. I could see it in the CEO's face, he was desperate to know more."

"And?"

"What do you mean 'and'?! I've been working on this my entire life and now, at last, I've got their attention. I just thought you'd want to know that all your hard work has not been for nothing."

Hamilton banged his hand on the table and stood up, towering over them all.

"Enough of this!" he shouted. "We're here to talk about your plans, and my money, not this rubbish!" he directed his anger at Rene.

Amos sat back in his chair, stunned at how quickly the man had suddenly changed the tone of the meeting.

Dan stood up as well, putting his hand on Hamilton's arm.

"Not now," Dan whispered to him.

Hamilton looked down at Dan's hand on his arm, causing Dan to withdraw it immediately. They stood a moment longer, before both sitting back down.

"I don't understand," Amos said to the big man. "And I don't even know why you are here, you have no involvement in my charity. Rene, what is this about?"

"We have one thing in common, Amos, we both want the oil industry to stop the damage it's causing to our planet. But we want to do it in different ways," Rene said.

"What do you mean?" Amos replied, the worry in his voice palpable for everyone to pick up on.

"How much did this little demonstration cost us?" Rene asked, without answering Amos's question.

"I don't know exactly, but what does it matter?" Amos stuttered. "I had to finish the prototype and then create the film I showed them, and work out how to break into their sound system…"

"How much?" Rene snapped.

"About three million rand," Amos said, feeling embarrassed saying it out loud.

Zara couldn't help herself laugh again, whilst Hamilton was ready to tear the man's head off his shoulders.

"You spent three million rand just to get their attention?!" Rene screamed at him.

"And to finish my prototype!" The frustration and confusion was clear in Amos's voice.

"I think it's time we told him the truth," Zara said to Rene, a childish grin etched on her face.

"What truth? What are you talking about?" Amos said, turning to her, before moving his attention back to Rene. "What don't I know?"

"Why do we need to do this today?" Karly asked, trying to keep herself from looking directly at Amos.

"Because now we are almost ready to move to the final steps and everyone, including him, needs to be ready. The next payment has to be completed, and we are going to need his direct cooperation. His bank will need his authorisation for the transfer, and only he can do that. So, it's time he knew where the money is actually going."

"What are you talking about?" Amos asked once again in frustration.

"Tell him," Dan said to Rene.

"We are going to wait until Adesco deliver their new oil platform, Neptune, and as the world's press are watching, we are going to bring it crashing down into the sea. Then we are going to bring the entire oil industry to its knees. And it all starts with your friends at Adesco Oil."

Amos went quiet, trying to take in the news as Rene carried on explaining.

"And you are going to help us move the final money over, so we can pay Hamilton's men for what they need to do, and we can pay Dan for the last set of explosives that need to be delivered to site."

"How could you do this to me?" Amos said, looking at Karly.

She looked at him sadly. "I didn't want you to know," was all she could think of saying.

"You didn't want me to know?! You've hijacked my charity with the intention of destroying the same industry I am trying to change; how many people will you kill in the process? God only knows, and you didn't want to tell me?!" he screamed at her as if the entire plan had been hers all along. "And you're starting with the one company who are actually trying to make a difference, how could you do this?!" he screamed, directing all his anger at the one person in the room he actually cared about, the only person in the world he would have risked his own life for.

"Don't be so naïve," Rene said, drawing Amos's attention back to him. "They have no intention of stopping what they do, and they will never put your invention into their plans. They talk about using renewable energy to run their platform as some way of saving the planet, when all they are doing it for is to save themselves millions of dollars in running costs. Money that they will use to pay their shareholders more dividends, and more money to spend on building even more of their platforms."

"You're wrong!" Amos shouted back. "Their CEO is not like the rest of his family. He is a visionary. He has seen what their industry has been doing, ruining our oceans and destroying the planet and he is going to change all that. Neptune is going to be the first of his platforms to go fully green and one day all the other companies will follow, they have no choice, and it's all because of him. The man is trying to save the planet, not destroy it."

Rene turned from Amos, ignoring his pleas, and spoke directly to Dan.

"Where are we with the explosives?"

"Explosives?" Amos said, alarmed at where the conversation was now going.

"They have already started to be delivered to the site," Dan said. "We have over twenty barrels already in place, but we need the rest of the money now if we are going to deliver the final ones, the ones that will bring it crashing down."

"Good. And your men?" Rene said, turning to Hamilton.

"Don't you think this conversation is perhaps for another time?" Karly cut in.

Rene turned to her. "It's time Amos knew it all," he said, looking from Karly to Amos.

"Hamilton," Rene continued, "an update on your men, please."

"My men are always ready. But I can't send them to the site until we pay them. I told you that from day one. Without the cash, they won't do anything, not even if I tell them to."

"I thought you were in charge," Rene said to him.

"You can't be in charge of men like that. We pay them or they will walk away, and then you embarrass me, and that will not end well for any of you."

"Karly, an update on the money please," Rene said, looking to Hamilton's left, and ignoring the threat that had just been levelled at him.

"The insurance money came in on all the claims as predicted. They were all paid to Adesco by the insurance company and then I managed to cover my tracks before sending them from the Adesco account into Amos's charity account, before Zara then transferred them from there straight to Hamilton."

"And no one at Adesco queried it?" Rene said, relieved, but also astonished.

Karly picked up on his meaning.

"After I made the first payments, I expected them to be flagged up by the CEO. But nothing was said. I had an explanation ready, that we had suffered some leakage in the tankers, but I was never asked. Then I was sure that Gavin would spot the payments when I gave him the end of month accounts. All he seemed to do was to go straight to the bottom lines, and of course, nothing had changed on them, all the columns still balanced. So, he just signed them off."

"And no one else but him sees them?" Rene asked.

"Only Caroline, his assistant. She collects a hard copy from me and takes them to his brother Tony as he doesn't trust computer files. But she has stopped coming for them since we started this. I have no idea why, it's so unlike her. I didn't want to cause any suspicion, so I just never asked her."

"So, it seems I was right, then. They are so fixated on building their new platform that they have totally taken their eyes off the ball on their day-to-day business."

"I guess you were," she replied, bringing a smile to Rene's lips for the first time since the meeting had started.

"Did you send the funds Dan needed for the explosives?" he said, turning to Zara.

"Yes, that's the easy bit. Once Karly sent the money to the charity account it was simply a case of getting Amos to agree the transfer."

"But I never agreed any transfers," Amos said.

"You certainly did," Zara replied. "You just didn't know. I now have full control over your accounts, I don't need your help to move money around."

"I never gave you any control over my charity accounts."

"Of course you did, sweetheart, you just never knew," Zara said, giving him a wink.

"How could you let them do this to me?" Amos said to Karly.

"Amos, my darling, there isn't a bank account in the world I can't hack into. Your little charity one was so very easy," Zara said to him, a smile sitting on her very beautiful face.

"So, why do you need me now if you have everything you need?" he said, throwing up a challenge to her.

"Because, unfortunately, only you can make larger payments, even I can't do that. If I could, then we'd have no need for you anymore."

"Zara," Rene said to her. Then, turning to Amos, said, "We need your charity, but we never had plans to hurt you, we are not murderers."

"But people will die if you blow up the new platform, won't they?" Amos challenged him.

"Yes, they will, but only Adesco people, and we can't help that, there is always collateral damage. But we are not murderers," he said again, more to convince himself than anyone else.

"You only sent me half the money you promised me," Hamilton spoke up, bringing the conversation back to where he needed it to be.

"Me as well, and I need the rest of mine urgently," Dan joined in. "The bombs we currently have will be enough to disrupt them, but they won't be enough to completely sink them. I need the rest in place before the platform is opened for business. At the moment, they have hardly any security stationed there at all, so Hamilton's men will outnumber them by three to one if we do it now, but once they make the platform live, the onsite security ramps up and it will be impossible for us to do this. And, if you want to limit the people who are hurt, then we can't wait any longer, so it's literally now or never."

"Why have we only paid over half the money?" Rene turned once again to Karly. "I told you we needed it all transferred over."

"It's the last claim; it's been held up at the insurance company. But it will come through, it's just been delayed," she replied.

"Is there a problem I need to know about?" Rene asked her.

"Not a problem, just a delay. A claim this size was always going to be looked at more closely than the others. I told you from the start that small claims will be easy, the boss just lets his team sign them off. But as soon as you started to double the numbers, he was always going to be alerted to it. That was always a risk, I told you that at the start."

"But it will be paid, you're certain about that…?" Rene said, trying to keep the worry from his voice.

"It will definitely be paid," she replied, "I promise you."

"Good," he said, giving both Hamilton and Dan a nod of satisfaction.

He then turned his attention back to Amos.

"So, let's be clear, shall we? We needed a private little charity to move our money around without being challenged by the authorities and yours was the perfect fit."

"But why mine?" Amos said in despair.

"Because you are small enough to go unnoticed, and with the amounts we are moving around, we can't risk the authorities looking into us. Also, you work against climate change, and that is not something the banks want to disrupt, especially not at the moment with all the disasters the world is experiencing, so yours was, and still is, the perfect fit."

"Well now you've told me, there's no way I can let it go on, is there?"

"And what do you think you can do to stop us?"

"I can go to the police and tell them everything."

"But our names don't appear anywhere. So, if you do that then the only name they will find will be yours. Zara can be very creative with what is seen. There's absolutely no proof of anything, other than perhaps you laundering money. So, do you really want to risk going to prison for money laundering, which is a major crime by the way, and will mean years in prison? And then, not only will you spend the rest of your life rotting in a cell somewhere, but your batteries will never see the light of day. Or you can keep your mouth shut and we'll leave some of the cash back so you can finish your own plans and find another company to partner with. If they work as you keep telling us they do, then someone else will be able to use them and you can go on saving the world in your little way."

"Please," Amos begged him, "don't do it. My batteries work, I've tested them, you know that. No one needs to get hurt for us to do this. I just needed your help to build my models, that's all I ever asked you to do, and they work, I promise you, and after the AGM, I've even got Adesco ready to listen to me. We can make a real, positive change, together, all of us." He looked around the room, trying to bring everyone on side. "Why destroy things when we can make them better? This is our one chance to help the world, and no one needs to be hurt, or be killed…"

Rene hit the table with both his palms before Amos could

finish his plea. "Whilst you continue down the road of trying to turn water into wine, the planet continues to die. You can play inventor all you like, but the war has now started, my friend, and like it or not, you are right in the fucking middle of it."

With that, the five of them got up and left, with only Karly turning back at the door. "I'll catch you up in a minute," she said to the others as they left, before closing the door and walking back to Amos.

"I can't let them do this," Amos said to Karly as soon as she walked back to him.

"Please don't do anything stupid, Amos."

"I can't just turn the other way whilst they do this."

"You can, and you must. They are dangerous people, you can see that. If you do anything silly, I can't protect you."

"I might have been taken in by them, blinded by their promises of the money, but you've known all along who they are. How could you get tied up with people like this?"

"They might have a different way of approaching the problem, but deep down, they are just like you and me. All they want to do is save the planet from the destruction caused by the oil companies, and maybe they are just brave enough to do it."

"They are going to kill people, Karly. You heard them, they'll do anything to get their own way, and that Hamilton, you can't convince me he gives a damn about the planet or the oil companies."

"No, he doesn't, you're right. But they need him and his men, and they will pay him, and that's all he's there for. But Rene is different, he spent years fighting to keep the planet safe. He did what all the others out there in the world are doing, he's been on marches, he's stood for hours on end in the rain trying to be heard above the noise, he's given up his life to save the planet and stop climate change. And all he has ever had for his troubles are arrests, abuse and prison time. Nothing has changed, has it? So, now he's taking real action. He's putting his own life on the line to save us all, to save everyone."

"And he's willing to murder to do it."

"Whatever he says, he is not going to kill anyone. He's so passionate about this that he'll say anything he has to say to get the attention he needs. But he's not going to kill anyone, he just couldn't do that."

"You heard everything I heard. And you're being naïve if you really believe that."

"You need to trust me, Amos. Please. Just don't tell anyone, okay? Please, trust me."

"Of course I trust you. You know how I feel about you."

Karly stepped forward and kissed him on the lips.

"I know. I feel the same. I won't let them do anything to you, or the charity," she said, having stepped back and opened the door again. "I'll make sure no one gets hurt."

She closed the door behind her, leaving Amos all alone with his thoughts, wondering, and totally unconvinced that Karly had any more sway with the others than he did.

CHAPTER 11

The doorbell rang for the second time before he got up to answer it. Gavin had been waiting for Tony to arrive and was ready at the first ring, but it took all his energy to get up from his chair in the lounge and walk the ten metres to the front door.

Every month, the brothers would meet at Gavin's house, just the two of them, to discuss the family business. It was something that their father had insisted upon when he stepped down from the business just a few weeks before his death. He knew his sons had completely different ideas on how Adesco would run without him at the helm, and whilst he could not manage them from the grave, he was damn sure he would do what he could before he died to keep the family business, and his legacy, alive. He had toyed long and hard with who to leave in charge, as there had to be one ultimate CEO, as no business can be effective with a split leader, but equally, he wanted both his boys to have a say in how things would be done. The decision to appoint Gavin to the lead role was in the end one of age over ability. He knew that both of them were capable of taking the helm. Gavin, whilst spending less time in the firm, was well travelled, and because of that understood world politics and had a feel for the changes that they would need to make if they were to survive another hundred years. He did worry about Gavin's obsession with the environment and the damage that fossil fuels were doing to the planet, but he also saw that as a strength, as their core business was based on a substance that had a shelf life. At some point, Adesco would have to find something more sustainable than oil exploration if it were to survive, and Gavin was by far the most knowledgeable in that field. The downside to making him CEO, though, was obvious. His travels around the globe had brought him into contact with some of the most fervent climate activists and scientists in the world, and his focus had become so much about climate change that there was a danger he would sacrifice the company in his pursuit of climate perfection.

Tony, on the other hand, was in some ways the perfect CEO for an oil company. He had no desire to travel the world, South Africa was more than enough for him. And oil ran through his veins like blood. The smell of it, the feel of it, and the opportunities it gave him were everything he ever needed. Unlike Gavin, who was married with four teenage children and spent his life worrying about the future he was leaving them, Tony was fully focused on the family name and the power that true wealth delivered. Just like he had been, his own two sons were being groomed to one day take over the family business, and just like him, they believed that climate change was a natural phenomenon and had nothing to do with the business they were in. The threat he saw for this own family came from his brother and not the oil under the ocean floor. But Tony's complete and utter dismissal of climate change worried their father more than Gavin's desire to solve the problem did. For Adesco to survive, they had to believe that there was a problem and that they were part of it. It was imperative that they adapted to the new world; if they stayed in their own bubble and shut the world out, then their days were surely numbered.

So, the choice their father had was, in some respects, one of the devil or the deep blue sea. So, finally, he went old school on his decision and made Gavin CEO due to him being the oldest, but made Tony his COO, the second-in-command. And he did that with one condition, that every month they meet up, just the two of them, and work through any problems that they have, always balancing the needs of the company with the needs of the planet in equal measure. It was their father's dying wish that his sons find a way of working together to preserve all the family had built and this was his only workable solution. It was, of course, an unworkable solution, but it was all he had.

Tony knocked on the door as hard as he could, knowing that whilst the bell had worked, his brother was ignoring it and making him wait. Eventually, he was let in.

"Morning, brother," Tony said, pushing Gavin out of the way and heading to the lounge. "Still playing these silly power games, are we?" he said, as he stopped by the drinks bar and poured himself a large bourbon.

"No games, brother. I just needed to compose myself before we started our usual dance."

"Drink?" Tony offered him.

"Sure, it might take the edge off."

Gavin sat back into his favourite leather armchair and took the glass his brother offered him.

"If all we are going to do is sit here and insult each other, then surely it's about time we ended this charade and called a halt to these get-togethers."

"It was what Dad wanted," Gavin said.

"It's been almost ten years since he died, I'm sure he never expected us to last this long."

"All the time I'm CEO we'll respect his wishes."

"Then it's time I took over."

"Not happening, brother."

"Go on then, let's get this done. Tell me all about your plans for the new platform, then I'll tell you how I won't support them, and we can cut to the chase and let the board decide."

"And they'll follow me as they always do."

"Maybe, brother, maybe, but not forever. At some point, they will understand what your plans are costing us and then, hopefully before you've done too much damage, they will let me take over and turn it all back to what Dad had wanted us to do."

"Dad put me in charge because he knew I have the future of the company in mind."

"Then he was a fool, as you are slowly bankrupting us."

"I'm saving us, Tony. At some point, the oil reserves will run dry and what will you do then? And look at the way the planet is changing, just look at the oceans we are working in, the damage we are causing to them. We need to find a better way of lighting up the world, we can't rely on oil forever."

"Forever is a long way away. There's enough oil under the ocean for another two hundred years."

"And what if the planet doesn't have two hundred more years for us to rape it, then what?"

"But the planet will repair itself, it has for thousands of years, it always does. The changes we've been seeing over the last decade are all natural. Man-made climate change is the greatest con since organised religion. And think about it, are humans really so powerful that we have the ability to effect the natural changes that the planet has to go through, changes that were happening before humans even existed, and will happen again long after we are extinct? If you think that then you're not only naïve, but you're dangerously stupid."

"Listen to yourself, Tony, and you call me naïve?"

"And if you think I don't know how much you have spent on the new platform then you really have lost touch with reality. But it stops now. You'll not be wasting another rand of our money on your bloody wave generators or your hippy universities. From now on, every dollar spent will go on making Neptune the most efficient oil producing platform in the world. I've already spoken to the board, and they are cutting you off. You can stay as CEO, but the money stops now."

"You don't have the authority to do that."

"Just watch me."

"The board will not agree to that. They know exactly what I am doing and why, and I have all their support."

"Looks like we're done for another month," Tony replied, lifting his glass into the air in a mock salute. "Thanks, Dad, you really did us proud giving the top job to this clown."

With that, he placed his glass back on the table and left.

As soon as he heard the door slam shut, Gavin hurled his glass into the fireplace, shattering it and causing the bourbon to splash back all over the wooden floor.

"Fuck, fuck, fuck!" he shouted to no one.

He picked up his phone and called Caroline. It went directly to voicemail.

"I'm heading to the office now, meet me in the boardroom," he said before slamming the phone back onto the table. "Fuck!"

CHAPTER 12

The days since she took Tyrone's call had been frantic, trying to get everything in order at home as well as trying to clear up all the loose ends on her existing workload. It had left her no time to really think about the fact that she was about to fly to the other side of the world for a job she knew little about.

The first job was to get her in-laws to agree to move in, and that had proved easy. Judy hadn't needed to be persuaded at all, she had said yes even before Kiara had finished saying good morning. Kiara had always been close to her in-laws. From the moment Asher had introduced her to them, they had felt like family. Her own parents had both died when she was still a teenager, so Judy and Peter had quickly become much more than just in-laws to her. They had always treated her like a daughter and loved her as if she had been their own flesh and blood; she felt the same towards them, so nothing was ever too much trouble for them.

Asher's death a few months before could easily have driven them all apart, like it did to so many families when a sudden loss happened, especially such a horrendous one as his was. But it had seemed to draw them even closer, if that was even possible. Sometimes it just happens like that.

The twins were the same. Since losing their dad, they had stuck to their mum and their grandparents like glue. Mia and Jasmin adored Peter and Judy, and even though they would complain about them as every teenager did about the older generation, they still chose to spend as much time with them as they could. It was true in reverse as well. Judy would revel in the fact that the two girls wanted her to go clothes shopping with them and she loved it when they would join her on the weekly walk around Waitrose to fill up the fridge for the week ahead. As for Peter, he simply doted on his girls. Whenever Kiara wasn't watching, he would slip them a few extra pounds pocket money each, and he was literally on speed dial every time one, or both of them needed a lift somewhere.

The next few days, Kiara spent clearing up all her work and making calls to her various clients explaining that she was going to be away for the next week, but she was happy for them to send over any new cases for when she was back. That left her two full days to look over Tyrone's files to make sure that she really knew what she was going to be facing when she arrived.

There was a dozen claim files in total. The first few contained hardly any information at all. They listed a claims date, the amount of oil missing and the name of the tanker where the losses had supposedly happened. And the amounts were all relatively small, considering the total value of the cargo being insured. Each one was just a few thousand dollars, rising up to no more than twenty thousand. For most insurance companies, they would have been big enough to warrant further investigation, but it seemed that Tyrone had not even bothered to look at them, he had simply left his team to sort them out with the client. He was either a fool or someone who trusted his staff implicitly, and she hoped it was the latter.

It was not until a claim dated at the tail end of the previous year, one that had jumped in value to over a hundred thousand dollars, that his initials had started to appear on the documents. This file had a lot more pages than the earlier ones, but still, for such a large singular claim it seemed unusually light. *At least he had now started to take an interest in what was happening,* she thought to herself. If this was fraud, as she suspected, then the thieves had done the classic mistake of getting too cocky too quickly. They had been getting away with the smaller claims for so long that they decided they could up the numbers and still not be noticed. It was something Kiara had seen so many times and was usually the reason why they were eventually caught out. They always got sloppy just when they thought they were safe.

All she had to do was read between the lines, speak to the various people involved in the claims and then she would discover the grey areas, which always existed, but were generally ignored. This ultimately would lead her to the person, or persons who were committing the fraud. There were always little clues and trails they left for her to follow. Fraudsters, in Kiara's experience, were rarely as smart as they believed themselves to be, and they left crumbs all over the place. Usually, the first few thefts were the hardest to figure out, but by the time the fourth or fifth one was being done, the perpetrators thought that they were invincible and would start taking more and more chances, and that was when Kiara would be able to spot the cracks. Her job was much more about following the crumbs than following the clues.

To have such little information on a file was suspicious in itself, and that made her think about who in Tyrone's company was in charge of the claims department. The fact that the claims were even paid out without proper checks being done was like a red rag to a bull.

Of course, she had to reason with herself, she was looking at a South African incident file rather than a UK based one and perhaps their way of recording things would be very different to how she was used to doing things. Working on the other side of the world would bring many challenges, including cultural differences that she would have to contend with.

But, if Tyrone wanted her to work on this for him then he would also have to do it her way, which meant him hiding nothing from her and crossing every t and dotting every single i. He and his team would have to deal with the cultural differences with her as much as she would with them.

She clicked onto the next file.

It seemed that this file was not only limited by the number of pages it contained, but it was basic to its core. She quickly clicked through the file to get an idea of how it was ordered. The majority of pages were very poorly handwritten forms instead of typed-out ones, and they were signed so badly that there was no way she could discern who the author was. She wondered if the quality of the copies may have suffered when they were scanned in, so she would have to ask for the originals when she got to his office.

Despite this, she carried on trying to make sense of what was in front of her.

This claim itself was, however, very simple to understand. An oil tanker called the Aframel, owned by Tyrone's client, Adesco Oil, had left its destination point at the Waterfront in Cape Town and made its way across the Atlantic Ocean towards the North Sea to its final destination port in Rotterdam, in the Netherlands. At the original loading port in Cape Town, the ship had fifteen thousand tonnes of oil in its tanks, which was approximately seventy-five thousand barrels. However, when the ship arrived at the port in the Netherlands and unloaded its cargo, there was only fourteen thousand tonnes. That meant that, somewhere between Cape Town and the Netherlands, one thousand tonnes, or five thousand barrels, had vanished. Kiara went onto Google on her phone and looked up the price of oil. At today's price, eighty-two US dollars per barrel, it meant that the total loss came to about four hundred thousand dollars. This was about ten times the value of the first claims made on its own. They were clearly ramping things up now. The file simply showed the difference between the amount of oil at the starting port compared to the destination port, but it said nothing about how the loss itself had happened.

Surely oil does not just evaporate?! Worldwide Marine Insurance, her new employer, had simply paid the claim without asking where the oil had gone. There was no investigation to talk of, no questions asked, or certainly if there were it had not been in the file she was sent. It seemed to suggest that they simply accepted the loss of almost half a million dollars, paid the claim and then insured the ship for its next journey.

She closed the file and clicked open the next one.

This one had a similar amount of paperwork as the last one did and a very similar claim profile. It was even the same oil tanker, and it left the same port in Cape Town, but this time its destination was Houston in the USA. Judging by the writing on the forms, the same person had completed the paperwork and signed it off. Once again, she couldn't work out the name of the signature, and it was not even clear to her if the person who had completed the forms worked for Adesco Oil, Worldwide Insurance or even for one of the ports. Almost everything about the claim, barring the destination, was the same, except for the amount of the loss. This claim, which was just two months after the last one, suffered a much larger seventy-five thousand barrels. She opened the calculator on her phone again and did the maths. Eighty-two multiplied by seventy-five thousand. She took a deep breath when she realised this time it was in excess of six million dollars. Twice the size of the previous claim. Whoever was stealing this oil was upping the numbers out of all proportion. They were either getting very greedy, which was a dangerous thing for them to be, or if they were stealing the money for a specific purpose, it was coming around quicker than they'd anticipated and they needed to get the money in faster than they had planned. Once again, Worldwide had seemingly just paid the claim without asking for anything more than a few forms to be completed and Tyrone's initials added and still no one seemed to be asking where all the oil had gone.

Where the hell was Tyrone when all this was happening? she thought to herself.

She opened the last file he had sent her and wondered what she was going to find.

Again, it occurred on exactly the same ship as the first few, the Aframel. The fraudsters were getting much sloppier now, not even choosing a different tanker, which proved to her that they thought they were invisible.

She smiled to herself. *I'm definitely going to find you,* she thought, *all I have to do is follow those crumbs.* "And surely someone at Worldwide should be asking what's happening on that tanker," she muttered to no one.

For this claim, the Aframel had sailed to yet another destination. The port it ended up in was Qingdao in China. The loss they suffered was even greater. The Aframel was classed as a supertanker and had huge storage tanks. Unlike her previous shipments, this time she had almost a full cargo of two million barrels of oil. The loss that was reported to Worldwide a month after she had set sail was a massive two hundred and fifty thousand barrels, almost a quarter of her cargo. This meant that the claim came to over twenty million US dollars.

The size of the loss was staggering, far bigger than anything Kiara had ever come across in her fifteen years in the job. No wonder Tyrone sounded so worried; this would have an impact on any business, no matter its size.

She sat back in her chair and let out a whistle when she realised the amount now claiming to have been lost.

She was relieved to see that this time Tyrone had had the sense to appoint an independent loss adjuster and had put the claim on instant hold. The fraudsters had at last overstepped the mark enough to get his full attention. He had appointed a company called Bluepage, who were a specialist forensic claims company. They had sent a team of three people over to the destination port in Cape Town and another two to the port in China. Five people seemed a decent number to have working on this, so she had to wonder why she was now being employed as well. Surely between them they would have been able to tell him how the losses had happened.

She clicked forward until she came to the report that Bluepage had put in. She moved past their introduction and went straight to the conclusion:

> … the AIS, the automatic identification system on the tanker, had been temporarily disabled.
> ★ We can confirm that extreme weather conditions can cause the AIS to become temporarily offline.
> … We have interviewed the crew of the Aframel and can confirm that the ship completed its journey port to port without encountering any other ships or attacks from unknown vessels.
> ★ We can confirm that no incident report was filed to show the Aframel might have stopped mid-journey
> Conclusion – the AIS system on the Aframel shows the same level of oil within the tanks as the AIS system from the originating port. However, the AIS at the port in China presents a much lower weight. We can evidence no leakage in the tanks during the journey. We can evidence from the GPS on the Aframel that the tanker did not stop mid-journey.

Kiara clicked on the document again and moved to the final page, which simply listed the investigators' contact details and nothing more.

Nowhere within the document from Bluepage did it suggest how the oil could have vanished. It simply stated that the tanks had not leaked oil into the ocean and that pirates had not stopped the tanker and syphoned off the oil, which really were the only two ways she could think of to cause a loss of this nature.

No conclusion seemed to have been offered. No wonder Tyrone had not settled the claim.

She went back to the front of the claim file and re-read the file note from Tyrone's office:

> … we have been unable to establish the reason for the loss of oil, other than the possibility that the AIS system being incorrect or faulty at the time of leaving the port. There was the suggestion made by Bluepage that someone from outside of the port may have altered the loading numbers on the port's system, however, I have interviewed the head of IT at the port and also the architects of the AIS system and both confirm that the system is not accessible from outside the port's own servers and that once loading or unloading numbers are entered into the system, they cannot be altered, even from inside the port's servers themselves. Finally, the AIS system would record any additional entries in respect of those shipments if someone had to load on a change to the numbers post a loss, such as oil leakage or theft. No additional entries were made. Because we cannot establish the cause of the loss, we have no option but to settle the claim. I will refer the claim file to Bea's department for future underwriting as she may well determine that we no longer wish to retain the client post this claim.
>
> Jan – Head of Claims

That was it? They simply wanted Tyrone to accept that they had no idea where the oil went or how it was taken. And they suggest he pays out over twenty million dollars. Kiara was furious, she hated lazy people, especially people who worked in her industry. These people were beyond lazy. Someone, maybe even someone at Worldwide, was committing major fraud and she was determined to find out who it was.

Without even meeting these people, she knew that one, or even more of his staff, were trying to pull the wool over Tyrone's eyes. And she hated this shit more than anything. He had already paid out millions in fake claims and she was not going to let him pay out any more.

She closed the file and slammed her laptop shut in anger. She headed up to her bedroom and pulled the case from under her bed; it was time to pack. She was definitely taking this job, and she was going to find whoever it was that was stealing Tyrone's money, if it was the very last thing she did.

CHAPTER 13

Gavin stood in the small meeting room on the top floor of the Adesco Oil Cape Town office. The meeting room overlooked the commercial docking bay at the Waterfront where his two largest tankers were undergoing maintenance before their next journeys. The room also had the largest TV screen in the building, taking up a whole wall. It currently displayed the schematics for Platform Neptune, their newest and largest oil platform. Gavin stood still, facing the wall, looking intently at his two-billion dollar investment.

The door to the room opened and his assistant walked in.

"You called for me," Caroline said to him.

"I told you to make sure the money gets to him, but I never told you to let him have the full plans for Neptune and I said to keep my part in this quiet. If Tony knows what I'm doing, he'll turn the entire family against me."

He kept looking at the screen for another minute before turning to face her.

"I never sent him the plans," she said. "And why do you think he suspects you're helping him? There's no trace back to you at all."

"It was me he specifically spoke to at the AGM, wasn't it?"

"You're the CEO, and you're the one pushing the green energy agenda, so it was obviously you he wanted to impress."

Gavin thought for a moment. *Maybe she's right, perhaps I'm overthinking this?*

He just had to keep his involvement hidden until everything was in place.

"I suppose so, but his film had the exact set up of Neptune. It was almost a perfect replica. So, if it wasn't you who gave him the plans, then someone else must have leaked them to him."

"There's been a lot of press around the opening, TV crews from around the world have been beaming photos and video content for months now. We were able to hide it as it was being built, but as soon as it was towed into the ocean and finally anchored in place, it became impossible to keep it hidden."

"I don't mean the platform itself. I mean the underside, where it sits under the sea, where our tidal turbines are. You can't see them unless you are under the water, deep under water. That detail is not in the public domain at all."

Caroline wasn't sure what to say to him. She had no idea how Amos had seen them.

"You're right, someone must have sent the drawings to him," Caroline agreed. "It could only have been one of the senior executives, but none of them even know he exists, do they?"

"It could be someone senior in the accounts department. Who there would have access to the plans?"

Caroline thought for a moment. "Karly," she said. "She worked with us on costing the platform from day one, so she must still have access to the entire plans."

"And she's the one who is sending the claims payments to him each month?"

"Yes, she's smart, but it seems not that smart, after all. She hasn't even questioned how she has been able to send the claims money from our account without it being spotted. I would have thought by now she would have realised we were letting her do it."

"She thinks she's stealing from us, but she has no idea it's given me a chance to fund his project using someone else's money, and it's the perfect way to keep it hidden from my brother. But if she's shared our drawings with him as well, then she's clearly getting more daring now, and that is dangerous. This could compromise everything I'm doing and could give Tony the leverage he has been looking for."

"What do you need me to do?"

"I need you to keep an even closer eye on her. Let her keep making the payments, for now, but that's all. If she starts poking around any more than that, then let me know right away."

"Of course."

"So, do you think his batteries actually work?" Gavin said, more to himself than to her.

"Well…"

"I mean, just think about it," he said, cutting her off before she had a chance to finish her sentence. "Our turbines are capable of producing enough energy to power the entire platform, all its facilities, including the houses, our universities, plus all of the external plug-ins, such as our tankers, our helicopters, our safety boats, as well as run the engines for our oil production. We literally can run Neptune at zero cost. And still, we'll only be using about a third of the energy we produce. Can you imagine if we can then store the rest in his batteries and transport them around the world? We could power entire cities with free, clean energy." He turned to face Caroline so that she could understand fully what he was saying. "And that is just with Neptune. What if we attached them to another one of our platforms, or even to all of them? We could generate enough free energy to power every major city in the world just from the power of the tides."

Gavin turned back to the big screen and gazed at it again. "It's what Neptune University is for. To enable the greatest minds in science to spend time in the middle of the oceans and find a way to not only harness its power, but to find a way to store and transport it." He turned back to face her again. "Do you know the oceans make up more than seventy percent of the surface of our planet. And every twenty-four hours, there are two high and two low tides, all the time, never stopping. And twice a month, when the earth, sun and moon are aligned, we get gravitational forces creating neap and spring tides. Twice a year when the sun is directly overhead at the equator and there is a full moon, we get storm surges caused by the high winds. Just think of the energy produced by all that movement. Free, clean energy." He looked closely again at Neptune up on the screen. "If his batteries actually do work…"

"You and your fucking climate change!" Tony had entered the room without Gavin and Caroline hearing him. "You spout that shit like you're a fucking professor of science rather than an oil barren. Do you think Caroline doesn't already know all that stuff? You're like a broken fucking record…!"

Gavin turned to his brother. "What do you want?" he said, his anger still present from their meeting that morning.

"I already told you what I want, the same as all our shareholders want. The same as you should want. What our grandfather and father built this company for: to drill for oil and to make money for the family."

"And where will that end? I told you, we need to have an alternative source of energy, and this is it," he said, waving to the screen. "And that's what I am going to deliver."

"And bankrupt us in the meantime. I've told you, Gavin, the board are with me, every one of them. Neptune had better open soon, and it had better start producing oil right away, or, brother, you are toast."

Tony turned and left the room, slamming the door behind him with such force that the entire room seemed to vibrate.

"I need to know if his batteries work, if they will actually store the energy we create," Gavin said to Caroline.

"Maybe it's time to bring him in to show us," she said.

Gavin thought about that; maybe it was time he took ownership of this project. If it actually worked, then it would bring his plans forward by years, and he could prove to his brother and the family that everything he had been saying for years was true, that producing green energy was not only good for the planet, but could generate fortunes for their company as well.

"Do it, make contact with him, but don't bring him here, and don't let him know it's me just yet. Before we reveal everything to the board, I need to know that his batteries actually work, otherwise I am truly screwed. Then, we can bring him in on a fucking white stallion if he wants. And get me Karly up here."

Caroline turned to him in surprise. "I thought you were not going to let her in on your involvement?"

"I'm not. Tell her to bring the numbers, specifically for the new tidal turbines. Once Neptune is online, I want us to put turbines on every other one of our platforms. Every single one. And I need to know what it's going to cost us."

"Okay, boss," Caroline said, "I'll send her up right away."

Caroline left the room and almost walked straight into Tony who had been waiting for her in the hallway.

"I want to know who that man from the AGM was. Has Gavin got you looking for him yet?"

Caroline tried her best to keep her face neutral, but with little success.

"So, he has then," Tony said. "Well, when you find him, I want to know first, and right away, you understand me?"

"Yes, Tony," she said, meaning it.

"What else is that brother of mine up to?" he asked her. She turned back to the door to make sure Gavin had not come out and was listening to them.

"He's asked me to send Karly up to him. He wants her to price putting tidal turbines on all our platforms."

"Tell her I want the figures before she gives them to him. I'll make sure that the board stop that idea before it even starts. And Caroline…?"

"Yes?"

"Remember our agreement. When I become CEO, you will become a very, very rich lady."

"I haven't forgotten."

"Good girl," Tony said, before turning and walking away.

Caroline watched Tony leave before turning back to face the office where Gavin was inside still pacing around the room.

"Bloody maniacs!" she whispered to herself, before heading off to the accounts department to find Karly.

CHAPTER 14

Glancing at the board, she saw that she still had a good ninety minutes before her flight was going to be called. She needed to calm herself down. It would do her nerves no good getting on a plane for twelve hours feeling so unsettled. She still had enough time to take advantage of the free food and drinks in the lounge, which meant she could skip the airline meal and go straight to sleep. She needed to be rested and on her top game when she landed, as going by Tyrone's last message, she was going to be taken straight to his office to meet his team, and so far, all she had for them were some tough challenging questions, which they were most likely to be offended by.

She used her mobile phone to click on the barcode that was printed onto the corner of her table and ordered a side salad and then the classic chicken burger with fries. She decided she would have just one drink to help her sleep later, so she added an amaretto sour on the side.

Before the food and drink came, she had just enough time to call the twins and find out how their day at college went.

The screen flashed for boarding just as she had finished her drink. Within minutes of take-off, she had already fallen asleep, and she stayed that way until an hour before landing.

As soon as the lights came on, she made her way to one of the empty bathrooms, changed into her clean set of work clothes, brushed her teeth, made her hair presentable into a bun on top and applied some moisturiser to her face. By the time she'd returned to her seat, it had already been turned back from a bed into a regular chair by the stewardess, who was hovering to take Kiara's order for breakfast. She settled back for the final hour, giving herself time to think about the meeting that was about to happen. She knew she would have to be brutally honest with Tyrone if it was one of his staff, as she sensed he was a deeply loyal person and he would not be ready to hear that someone in his team was defrauding him. Decent people rarely suspected someone close to them, which always made her job that much harder. She closed her eyes and tried to silence her mind until they landed.

As soon as the door was open, she was one of the first off and one of the quickest to reach security. She cleared customs without a hitch and collected her case on the first turn of the baggage carousel.

She walked through the departure exit, pulling along her case, and she looked around the hall. It was already full with families ready to pick up their loved ones, and chauffeurs holding passenger names on placards and iPad screens. The man collecting her didn't need a screen or a piece of card, he already knew what she looked like from the photo Nick Taylor had emailed him the evening before. He pushed through the crowds the moment he saw her coming through.

"Kiara Fox," he said, "you look like you've just stepped out of a beauty salon, not like you've been on a plane for twelve hours. It was a good flight, I hope," he said with a boyish grin.

Kiara might have looked like her picture, but Tyrone's online profile had done him no justice at all. On his website, he was sitting behind a desk wearing a suit and tie, his skin a pasty white and his eyes glazed over. In the flesh, though, he was dressed in casual clothes, jeans, white T-shirt and baseball shoes. And his skin was far from pale, it had that beautiful South African bronze that she had expected to see. He stood at just over five feet ten inches and had the physique of someone who could have been a professional athlete.

"I think it was the best flight I've ever had," she said back to him. "I caught up on a whole week's sleep in one go."

"Excellent, so you're refreshed and ready to crack on then?"

"Too right."

"If you're hungry, I've got some nice pastries and fresh coffee at the office. I've asked just my key people to join us, so we can quickly get on the same page," he said as he took the case from her and wheeled it from the airport exit before stopping alongside a shining white Porsche 911 Turbo Cabriolet. He popped open the small rear boot, which her case completely filled up, and then held the door open for her, the smile never leaving his face.

Kiara slipped into the low seat, wondering how someone who had recently lost tens of millions of dollars could smile so much.

"Do you mind if we have the roof down?" he asked.

"It would be perfect," she said, relishing the chance to have a few days enjoying the African sun instead of the British rain.

"Would it be possible to pop to the hotel on the way to your office?" she asked. "Just so I can check myself in and drop off my case before we start work."

"Actually, if it's okay with you, I'd prefer to just go straight to my office, as I've asked my team to join us before the day cranks up. I have a feeling they'll be having a busy one, what with their existing work and also your feedback to think about. It's close to the hotel and we only have to stay in the office for a short time, and then I'll take you right there and you can have the first day to yourself. Is that okay?" he asked her, keeping his eyes glued to the front as he navigated his car out of the busy airport.

"Of course," she said, "I'm on your time now, so no problem."

"*Lekker,*" he replied with a smile. "Perfect."

The drive to the offices of Worldwide Marine Insurance was short, as the roads were pretty quiet, and they spent the entire journey talking about their shared love of fitness. Tyrone, just like Kiara, had a passion for exercise. In fact, it sounded like exercise was a way of life for him rather than just a hobby. She marvelled at how similar they were.

"Mountain bikes are my go-to," he boasted. "I've done stacks of races, some real tough ones. I also spend hours on my Wahoo spin bike at home, racing total strangers on Zwift. I do a fair bit of weight work as well. But I couldn't do triathlons like you. I swim like a lead balloon."

"The swimming's the best bit," Kiara replied, defending her chosen sport. "If I lived in a climate like this, I'd be in the sea every minute I had."

"Not in Joburg, you wouldn't!" he laughed. "There's no sea around here. Cape Town is different, though. I do have a weekend house there and I take my twins down to the beach every other weekend, they love the ocean, as most kids do."

"You have twins?" Kiara replied in surprise, looking at him with a new respect. "Boys or girls?"

"Boys. Matty and Troy."

"How old?"

"Just about to turn ten. Nick told me you had twins as well."

"Yes, I have girls, Mia and Jasmin. Almost seventeen, going on twenty-one!" Kiara said, smiling to herself.

"I bet they didn't like you flying all the way over here so suddenly. No wonder you hesitated when I first called."

"It's hard for them, me not being there. I lost my husband recently, so they try to keep me as close as possible now."

"Yes, Nick did tell me, I'm so sorry."

"Are your boys close to their mother?" Kiara asked, moving the attention away from herself.

"I guess so," he said. "We divorced a couple of years ago. The boys were always our focus, though; we made sure that it didn't have an impact on them too much when we split up. My wife and I met too young to be honest. We started dating in primary school, can you believe that? So, neither of us had played the field, if you know what I mean. We'd kind of got into a routine with each other that was much more about friendship than anything else. So, we decided to call it a day. We are still good friends, which is healthy for the boys; it's much better than the alternative, isn't it?"

"Where do your boys live? Are they with you?"

"Yes, they stay with me most of the time. I have a couple of live-in nannies to help, and they are with their mum every other weekend."

"Wow. I couldn't imagine not having my girls with me all the time."

"It seems to work for us."

"They are lucky to have a dad like you," Kiara said.

"I'm lucky to have boys like them," he replied honestly.

Kiara was pleased that Tyrone was such a family man. It meant that their time together could be an honest and open one, which was vital if he was going to be able to take the news she felt sure she would be having to give him.

"Here we are," he said a couple of minutes later.

He had pulled up to a set of large white gates and waited whilst the security guard came forward, saw who it was, and waved them through. Kiara noticed that everything in Johannesburg seemed to be surrounded by gates and armed security and it made her realise how lucky she was to live in a safe place like England.

Tyrone parked outside a three-storey box-like building that proudly displayed his company name in shiny silver letters across the front, breaking up the white of the brickwork. There were no other offices in the courtyard, just Worldwide Marine Insurance. The car park outside the office was extremely clean and well looked after and filled with expensive-looking cars that were parked neatly side by side, each with their own canopy over them to keep the sun from blistering the paintwork. *He clearly pays his team well and likes things to be kept in order*, she thought to herself. *Another positive sign of a decent person.*

Before she could open her car door, another security guard sprang forward from the office block and opened it for her, likewise for Tyrone. Another waited at the front door to let them in. Tyrone greeted his receptionist like a close friend before leading Kiara up a flight of stairs to a large boardroom at the top.

Currently there was no one else in there. The long table in the middle was made from a single piece of polished marble and was surrounded by twelve chairs. The artwork that covered the wall consisted of signed photographs from South Africa's winning Springbok rugby team, stars from leading cycling teams, top tennis players and even some of the world's most iconic bands. She noticed that each one contained a personal message signed to him, as well as a couple that said *to my good buddy.* He was clearly someone very respected in his community. At the end of the room were sliding glass doors that led outside onto a large patio, which was already been warmed up by the morning sun.

"Grab any seat," Tyrone said to Kiara. "Lesedi will bring out the coffee and pastries in a minute. I'm just going to check my emails and then I'll get the others to join us. Do you want some water meanwhile?" he asked.

"Actually, that would be great, thank you," she replied.

He walked over to the glass doors and slid them back.

"Help yourself," he said, pointing to the beer fridge, which she could see also contained bottles of water. "I'll only be a few minutes." And, with that, he continued onto the balcony and took a right to go through another set of outside glass doors that led back into the building, into his own private office directly adjacent to the boardroom.

Kiara walked out into the sun and grabbed herself a bottle of water. She went to the end of the balcony and looked out over the gardens at the back. It was a decent sized area, especially for being in the middle of a financial city where space would be at a premium. She looked up at the clear blue sky and enjoyed the twenty-eight-degree warmth that enveloped her and wondered on the madness of suddenly being on another continent so far from home.

"Hi there!" Bea entered the room, followed by Lesedi who carried in the first tray of goodies and placed them in the middle of the table.

"I'm Bea, I'm head of underwriting on our marine books."

Kiara walked back inside and shook the hand being offered to her in friendship. Bea was only a year or two older than Kiara, but dressed like she could be her mother, in a long-patterned dress and sensible flat shoes. She also wore her hair in a school matron bun tight on the top.

"It's really nice to meet you," Kiara said as Bea took a seat and beckoned Kiara to join her.

The door opened again, letting Lesedi out and letting Jan in. He stood at a couple of inches shorter than Kiara at around five foot six, but carried twice as much weight as someone of his height should. Much like Tyrone, he had a kind smile on his face that instantly drew Kiara in.

"Hi there, I'm Jan, I'm head of claims at Worldwide. I look after the entire claims book for the company," he said.

The last person to enter the room before Tyrone came back was a very striking lady, dressed in a multicoloured dress that reached all the way to the floor and long black hair that curled past her shoulders. She introduced herself as Mufuka, the company CFO, the person in charge of the flow of money and the most senior person at the company except for Tyrone himself.

"So, you've met my key people, then," Tyrone said, walking back into the room, helping Lesedi carry the last tray of coffees back in. "Thanks, Lesi," he said, showing her back out of the room.

"Kiara, would you mind starting by telling us your thoughts on the claim files I sent over?"

She hesitated a second, not sure how honest she could be in

front of all these strangers. Tyrone picked up on what she was thinking and decided to say it as only he could. "There's no point you being here if you start pulling punches on the first day," he said. "We are all adults and have broad shoulders. So, tell us honestly what you thought when you read the files."

Kiara took a breath before letting rip. "Well, all the files you sent me were pretty poor, if I'm being honest," she started with, to the surprise of the people around the table, especially Jan.

She decided to ignore the looks she was being given and carried on. "The paperwork, what there was of it, was mostly handwritten and illegible. To say there were holes in the information is an understatement. I honestly can't believe you paid them out based on what you had. At least for the largest one, you sent in a team of forensic accountants, but from what I could see, they reported back on the facts, but came up with no solution beyond that, and still the recommendation was to pay it."

"You do know this is South Africa, yar?" Jan said, trying to protect his department. "Things work differently here. Paperwork is simply not that easy to get done, and the authorities, such as the police and the coastguards at the ports, barely show up to do their own work, let alone taking time to help us with ours. If we waited for the police to do a report before we paid a claim, then we would have no clients left. But that doesn't mean we are not diligent in what we do."

"And if my clients don't get their claims paid, then I will lose all their accounts," Bea joined in, defending her department as well.

"You asked my opinion and that is what I've given you," Kiara said, as kindly as she was able to, trying hard not to sound aggressive, but knowing that there simply was no way to say what she needed to say without it coming across like that.

"And you're not blameless in this, either," she said, looking to Tyrone.

"Go on, let me have it," he replied with a smile forming on this face.

"Well, why would you let your office pay claims like this without you insisting on doing a full investigation first?"

"I hold my hands up as well, I should have kept a closer eye on everything, I get that. This is exactly why you are here," Tyrone said, acknowledging his own mistakes before turning to his team. "Let's just indulge Kiara and let her do what they do so well in the London markets. If we don't and these claims keep coming in, then we are in deep trouble."

Both Jan and Bea sat back in their chairs and sighed. They knew Tyrone was right. But it still irked them both that this British woman could stroll in there and within a few minutes pull apart all the work they had both been doing.

"Go on, Kiara," Tyrone encouraged her.

"I'm sorry if you think I'm being rude, it's honestly not my intention to alienate any of you, I promise, but I just don't think any claim, no matter the size, should just be paid unless it is clear that the loss was caused by an insured event and there is no evidence of fraud taking place. The problem here is that the reasons for the losses should be pretty easy to find. It's either contaminated stock, leakage of oil from a damaged tank or theft by piracy of some kind. There's only so much that can cause a loss of this type. And surely your client, the owners of the ships whom you are insuring, should be held responsible if their own security is so lax on the job. From what I can see, assuming you have not held anything back, no one has even challenged them yet."

"Of course we have. I'm in constant contact with their head of accounts, who also handles all their claims. We are speaking almost every day…" Bea cut in.

Kiara ignored her and carried on. Her boldness brought a smile to Tyrone's face "… the first thing I want to do is talk to someone senior at both the client's and at the ports."

"I can arrange a call with Adesco," Bea replied curtly. "Although you should know I work closely with our clients, all of them, and I would put my reputation on the fact that they are all well run and take security and the shipping of their products very seriously indeed."

"And can I please see the full financial records of both Worldwide Marine and Adesco oil?"

"That's down to me," Mufuka said. "But why do you need to see ours?"

"Thanks," Kiara replied, not giving an answer to Mufuka's question, again drawing a smile from Tyrone. "I'm only here until Friday night, so if you could arrange them right away, I would be ever so grateful."

"Do you need anything else?" Tyrone asked.

"Just a desk, a computer and another coffee please. And maybe a lift to my hotel at the end of the day would be great," Kiara replied.

"I thought you wanted to go straight to your hotel after this meeting?" Tyrone asked her.

"Actually, now I'm here, I think I'd like to just get on if that's okay?"

"You got it," he said, pleased that he had been right to bring her straight to the office rather than to the Saxon Hotel where she would have been far too comfortable to have wanted to get to work straight away. "Thanks, everyone," he said to them. "Listen, Kiara is now leading on this, okay? So, full cooperation from everyone please."

They all nodded in agreement.

The tension around the table was palpable.

"Right then, Mufuka please pop Kiara down to the office next to Jan," he said. "And can you ask Lesedi to get Kiara and me some fresh coffee?"

"Sure, boss," Jan said, holding the door open for Kiara to follow him. "This way."

"I'll see you in reception at three o'clock, if that's okay, and I'll drop you to the hotel. Maybe if you've no wish to be on your own tonight I'll pop back to join you for dinner, at about seven thirty. The Saxon do the best steaks in the city."

"Sounds perfect," Kiara said, following Jan down to her allocated office.

CHAPTER 15

A mos stood alone in his office the next morning and gazed out of the window over Camps Bay as the early morning stalwarts from the Polar Bear club returned once again, this time just a handful of them. He envied them their simple start to the day.

He thought back to yesterday's meeting, to the people who had been sitting around his table, Rene, Karly, Zara and the two strangers, Dan and Hamilton. He had always suspected that Rene had his own agenda, and he had obviously become more and more worried as the money started pouring in, but he simply didn't have the heart to call Rene on it and potentially upset the man enough to stop the flow of cash before his batteries were completed. And, ultimately, he believed that Rene wanted what he wanted, to stop the oil companies destroying the planet. Deep down, he still believed that this was Rene's aim, even if the other man was far more extreme than he was in his methods.

He had assumed when Rene had first approached him that he would be just like all those other couch protestors. That he would rant and rave about the evils of big businesses, that he possibly would bring in a small amount of money and then eventually would fade into the ether as all the others had over the years.

He had certainly never expected that Rene would be prepared to kill people for their cause, which was something that had shaken him. Ever since the revelation that they were planning on destroying Adesco's new oil platform, he had felt sick to the stomach. That his little charity could be complicit in the murder of innocent people was shocking to the core. All he had ever wanted to do was save lives, not take them.

Once the swimmers were in the water and the beach was once again empty, he turned away from the window and walked down the tight spiral staircase that led from his hallway all the way under the main house to his workshop below. The room itself ran the entire length of the downstairs, giving him around two thousand square feet of workspace. It was jam-packed with work tools, models in various stages of being built and a bank of computers running various simulations on the tidal movements around the world's biggest oceans. Dead centre in the room stood a huge pool. It was around ten metres square and sunk over ten feet into the ground. It had taken the bulk of his inheritance to not only dig that deep into the ground but to also bribe the local planners to look the other way.

Attached to one end of the pool was a water propulsion unit that allowed a steady set of waves to be sent across the water, much like what was used in the endless pool set-ups that elite swimmers trained in. In the middle of the pool was a miniature version of Adesco's own tidal generator that Amos had painstakingly built from the plans of the Neptune platform that Karly had managed to steal from Adesco's head office. And then, underneath the generator, a few feet under the water, Amos's own tidal battery was attached. There was space for four of them in total covering the entire area underneath the generator, but only one was attached, being charged up for his personal use.

He walked to the pool and gazed down lovingly at his invention. It was all he had thought about since he had first conceived the idea of storing free energy in a portable transferable unit. The water was so clear that he could see the battery in all its glory, gobbling up the energy units from the waves and storing them in its belly ready to bring to the surface for sharing. He smiled, allowing himself a moment to bask in his own brilliance. *This is going to change the world*, he thought. Then he corrected himself, *No, it's not going to change the world, it's going to save the world.*

He walked over to the end of the pool and switched off the wave machine, causing the room to fall deathly silent. He had switched on the wave propulsion before going to bed the previous evening, so it had been delivering a steady stream of waves to the battery now for just over twelve hours. At last it was ready to test.

Once the waves had stopped and the pool was flat again, he held the button that controlled the winch and raised the entire generator up and out of the pool, exposing his battery. He carefully pulled the unit closer to the edge using an old garden rake that he had kept for that purpose and then unclipped his battery unit. Because it had been submerged in water the entire time, the battery remained cool to the touch, which was a fundamental part of his decision. And because the battery was only the size of a computer monitor, twenty inches by twelves inches square, it was easy for him to unclip it and lift it out on his own. The actual batteries that would eventually be attached to the underside of the Neptune platform were each designed to be the size of a London double-decker bus, and Neptune would be able to hold twenty of them side by side under its belly. Another smile came to his face as he pictured the scene. Twenty massive batteries sitting deep in the ocean underneath the world's largest oil platform gathering enough energy to power dozens of cities, supplying an unlimited amount of free energy to millions of businesses, hospitals, farms, schools and homes. And then, expanding that even further, by attaching his batteries to every oil platform around the world, and not just Adesco's, until eventually the oil platforms themselves no longer needed to drill down into the seabed to extract the black gold that had been building up over the centuries, but instead were there solely to collect the free energy that the waves surrounding them produced. The picture in his head caused a shiver of excitement to run down his spine.

He carried the small battery over to the power generator that he had set up to power his home, and plugged it in. He held his breath as he always did at that point. He felt like Mary Shelly as she penned *Frankenstein* and gave the monster the gift of life.

He pressed the switch on the small generator and immediately the power indicator shot up to a hundred percent. There was enough power in this one small battery to run his entire house, including his workshop, his electric car, all the heating, hot water, appliances, TV, literally everything, For the whole of the following year.

This was to be the future of free green energy. But only if he could get Adesco on board to roll it out and help him show it to the world. And only if he could stop Rene from carrying out his plan to send it all crashing onto the ocean's floor.

Before leaving the room, he attached a new battery to the pool generator. He ran his hand over the unit slowly and carefully, almost caressing it as if it were the wife he had never found the time to find.

Once fully charged, he would take the battery to Rene, and together they could go to Hamilton's township and show him how they could bring free electricity to everyone living there. What better way to get them all on his side than by demonstrating to Hamilton how his small invention could change the lives of everyone living in the isolated township outside of Cape Town, how, because of him, the millions living there would no longer have to live in darkness or suffer the cold of winter.

He pushed the unit into the centre of the pool and then lowered it into the water, before switching on the wave machine. He smiled one last time to himself and then turned out the lights and headed back upstairs to the main house.

Once he was back in his office, he settled at his desk and turned on his computer, logging into his emails, ready to share the news with Karly that his batteries really do work. He looked at his inbox and saw that there was already a message waiting for him. He clicked on it. It was from Caroline Beazley, PA to Gavin Adriaanse, the CEO of Adesco Oil. *Could this day get any better?* he thought.

He sat back in his chair. *So, my little stunt did get your attention, then.*

CHAPTER 16

"I've contacted him," Caroline said to Tony as she entered his office uninvited and took a chair facing him.

"The man from the meeting?"

"Yes. I traced him from the video at the AGM," she lied, having already known his whereabouts all along. "I've emailed him for a face to face. I'm pretty sure I can get a copy of his plans as well, if you need them," she carried on.

"Why the hell would I want those?!"

"Sorry, I just thought you might be interested to know if there was any substance to what he was saying about his invention."

"I couldn't give a damn about what he has or has not invented. We just need to stop him in case whatever it is he's done actually works and my brother parades it in front of the board and the investors. Do you have his address?"

"Not yet," Caroline replied.

"Get it then and I'll deal with him personally. So, what are you going to tell my brother?"

"What do you want me to tell him?"

"Tell him you haven't found the man yet. I'll handle it from here on."

Caroline left the room and headed back to her desk to send Amos another email and told him they would be in touch again soon.

Part of her felt bad for doing this as she fundamentally agreed with Gavin that long-term they needed to do something about switching to a more sustainable business model, and his work on the tidal generator was astonishing, it really did generate huge amounts of energy to power Neptune in its entirety. But, like Tony, she was so heavily invested in Adesco that her whole future was based on the dividends that the company paid annually, dividends that had stopped coming since Gavin had started investing in the green programme.

Over the years, she had sunk over half her salary into the company share scheme and always reinvested the dividends back into the company pension, purposely living a frugal lifestyle, never even taking a holiday abroad or going out for meals, which was all on the expectation that she would be able to retire super early and travel the world in the finest style possible. Her retirement dominated her thoughts and was the reason she got up every morning and worked for people like Gavin and Tony. But, if the dividends were not reinstated, and if the share price dropped any further, it would all have been in vain. All those years of being careful would be for nothing. And that trumped everything else she felt about the people she worked for and what the company did.

And, quite frankly, she wasn't a hundred percent convinced that drilling for oil was really the worst thing to do, anyway. *Sure, it's a contributor to climate change,* she reasoned with herself, *but even if they stopped drilling for oil, all the other fossil fuel industries, such as coal, gas and plastics, would continue to do their thing, so does it really matter if Adesco carries on for a few more years doing what it was designed to do?*

CHAPTER 17

Amos replied to the email from Caroline, accepting her offer of a meeting and asking for it as soon as was physically possible. He knew that his stunt at the AGM had had an impact, but he wondered if Karly had maybe also spoken to Caroline for him. He had asked Karly in the past if she would talk to Adesco's board and have him come in to present his project to them, but she always put him off with the excuse that his batteries were not yet ready to show and that she never had direct access to Gavin other than to present the monthly accounts to him.

Amos always felt that she was being less than honest with him about that, and that perhaps there was something more that she was unable to tell him, so eventually he gave up asking. She had managed to get hold of the schematics for Neptune for him earlier in the year and that had been a massive help, but now, with a face-to-face meeting being offered, he assumed that she must have been even more emboldened by what he did at the AGM and had actually put him forward to them. He needed to tell her that he had tested his battery, that it worked and thank her for having this meeting arranged.

He thought about Karly a lot. He once had even plucked up the courage to ask her out on a date, but before he could do so, she told him that she had reconnected with her ex-boyfriend, and she had seemed so excited about it. He had been devastated by that news.

What he didn't know was that her feelings towards him were as strong as his were towards her. But she wasn't able to act on them. She couldn't tell him that her ex worked at Worldwide Insurance and was the conduit needed between all the parties that would allow Rene to commit his fraud. Rene has left her in no doubt that she needed to restart the relationship with her ex for the good of their plans, that the future of the planet was more important than any feelings she could be developing for Amos.

Theirs was a love story that was destined never to be played out.

Amos made the call.

Karly picked it up as soon as she saw it was Amos calling.

"I can't really talk," she said quietly into the handset, "I'm still at work."

"I just wanted to thank you for putting a word in for me."

"What word? What do you mean?"

"The meeting, of course. I had an email from Gavin's PA asking me to meet with him. I know my stunt at their AGM had an impact, but I figured you must have put in a word for me as well."

"Me? No, I didn't say anything to anyone. I don't usually get to see any of the senior management, especially not Gavin or Tony, unless I'm delivering the quarterly accounts, and these days, even those are collected from me by someone else."

"Oh, that's strange. I guess it was just the AGM, after all. Wow, I really must have made an impact then."

"You must have done. Look, I have to go, but maybe we can speak later, if you're free?"

"That would be nice," he replied, his heart skipping a beat as it always did when he spoke to her.

After the call ended, he decided to leave the office and go for a walk along the beach to clear his head. He needed to focus on two things now: one to get in front of Gavin Adriaanse and the other to stop Rene destroying all his plans.

As he walked down the beach, his mind took him back nearly two years to the meeting that changed everything for him.

CHAPTER 18

A mos has been at the University of Cape Town giving a lecture on the effects of climate change on the world's oceans when he had first met Rene Bester. The lecture had attracted a full house of eager students keen to know more about the subject, and the entire auditorium was full to the brim with standing room only by the time Amos had stood at the lectern.

But by the mid-point of his talk, there were three times more chairs left than people, and by the end, there was no more than a splattering of people left.

"The subject is fascinating, but sadly the delivery was somewhat less so."

Amos looked up to the man who had been sitting throughout his lecture in the middle of the front row, one of only half a dozen who had stayed until the end. He looked from the man to the now empty hall.

"I am more of a doer than a talker, I guess."

"Then why did you put yourself up on that stage?"

"Because people need to know what is happening out there, it's important."

"I agree, but there are plenty of people delivering similar messages to yours and doing it very successfully."

"But all they are doing is talking, none of them are taking the action I'm taking, are they? Sorry, who are you?" Amos asked, feeling ambushed by this stranger.

"Sorry, I'm Rene, Rene Bester," he said, offering his hand. "I didn't mean to come across so rude. I've been following you online for some time now and I'm fascinated by everything you have been posting about climate effects, especially those caused by fossil fuels. I just think that your talk should be more about the work you are doing to reduce it. Your project to store wave energy into portable batteries is fascinating, and if you can actually get it working, it could be a game changer.

"I know it will work; I've tested it in my home lab on some small batteries and I almost got it to hold the charges, it was so close."

"So, what's stopping you completing it?" Rene asked, hearing the excitement in Amos's voice.

"The usual thing, money. I have already exhausted my own funds, and my charity barely raises enough each year to keep the project going."

"Tell me more."

"What's your interest?" Amos asked.

"I want to help you."

Amos was always sceptical when people started talking to him after he had delivered a talk. Usually there were one or two people who wanted to keep the conversation going, and one of them always ended up promising the world but delivering nothing.

"Everyone wants to help me, but here I still am, on my own, trying to change the world."

"Perhaps I'm not like all the others you have met. Maybe I'm the one who can actually do something."

"Perhaps," Amos said, not truly believing him.

"Let me help you box everything up and then let me buy you a coffee."

"Sure," Amos said, happy to at least let the stranger help him carry everything to his car.

"I mean it," Rene continued, "come for coffee and tell me your story."

With nothing else to do for the day, Amos took him up on the offer. Over coffee, he told Rene his story.

"I studied at Cape Town University, marine biology. It seemed the most natural subject to me. I graduated top of my class with honours, finishing the course a year early. I then moved on to engineering, with my focus on tidal plants. I even spent some time as a residency at the Lake Sihwa Tidal Power Station in South Korea; it's the largest of its type in the world. It could generate over five hundred megawatts of clean free energy, enough to service in excess of a hundred and fifty thousand households a year. Can you imagine that power? And it's free, and never ends."

He found Rene eager to listen, so he told him everything.

"My dad made his fortune investing in the fossil fuel industry, particularly oil. He was an original shareholder in a local startup and yet there I was putting all my time into something that was designed to destroy it. It pretty much ended our relationship. I spent my final year studying the engineering behind energy storage, and I was struck by the fact that there were so few tidal plants anywhere in the world and that none of them had yet been able to design a battery small enough to enable the stored energy to be transported without physical connections. It was the missing part to their puzzle, even though they never realised it. It has been my sole focus ever since."

"How far away are you from finishing?" Rene asked.

"That's a piece of string, isn't it? I know I am not far away, but I've exhausted all my inheritance now; all I've got left is the house I was left. My mum made sure when Dad died that she rewrote her will to bring me back in, but by the time she died, she had spent her last years in a nursing home, which took half of what he'd left. The rest I spent setting up the charity and building my models. I am so close now, I can feel it, but the next phase, which is building the generators, adding a test pool into my workshop and creating a set of working batteries is going to take more than I can possibly find. I have spent the last two years going around universities and investment houses to try to get support, and I have been successful in some small wins, but basically, I'm running out of cash fast now and I was on the brink of having to close everything down…"

"And then…" Rene asked, seemingly caught up in the story.

"The head of Adesco Oil, one of the largest producers in the region, put out a statement that they will be building this new, huge oil platform, which is going to be powered completely by wave energy. I mean, it's everything I have been talking about. He even said he was going to be building a university on site to shape the newest minds to find a way to one day gather the energy and export it. It was basically everything I have been doing, and he was out there talking about it."

"Amazing. So, you have contacted him then?"

"Of course I have. But I can't seem to get through to him. At every try I am blocked. They seem to view me as some mad scientist, which I am absolutely not, and they just keep pushing me away. I have even changed my designs to show that my batteries can be retrofitted to the underneath of any oil platform. It'll cost millions, I know that, but as an investment, it'll remove all their running costs and they can even sell on the energy in place of oil – and I estimate it'll make them the same, if not more, in profits."

"So, what will it take for them to take you seriously?"

"I need to finish my batteries and somehow get in front of their CEO."

"It's genius," Rene admitted. "Unlike most other climate organisations who want to pull the oil industry down, you actually want them to build even more platforms. You see the oil companies as your future partners."

"Exactly! They already have the platforms I need in every ocean in the world, but they also have the money to make my plans come alive. Then, by allowing the oil companies to sell the free energy they will be producing to the richest countries in the world, they could effectively stop drilling for oil and still retain their profits. Companies like Adesco Oil don't have to be the enemy of the planet, they could be its saviour. Surely, in a world of greed and capitalism, it's got to be better to work with the devil than try to cast them out?"

"So, let me help you," Rene said.

"Help me? How exactly can you help me?" Amos replied, suddenly exhausted by his own enthusiasm.

"I used to work in the oil industry, and I saw firsthand the damage they were causing. I left them, along with my closest people, and we formed our own climate group, focusing on bringing down the whole foul industry. But you are right. Why bring them down when we can work with them? We are very connected with the money markets and we work closely with a huge number of climate activists who I know would see your plans just like I am, as a way of saving the planet without destroying an entire industry. Let me and my people join your charity, and I promise you we will bring you in all the money you need. You can focus on your project and, whilst my team find you the money, I will make contact with the CEO of Adesco Oil and we will get you in front of them."

Amos knew he should have said no to the stranger. It all sounded far too good to be true. And the words 'climate activists' scared him almost as much as the oil people themselves did. But he needed help. Without the money or access to the Adesco CEO, he would still be here, making speeches to universities with the hope of raising a few dollars at best.

Against his better judgement, he shook Rene's hand.

CHAPTER 19

After the meeting at Amos's, Rene convinced Hamilton that the rest of his money would be with him soon. He also told Dan the same and to press ahead and get the rest of the bombs in place. When they left, he turned to Karly.

"What do you mean the money has been delayed?" he spat out the words. He could hardly contain his anger.

"All I know is that the last claim is being investigated further. I'm a hundred percent certain it'll be paid, but it's just going to take a little more time."

"We don't have time, do we? You heard Hamilton and Dan, we need the money now. We have to get another insurance claim in quickly." Turning to Zara, he said, "I need you to go back to the port and create another loss."

"Hamilton can get me back into the port."

"How large can you make this one?" Rene asked her.

"As large as you want. But if they are already refusing to pay the last one then maybe make this one smaller, so it just goes through?"

"Time is running out, we have to be ready when Adesco launches the platform. We need to have some big pay days now, otherwise the whole thing falls apart." He thought for a moment. "Get us about forty million dollars."

"We can't just keep doubling the numbers," Karly said.

"You just make sure your boyfriend knows that this one has to go through, or else." He left the threat hanging in the air.

"Can you do it?" he asked Zara.

116

"Of course I can. If Hamilton can get me back into the port's office, I can break into their servers no problem. It's only numbers on a screen, I can change them to anything you want," she said.

"Will Amos's bank be a problem if a payment that big comes in?" he asked her.

"I'll tell Amos exactly what to say to them. I'll need him on hand to accept the payment and then authorise it out. I can then do the rest."

"Actually, we might have another little problem as well," Karly cut in nervously.

"What now?" Rene said, daring her to deliver him even more bad news.

"My contact at the insurance company told me about this woman that his boss has just brought in."

"What lady?"

"I told you that Worldwide Insurance haven't agreed the last claim, but what I didn't tell you is that they didn't settle everything on the claim before that, either," she said, waiting for him to explode. When he stayed quiet, she carried on. "They only paid a small part of it, and the owner contacted this woman, she's some top-end fraud specialist from the UK."

"How much did they hold back?" he asked, incredulous that she hadn't told him before this.

Karly took a breath in before telling him. "Just shy of two million," she said. "That's why the rest of the claim is going to take longer. They have brought this woman in to investigate what's been happening. That's why I'm frightened of you putting in another claim right away, especially such a big one. I am told that she'll find nothing to prove the fraud, but we've still got to be really careful to cover our tracks. I know that they will pay the full claim eventually, I am one hundred percent sure of that, but now that they are looking at this, we probably have limited chances to keep doing it for much longer."

"Tell me about this woman they have hired," Rene said to her.

"Apparently, she's got a serious reputation for getting the job done. My contact has been really thorough, but if she is as good as I have been told, then she might just make it harder for us to get some more through whilst she is still here."

"Then we need to stop her before she realises what we have been doing," Rene said. "What have you been told about her?"

"Her name is Kiara Fox. Tyrone, the boss of Worldwide Insurance, has put her in charge of investigating all the claims. And he's told everyone that until she has finished, no more claims will be paid, not even smaller claims."

"Fuck, why didn't I know about this until now? We need to get rid of her," Zara cut in. "If we don't get the last payment in a few days, then Hamilton will come for all of us, and I for one do not want to be here if that happens."

"Let's send her a message, then," Rene said.

"What do you have in mind?" Zara asked.

"They must have her details at the office. Karly, can you get her contact there to log into their system and get them? Then I'll call her up. And Zara, you find me her home number in the UK, it must be on a database somewhere. And find me everything you can about her family, especially if she has a husband and any children. Search the London insurance markets, and the UK trade papers, if you have to. If she's some hotshot investigator, then there has to be some stuff about her on the internet."

"You're going to threaten her family?" Zara said with a smile in her voice. "If that doesn't send her running home, then she's crazier than even I am."

"Exactly," Rene said, "exactly."

CHAPTER 20

T yrone dropped Kiara off at the Saxon Hotel in the early afternoon. The hotel was incredible, certainly nothing like she had ever stayed in before. Originally, it had been a huge family estate owned by one of the richest men in South Africa, before being expanded and turned into arguably the finest hotel in Johannesburg.

She followed the bellboy from the main entrance into a small glass lift that went up just one stop, opening onto a covered walkway bridge, which gave views around the entire ten-acre estate. The bridge itself, whilst being solid and unmoving, was made purely of bamboo slats, with a glass curved roof and covered in native plants that ran all over and along the outside. It truly made her feel like she was in Africa, but more like being in the African Bush than a luxury hotel in the middle of a thriving city. At the end of the bridge, the bellboy led her through a set of huge wooden doors into another lobby area that contained a dozen sofas spread around and a grand staircase that led from the ground floor to the upper floor to the suites. The bellboy stopped at the first room by the top of the stairs and let Kiara in.

Her room was enormous. The main sleeping area had a triple king size bed with enough pillows and cushions to create her own children's play park. There was a huge walk-in shower with separate toilet, an oval bath set behind the bed on a wooden plinth, yet another bathroom with a toilet and a balcony overlooking the outside restaurant. On the wall opposite the bed there was a television set that must have been seventy-five inches. Then off the main room, there was a lounge-office area, twice the size of the bedroom with a twelve-person dining table, a huge office area with desk and screens to plug her laptop into, plus a separate seating area with a coffee table and small flat television. Kiara could not understand why anyone staying at a hotel for a few days would really have need of all this space.

After the bellboy had left, she unpacked the small amount of clothes she had brought, which filled up only a fraction of one of the six wardrobes, and then she sat down on the bed, her mobile phone in hand and pressed on the FaceTime app to call the twins.

Mia was the first to pick up.

"Hi, darling," Kiara said as soon as Mia's face appeared on the screen.

"Hey, Mum. What's it like there? Is it hot?"

"Is your sister there as well?"

"Jas!" Mia called out.

A few seconds later, Kiara was filling the girls in on the amazing flight she'd had on the way over and the incredible hotel.

"Why do you need so much room?" Mia exclaimed when Kiara had finished the tour.

"I don't!" Kiara agreed, confirming her own thoughts on the matter. "Are your grandparents there?" she asked.

"I'll go get them. Love you," Jas said as she left the screen.

"I hate you being away, Mum," Mia said as Jasmin went down to get Peter and Judy.

"I miss you guys as well. But it'll only be a few days. You two just be good for your grandparents, okay? Don't drive them crazy."

"I think it's the other way around," Mia said back with a laugh.

"Cheeky girl!" Judy said, taking the phone off Mia. "Go get your grandad," Judy called to her as Mia left the room.

"How are they?" Kiara asked her.

"They're okay. They were a bit quiet when they came home

from college and you were not here. But Peter took them to the village to get fish and chips and they were soon back to normal. How's things with you? Are you being looked after? Is the hotel nice?"

"It's all good, thanks. The hotel is insane. Tyrone met me at the airport, I spent the day with his staff, and he's going to come back here for dinner. So, I'm all safe and well if that was your worry."

"Well, you hear these things about South Africa, don't you?"

"Honestly, I'm fine. I doubt I'll be walking around anywhere on my own and, if I'm not picked up, I'll just get one of the hotel chauffeurs to drive me around and will bill it back to Tyrone."

"Hi Kiara," Peter said, joining in the conversation.

"Hi Pete, thanks for taking the girls for fish and chips earlier."

"They loved it. Mia, of course, was in charge of who had what. In fact, she's been in charge of all of us since you left."

"Of course she has," Kiara said, laughing. Mia was the boss even when she was home.

"By the way, we had a call this morning from someone you are working with. I thought it was odd that he called the house over here, considering you are over there."

"Really? That's odd. Was it Tyrone, or one of his staff?"

"No. He called himself Rene. His accent was quite strong, so I didn't get his surname. But it was definitely a Rene and not a Tyrone."

Kiara thought for a moment.

"I didn't meet a Rene today. What did he want?"

"I don't know. I was walking past your office, taking the dog for a walk near the pond, and your phone was ringing nonstop. So, I thought I should answer it, just in case it was new business for you. Anyway, it was this guy, he had a really strong South African accent, he said his name was Rene and he was an old friend of yours. He asked me when you'd left and said he was hoping to see you over there. He said it was a shame you weren't taking Mia and Jasmin with you."

"He knew the girls names?" she said in alarm.

"Sure. I mean, he said you and he were friends."

"But I don't know anyone called Rene."

"Who is he then?" Judy asked.

"I have no idea. The only people I know in South Africa are Tyrone and his staff, and only Tyrone knows my home number and the girls' names."

"You're sounding a bit worried, Kiara," Judy said. "Should we be concerned as well?" she asked her, remembering everything that they had recently gone through with the widows.

"I'm sure it's nothing. Look, don't worry, it must be someone connected with Tyrone, or with Nick Taylor. I'll call them both in a minute. Just keep a close eye on the girls for me, okay?"

"Do we have anything to be worried about, Kiara?" Peter had to ask, not for the first time since they became her in-laws.

"No."

Peter and Judy could both hear the slight change in her voice.

"I thought we were done with all this. After the last time, I thought you were going to just take some low-key jobs."

"There's nothing to worry about, honestly," Kiara tried to convince them, despite her stomach suddenly tightening.

"Are you sure?"

Kiara was sure. At least, she thought she was.

"It's fine. Just keep a watch on the girls for me, okay?"

"We always do," Judy said.

"I'll be home in a couple of days. I'm not even a hundred percent sure I can help them on this job, to be honest, it's not exactly my area of expertise. I'll call you in the morning."

The call ended.

Kiara felt uneasy. She didn't know a Rene, she never had, but he had called her home, and he knew the name of her two daughters;

she didn't like that, not one bit. She picked up her phone again and dialled Tyrone's number. He answered on the first ring.

"You missing me already?" he said before she had a chance to even say hello. "I'll be with you in a couple of hours."

"Do you know a Rene?" Kiara asked him outright.

He had to think for a minute. "Not that I can recall. Why do you ask?"

"It's probably nothing. I'll see you at seven, on the terrace, if that's okay, I'd rather eat outside, it's so warm and I want to at least take advantage of that whilst I'm here."

"Too right, see you shortly."

She ended the call and quickly dialled another number, this time to the UK.

Nick Taylor answered right away. It was still only four o'clock in the afternoon in England and he was at his London office dictating his notes into a voice machine for his secretary to type up later in the day.

"Hey, darling. You calling me from the other end of the world? Tyrone's looking after you, I hope."

"Yes, he's been great, and I'm staying in the most amazing hotel. I'm not sure how much I can help him, though, but I'll do my best, of course."

"I know you will. That's why I gave him your number."

"Nick, I just have a quick question."

"Fire away."

"Apart from Tyrone, do you have any other South African friends or business contacts?"

"Nope. As I said, I've never even been over there. Tye has talked about people, of course, but no one I've ever met."

"Has he ever mentioned a guy called Rene?"

"Rene? I don't think so. I'm sure I'd remember a name like that. Who is he?"

"That's what I'm trying to find out. Peter was walking in the garden this morning and heard my office phone, so he answered it and some African guy called Rene asked after me. Then he asked how Mia and Jasmin are."

"He knew you had twins?"

"Yes, and he knew their names. Before Tyrone, I've never had any contacts in South Africa, and now suddenly I've got this guy calling me on my home number. This case Tyrone has me looking at involves huge numbers – millions – so I'm just feeling a bit nervous, that's all. I'd come home now if I could, but it's only a few days, and getting a flight right away is probably not even possible. I'm sure it's just me being silly, but it is odd, right?"

"Yes, it is. I tell you what, I'll give TR a ring in a moment and just make sure he keeps an eye out for you, and I'll get him to rack his brains for a Rene, assuming that Peter got the name right?"

"There is that, of course," Kiara admitted.

"And I'll swing by the house after work, just to put your mind at rest."

"Thanks, Nick. That's great. I really appreciate it. I'll call you in the morning as well, you know, just because."

"Perfect," he said as the call ended.

Kiara laid back on the bed and tried to make sense of everything and plan her next move. If she were dealing with this at home, the next thing she would do was speak to the head of claims. She made a mental note to get some time in the morning with Jan and maybe ask to see some of the non-oil claims, just to compare the note-taking of his team. And then there was the oil company itself, Adesco, what did she know about them? Very little, as it happened. *So, a meeting with Bea, the client account handler, is also needed*, she thought.

The name Rene came back to her mind again, as well. Whoever he was, he had called her home number. She had no idea if he was someone else who worked for Tyrone and just called her at home instead of her mobile, or if he was someone sending her a warning to back off. Either way, she needed to ask Tyrone if this was a person he knew.

CHAPTER 21

After leaving Amos's house, Rene, Karly, Zara and Dan made the short flight back to Johannesburg, leaving Hamilton in Cape Town.

They went straight to a small office on the upper floor of the Sandton Mall in the middle of the financial district. Rene had rented an office on the lower floor, six floors under where Adesco Oil held a suite of meeting rooms. Rene always felt he should keep his enemies as close as possible, even if it was only in a physical sense.

He waited until the three of them were seated around the table. He opened the fridge in the corner and poured each of them a glass of water before he began. "I'm worried about these insurance payments. It feels like I'm losing control of the situation, which makes me very uncomfortable. And Hamilton is still the loose cannon; when he loses his temper, I don't want to be near him. And you don't help, winding him up like you do," he said to Zara, who in turn just smiled and shrugged back playfully.

"We need to get the money in, and quickly, or he will become a serious problem for us." The worry in Dan's voice was clear for everyone around the table to hear.

"Did you call her family?" Zara asked Rene.

"Yes, I did it before we got on the plane. You did amazing getting her kids' names and her number so quickly," Rene replied to her.

"It was easier than I thought it would be, actually," Zara said.

"She was all over the papers back in the UK. She was involved in some big case recently. So, it was pretty easy to find what you needed. Did you tell her kids we had their mummy here?" she said with a smirk.

"I wasn't going to speak to the kids themselves. I spoke to some old man, probably the grandfather."

"What did you say to him?" Zara asked, eager to know the details.

"It was what I didn't say that mattered."

Rene then turned to Karly. "Did you tell your partner we have a new claim going in that needs to be paid, no questions asked?"

"Yes, I did. But he said it's not as easy as that because the files are now being looked at more closely, they can't just do whatever they want at the moment. Also, I saw a message come in on my Adesco email that she wants to come in to talk to me and a few others about the claims. I'm pretty sure I can handle her, but if she asks to meet the directors then we could be in deep trouble."

"Well, this is your mess to sort out now you're in charge of what happens at the insurance company and at Adesco, that was the deal. Dan handles Hamilton, Zara looks after the flow of money when it reaches us, you deal with Worldwide and Adesco and I handle Amos and the charity. So, this is down to you, you need to clean up your mess or else you compromise us all."

"What am I meant to do? We never expected them to bring an investigator in, I never prepared for that."

"Well, you should have done, this is your area of expertise, not mine."

"If we had kept the claims small, under the radar, we wouldn't be in this position, would we?"

Rene ignored that comment, even though he knew she was probably right.

"I'll deal with the investigator, but I need that money paid." He thought about the flow of money for a second and had another idea. "If you really can't get your partner at the insurers to pay the claims right away, then you need to take it directly from Adesco's account."

"If I do that then I'll be found out for sure. At the moment, I'm only paying back out the exact money we have been getting in, so the bottom line on our accounts doesn't change. If I now make a payment without getting the claim money in first, then we'll show a loss in the accounts, and they'll be all over me in days."

"So, what's the solution then?" Rene asked her. "Because unless we pay Hamilton now, he'll be back, and probably with some of his men. So, you need to get us the money quickly from the insurers or you take it from Adesco, either one, I don't care which, otherwise we are all fucked."

Karly had nothing more to give him; both his options seemed impossible to her. Instead, she threw her hands up in mock surrender.

"We need to get this investigator out of the way, that's got to be our first priority," Rene said, turning to Dan. "With her gone, it might give Karly's person the opportunity to settle the claims again."

"What do you have in mind?" Dan asked.

"I've already sent a threat to her family, which she should know about by now if she has called home. But maybe it's not going to be enough. I think we need to give her a real reason to run back to the UK with her tail between her legs. I wish Hamilton were here, that would send her running back home," Rene said.

"Where is she staying?" Dan asked.

"She's at the Saxon," Zara said.

"You need to make sure she's not too comfortable," Rene said to Dan.

"And what do you need me to do?" Zara asked.

"I need you to get back onto the port's mainframe, find out when the next tanker is due to go and make sure you change those numbers. We need that big claim done and, once she's gone, Worldwide will have no excuse not to pay all the claims out."

"And where are we with the bombs?" Rene asked Dan.

"Some are already on the platform, and the rest are stored at Adesco's warehouses. They are in the empty oil barrels ready to be shipped. Hamilton's men will be on site when they are delivered. That is as long as they are paid! The next shipment is due to go over there this coming week."

"So, we know what we have to do then," Rene said to them all. "Dan, you make sure Kiara Fox knows that it's time she went back home, and don't take no for an answer… and Karly, you need to get your partner at Worldwide to get the claims paid one way or another. And Zara, get back to Cape Town and into the port's office."

"Isn't it about time we knew who this mysterious partner of your is?" Zara turned to Karly.

"I've told you, I won't ever give you that," she shot back at the other lady.

"Wow, so you do have some balls, after all," Zara said to Karly, having been surprised at how Karly had spoken back to her.

"I told you all from the beginning that I would never give them up to you." Karly suddenly felt the weight of the world on her shoulders. "I'll make sure that the claims are paid, I promise you, just keep my partner out of this, okay?"

"You get the claims paid and we'll never have to ask again," Rene said to her.

CHAPTER 22

Whilst everyone else was sitting inside the restaurant, Kiara and Tyrone had seated themselves outside, on the main terrace facing the large man-made lake. Even though it was already seven thirty at night and dark, the air temperature was a warm eighteen degrees. Tyrone was still wearing the zip-up he had arrived in and had no intention of taking it off.

"Would you prefer sitting inside?" she asked him.

"No, it's fine. It's nice out here."

"Can I bring you a heater over, sir?" the waiter asked as he set down on the table two glasses and a bottle of Pinotage, the hotel's signature red wine.

"Actually, that would be great, if you don't mind?" he asked Kiara.

"Of course not," she said, a smile forming on her lips as the tough South African was clearly not as hardy as she was.

"It's heading into our winter now," he said, picking up on what she was thinking. "We don't enjoy the cold like you crazy English do. I have no idea how you swim in that sea all year around, I'd freeze to death. What's the temperature at the moment?"

"The sea is about fifteen degrees right now, so not too bad to be honest"

"It's still madness to me!" he said, picking up his glass of red and savouring the smell, as the waiter returned and lit the gas heater next to them.

"Are you ready to order?" the waiter asked them both.

Tyrone looked to Kiara to let her order first.

"I'd like the tuna steak please, and seasonal veg."

"I'll go for the ribeye, medium, with the veg as well."

"Any starters?"

"I think just some olives, if that's okay, Kiara?"

"Perfect," she replied.

The waiter left them to put the orders in and Tyrone sat back in his chair and contemplated his guest. She was clearly beautiful, that was not up for debate, as far as he was concerned. All the waiters were clearly taken with her as well, as were some of the other hotel guests who had started to fill some of the tables around them. The little gazes, some lasting longer than they should, confirmed it. She was dressed in light weight trousers and a short-sleeved cotton top, which made her natural olive skin look like she had been on a recent beach holiday. Having washed her hair and towel dried it just before she came down for dinner, it sat just below her shoulders and had a natural wave going through. Whilst not being vain by nature, she hated the grey hairs that had started creeping in when she turned thirty-five, so she had it coloured every couple of months, the last time just before she came over, and it shone a beautiful brown. Finally, and not lost on Tyrone, was her shape. As a cyclist and weight trainer himself, he understood the time and effort it took to stay in such good shape. Kiara had told him she was a triathlete, which took serious hours of training each month just to be able to compete. The standard triathlon race consisted of a 1.5km sea swim, a 40km cycle and then lastly a 10km run. Tyrone doubted he could even finish the swim, let alone take on a cycle and run afterwards. He was impressed by the fact that she was clearly not only physically fit but focused enough to compete at that level.

"What are you thinking?" she asked him after the silence went on a fraction too long.

"Sorry, I don't mean to be disrespectful, but you really are impressive."

She was used to men hitting on her, but somehow his compliment struck her less as a come on and more as just his honest thoughts.

"Thank you," was all she could think of as a reply.

"So, how come you seem to solve so many more cases than any other investigator I've looked up? What's your secret?" he asked, having seamlessly moved the conversation back to business.

"Wow, you do jump from one thing to another, don't you?" she replied.

Tyrone laughed. "It usually throws people off enough to force them into an honest answer."

"Well, I don't need to be played like that. If you want an honest answer, then all you have to do is ask me an honest question. So, what do you really want to know?"

"Touché," he said, smiling at her response. "Okay, well, my question is the same, what's your secret for getting to the bottom of cases no one else can? I did my research before calling you and your record for cases solved is unmatched. So, what's your secret, and will you use it on my case?"

"My secret? I guess I hate to lose."

"We all hate to lose. It's something else; you've got something no one else has, and it's that I need if these claims aren't going to bankrupt me."

She couldn't help but smile. He really did have a way of being honest that made her want to answer him. "I call it my spider sense."

"After Spider-Man, as in the cartoon character?" he asked, disappointed that she was not being serious with his question.

He was about to find out that that she was deadly serious, though. "Yes, Spider-Man. His spider sense was his real gift, much more powerful than his super strength or spiderweb. His spider sense told him when something was wrong; nothing could get past him when it started to tingle. I'm the same; in fact, I would suggest everyone has a spider sense, including you, although I think you already use yours as well."

"Explain," he said, picking up his wine glass and leaning towards her, intrigued by where she was going with this.

"Another word for it," she continued, "is instinct. I trust it above everything, it's as simple as that. I get a feeling in my stomach and it's almost as if I already know something is happening. I believe we all get that, but the natural thing to do is instantly question it. The moment you do that, you have already removed its power. I used to do that all the time. Something would pop into my head and, rather than just believe it, I would brush it aside and look for another, perhaps more conventional answer. But almost every time, I realised afterwards that if I had stuck with my first instinct, I would have been right and not wasted hours, days or even months looking for the same truth that I had known about at the start. So, when my instinct kicks in, I now trust it in the first instance and try to push away any doubts I have."

"And it's always right?" TR asked.

"Of course not," she almost laughed. "But probably eight out of ten times I'd say it was. And once my instincts set me off on a course, I have the work ethic to see it through. And I'll do that for you if you let me."

He took a large swig of his wine and leant back into his chair as the waiter returned with their meals. Once the waiter had set the food and topped up Kiara's wine glass, he left them alone again.

"So, Peter Parker, what is your spider sense telling you about my problem?" Tyrone asked her, with a serious edge to his voice.

"Before I answer that, I have a question of my own."

"Ask away."

"Why did it take you so long to bring someone in?"

"You think I left it too late to sort out?"

"I'm not saying that. I'll find whoever it is who is doing this. But you paid out all those claims without really doing any real due diligence first and then you left it until now, when things are on a knife's edge for you, before you brought me in. You don't strike me as someone who is not on the ball, but it seems to me that you've let it slip."

He thought about her question; she was right, even if he didn't want to admit it.

"First of all, I trust my team implicitly. Most of my senior people have been with me for well over a decade and I trust them like I would my own family. So, it might look like I took my eye off the ball to you, but as far as I was aware, my best people were on it all along. But you are right, I should have got involved earlier as soon as multiple claims came in."

"There's something else I wanted to ask you."

"Feel free."

"Adesco are one of your biggest clients, perhaps even your biggest."

"Yes."

"So, why haven't you called them yourself about this? I think I would have called them before I even called me."

"I did call them, the moment I realised we could have a problem. I called Gavin, their CEO, but he seems to be avoiding my calls. He and I do clash a bit, so I leave that relationship with Bea to handle, but usually when I call him, I do get a call back. This time, though, I only heard from Caroline, his PA. Apparently, he is so tied up with the launch of their newest oil platform that he isn't around to meet me or take my calls."

"And you don't think that is odd? Surely if he's suffering so many losses on his main business, he'd find the time to talk with you?"

"If you know him, you'd realise it's not so odd. And to be honest, until recently, the claims have been quite small in comparison to the sums we are covering, so it's not really unusual that either him or me would not be taking such a close interest. It's only because the recent claims have spiked in value that I am now involved. And I suspect when he eventually sees my messages that I'll be the first person he calls."

"Okay," Kiara replied, the scepticism in her voice clear for him to hear.

"Maybe we just do business differently in Africa than you do in London," he added.

"Maybe."

"There's something else you want to say, isn't there?" he asked.

"I know you don't want to hear this, but my gut is telling me that someone from inside your company is doing a job on you, and that someone at Adesco, maybe not the CEO, but someone in a senior position, is helping them. It's simply been too easy for them to register the claims and get a payment…" She let that sink in before continuing. "Also, it just feels like there is much more to this than simply someone getting rich on the back of your losses. I'd stake my reputation on the fact that there is something much bigger at stake here. I just don't know yet what it is."

Tyrone put his glass down and looked her deeply in the eyes before speaking. "No one in my company is involved in this, and I would stake my life on that," was all he said.

"Is that your heart telling you that or your head?" Kiara replied seriously, returning his stare without blinking. "What's your instinct telling you?" she asked him. "What is that knot deep in your stomach telling you?"

He had to take his time again before he answered.

"You are good, Mrs Fox, I'll give you that. Yes, my first instinct was to find out who in Worldwide was fucking me out of millions of dollars."

Kiara smiled.

"But I pushed that thought aside, and I am pleased I did. My people are my family, they would never do anything to harm me or the business."

"And yet your spider sense gave you the true answer right at the start. And that is why you called me," she said, half smiling at him, before picking up her knife and fork and starting on her tuna steak.

Tyrone looked at her a few seconds longer, not sure what he should say, before also picking up his cutlery and starting on his steak, although he wasn't sure he had the appetite for it anymore.

CHAPTER 23

Rene picked up his phone on the first ring. He'd been
waiting for Dan's call.

"Can you see her?" Rene asked.

"Yes. She's on the terrace, having dinner with Tyrone
Waterstone, the CEO of Worldwide Insurance."

"Did you check with the chauffeur company at the hotel, has
she booked a car to the airport for the morning?"

"Yes, I checked. And yes, she's booked a car. But not to the
airport. She's being taken to Worldwide's office first…"

"What do you mean first?"

"The car is then booked to take her and Tyrone to the local
airport, where he keeps his helicopter. I checked the flight plan
with my contact there who can access all the flight logs for planes
or 'copters, and he told me that they are flying out to Durban to
the port offices there, where one of our claims happened."

"So, she didn't take my veiled threat to her family seriously
then. I'm not surprised, given what Karly told us about her. Okay,
stay at the Saxon and, when she is alone, pay her a little visit. I'll
call Zara and will tell her to meet you there."

"I can handle this one on my own."

"I have no doubt. But Zara has a certain way of getting my
messages across."

CHAPTER 24

"That was amazing," Kiara said, after finishing off her dessert.

"I think the Saxon still has one of the best restaurants in the area."

"It was perfect, thank you. You seemed to go quiet over dinner," she remarked.

"Sorry. I was trying to come to terms with the fact that you think someone in my team could be involved in this. Every one of them has been with me for years. They've all celebrated with me, been to my house, they all know my boys, and every year they buy them birthday presents. I just can't believe one of them could be involved."

"I'm sorry, you asked what I thought, so I had to tell you."

"Actually, I asked for you to find the facts and present them to me, not to make assumptions."

"Fair enough, but as I said, my instincts are rarely wrong, so sometimes I treat them as facts until I can prove otherwise. And if we find out that my hunch is right and I can prove it, what then?"

"Then whoever it is will have fucked with the wrong guy. But I don't think you will find anything there, maybe you will at Adesco, but not at Worldwide. I don't want you to make any of them think you suspect them, because I don't, and when this is over, I don't want to have to put it all back together."

"Okay, that's fair."

"I'll see you at the office in the morning. I've arranged the hotel chauffeur to bring you to us and then we'll take a short hop to Durban, to the port's local IT office, so you can see the operation firsthand and can talk to everyone who was involved in these transits. I assume you are okay with a short helicopter flight, and then if we need to, we can make a short trip to Cape Town to see the port's physical operation there."

With that, Tyrone got up and went to leave.

"I'm sorry, have I upset you?" Kiara had to ask as the dinner had come to such an abrupt end.

Tyrone stopped and looked back at her. "It's fine," he said simply, "you need to look at all options, I get that, but it doesn't mean I have to agree or like them."

He left without another word.

"Was everything to your liking?" the waiter asked once Tyrone had left.

"It was wonderful, thank you," she replied. "I think I'll head off to my room now, I'm a little tired."

"Will we see you for breakfast?" he asked as he helped pull her chair back.

"Absolutely. I'll do an hour in the gym before, so I can then order the entire menu," she said, smiling.

"I'll let the chef know," the waiter said, bowing to her as she left.

Kiara walked out of the hotel's main entrance and took the small elevator up to the walkway that led to her suite. She had been really surprised by Tyrone's reaction as he left. It was great that he trusted his staff and defended them so fiercely, it said a lot about his good character, but it was her job to tell him what she thought, and despite the lack of evidence so far, she was sure that someone in the office had to have a hand in the way the claims were being settled. But, she realised, he was right in that her job was to find out what was happening and who was doing it and provide the proof to him, it was not to make some off-the-cuff guesses and throw people under the bus without knowing for definite that they were involved.

The truth was that, ever since she had met him, just hours ago, she had been really comfortable in his company, and she had let herself think of him as a friend right away, rather than as a client. They had so much in common, both were successful in their respective fields, both had twins of a similar age, and both were single parents, her a widow and him a divorcee. Even in their hobbies they were very similar. It had meant that they'd gelled right from the off. She knew it wasn't a sexual thing, at least not for her, as she was not able to, or even wanting to have another partner after losing Asher, but there did seem to be a connection between them.

She reached the large castle-like front door that led into the private building that held her suite and had to give it a huge pull to draw it open.

As soon as she stepped into the building, a hand covered her mouth from behind, dragged her to the nearest corner and then pulled her outside through a side door that led from the building into an unseen area. She tried to resist, but whoever was holding her was clearly much stronger than she was and gave her no room to fight back or scream. She was dragged to an area that was even more hidden in wild bushes and trees, and thrown to the ground, her back striking a small tree and causing her to feel slightly sick. She instinctively tried to get herself up with the thought of surprising whoever they were by breaking into a sprint. She knew she was quick, and strong, and she thought the man who had grabbed her would expect her to be so shocked as to be subservient, that he wouldn't expect her to make a sudden run for it. But he was quicker and stronger than she'd hoped and was expecting her to do something like that. Before she had even got a step away, he grabbed her by the hair, flung her back into one of the trees, and followed that up with such a powerful punch to the stomach that she fell back down on her knees and instantly threw up her entire dinner.

"The next punch may well kill you," Dan said in a strong South African accent. "So, if I were you, I would stay where you are."

She looked upwards, still trying to catch her breath from the punch, and saw her attacker. He was well dressed, strongly built and standing at around six foot. His face was covered by a balaclava, but she could see his eyes, which watched her menacingly. When he was sure that she was not going to try to run again, he stepped aside, revealing another person standing behind him. She was clearly less worried about being seen, as she had not bothered to cover herself. Kiara looked at her as she stepped forward. She was a stunning black woman with long, plaited hair that ran down past her shoulders, a voluptuous mouth and she had the same athletic frame that Kiara had. Unlike the man, who radiated anger, the lady seemed to show no emotion at all. It was almost as if she simply didn't care one iota what was happening. It was like the whole thing was just a game to her.

"She's much prettier than I thought she'd be, I assumed these insurance investigators were all boring office types," Zara said to the man, clearly unfazed by the beating she saw Kiara get.

Dan ignored her comment and waited to see what, if anything, Kiara would say.

Kiara wiped the sick from the side of her mouth and pulled herself back against the tree, trying to stay as far away from the two of them as possible.

"Mrs Fox, you are a stubborn one, aren't you?" Zara said to her.

Kiara looked up at her and realised that the smallest of the bunch was the leader. It struck her that it was the perfect cliché, as every movie had the bad guy as being the smallest, weakest one. It brought a sudden smile to her face.

"You think this is funny?" Dan said, taking a step forward.

"No, I don't," Kiara shot back at him, "there's nothing funny about a man your size thinking he's tough just because he had the element of surprise." She then turned her attention to Zara "So, which one of you called my house?" she said, addressing them both.

"Then you did understand our message? I thought for a moment that perhaps you weren't as smart as I keep being told you are. And yet here you still are, poking around, making a nuisance of yourself."

"I understand the message now, I assure you," she said, meaning every word of it.

"Good. So, here's your choice, Mrs Fox. Get on the next flight out of Johannesburg back to London, go home to your lovely family in the UK and stay safe. You can tell your employer at Worldwide that you've reviewed the files and, as far as you can tell, the claims are genuine and that these things happen. And tell him to pay our claims, again, very simple."

"Or…?" Kiara asked, not sure why she was being so brave considering what the big man had just done to her.

Zara laughed out loud. "Oh my God, I love her, she's brilliant. Baby you need to join our crusade, we need people like you if we are going to bring down the whole oil industry. I have a feeling you'll love the fireworks we are about to let off. Let's keep her," Zara said to Dan with a laugh.

"Zara," Dan said sternly to her, "you've said too much."

Zara smiled and shrugged to him. "Oh, stop it, she has no idea what we are doing. But, if I were you, I really would do as he tells you, darling, he really does have a nasty little temper on him."

"There is no 'Or', Mrs Fox, go home," Dan said to her. "You do not want to be here when we press our buttons."

Kiara knew she shouldn't have challenged him. What the hell was she thinking? She didn't need this in her life. She agreed with him, she needed to get on the next plane home, as soon as possible.

Then Zara said the wrong thing.

"The last thing you want me to do is send my friend here over to the UK to meet your children in person."

Kiara had only recently had her girls' lives threatened. And back then, she discovered that the only way to keep them truly safe was to find out who was threatening them and take them down, which is exactly what she had done.

She looked the lady in the eyes and knew she meant every word she was saying.

"I get it," Kiara said, "I'll go."

Dan watched her for a few seconds to see if she was telling him the truth or not. He thought he could spot a lie a mile off, but Kiara had been an investigator for too long to give her true intentions away.

"Good choice. Let's go," he said to Zara.

"Shame," Zara said to Kiara as she was leaving, giving her a wink. "I think you and I could have been friends."

As they walked away, Zara turned to Dan.

"Rene is worried about your friend, he's too unpredictable."

"Hamilton?" Dan said, confirming that they were talking about the same person.

"Will he deliver what Rene needs him to?"

"He has enough men to do it, and he certainly has the balls. If we get the explosives on the platform, he'll have his men there and they can do what we need them to."

"You don't sound as convinced as you did at the meeting."

"He can do it, there's no doubt."

"But…"

"If we don't pay him, and soon, then it'll be us he takes down first. And trust me, I've seen how he works, if he comes for us, we will want to hide and stay hidden for a long time."

They were interrupted by Dan's phone ringing.

"Did you see her?" Rene asked him.

"Yes. We got our point across."

"So, she'll leave then?"

"She'd be crazy if she doesn't."

"Hamilton worries me," Rene said, backing up exactly what Zara had just said to him.

"What do you want me to do?"

"Go to Cape Town, tonight, see him in person and make sure he knows we'll get the money to him."

"Tonight?!"

"You heard me, go to the township right away and see the man in person, no more phone calls or fake promises," he repeated. "Tell him the money is coming, he'll have it within a few days. Convince him that he'll be paid, in full, but he needs to get his men on the platform right away. We are almost ready for the big day, and we can't risk missing it."

"What if I can't convince him?"

"If I were you, I wouldn't even think about that."

"If Zara can't get the money to him…"

"Then you'll be the first he kills anyway, and I'll be a dead man walking, won't I?"

CHAPTER 25

Kiara watched them vanish back into the bushes that surrounded the hotel grounds. Then she pulled herself up, using the tree as a lever. She let out a small moan as she moved, as the area where the brute had punched her was still tender. She made her way back to the side door and entered the building, before heading up to her suite. She felt totally lost as what to do or who to call. Being attacked is a shocking experience for anyone, but more so when you are alone in a foreign country.

She undressed slowly and put her clothes into the sink to rinse away the smell of her dinner. Then she climbed into the shower and turned it on as hot as she could bear it. The bruise where she had been hit had already started to purple and she had to take extra care when she washed it in the hot water.

She stayed in the shower for what seemed like a lifetime. She had a lot of thinking to do. She knew she could not just leave, not now they had threatened her family. If Tyrone chose not to pay the claim, which was well within his rights to do, then they might assume that she'd told him not to. And then what?! She was not going to spend the rest of her life looking over her shoulder just waiting for them to arrive on her doorstep. She had no idea if they would do that or not, but she could not take that risk. She needed to work out a way of making them believe she had taken the flight home whilst she stayed and exposed them to Tyrone, and to the authorities. What she needed to do now was find a way of stopping them and having them locked up. Stealing millions of dollars of

145

oil would definitely result in a long jail sentence, even in a country such as South Africa.

It then dawned on her what the other lady had said. She talked about bringing down the oil companies rather than just stealing their money. The whole conversation seemed to be about so much more than just dodgy claims, no matter how big they were. This was clearly not just about financial theft, it was not just about the money, exactly as she had said to Tyrone over dinner. Her brain started to piece things together. There were a few players in this. There was the oil company, Adesco, the ones drilling for the oil and who owned the tankers shipping it. There was Tyrone at Worldwide, the insurance company covering any loss of the oil during transit. And then there were the ones who'd just ambushed her. *So, who are they?* she wondered. Maybe they were climate activists, or terrorists might be a better description It had to be that; who else would want to bring down an oil company? There had certainly been some of those in the news in the last few years, stopping traffic on the motorways, splashing orange paint over works of art and interrupting events like the Super Bowl in America or the world famous Proms concert in London.

But to try to take down an entire oil platform in the middle of the sea? Now, that is on a completely different level, and it would take serious money. Tyrone was in the middle of something big and she needed to tell him.

Kiara, like most educated people, was fearful of global warming, and she always did her own small bit to try to protect the planet, from recycling to not using plastic bags, all the usual little things normal folk did. But she certainly would not sit in the middle of the motorway stopping people going about their business. And she wouldn't be travelling to Paris to throw orange paint over the Mona Lisa anytime soon. But that didn't mean she didn't deep down understand these people. And there was a large part of her that was relieved such people did what they did, for how else would the planet survive if not for these eco warriors? Her cutting down on a few plastic bottles wasn't going to reverse climate change, was it?

However, the line between eco warriors and eco terrorists was a very thin one. The people she'd just met were not throwing paint around museums. They were threatening her life and the safety of her children. And they were stealing millions of dollars for something that she couldn't even begin to comprehend. They were clearly people prepared to do anything for their cause, even if their methods destroyed lives to save lives.

She got out of the shower and took her time drying off before she decided who to call first. The first thing was to protect her family, and there was no one in South Africa who could help her with that.

She picked up her phone and made the first call.

"Judy, sorry to call so late, are the girls still up?" she said as soon as her mother-in-law answered from her home on the other side of the world.

"Kiara, darling, the girls thought you would call a couple of hours ago when they got back from college."

"I know, I'm sorry, something came up, which was unavoidable. Are they in bed yet?"

"No, it's only nine o'clock here, they don't go up until around ten. Let me call them."

"Just a second, Judy. Are you alone?"

"Of course, when aren't I? Peter is asleep in the chair and the girls are in the playroom."

"I just don't want to cause any concern, and I know you are always the level-headed one."

"What's going on, Kiara? I'm not sure I'm going to like the sound of this."

"I'm pretty sure it's nothing to worry about. But that phone call Peter picked up, from the South African guy, I think he's someone I'm now investigating. I have no idea how he found out the house phone number, or the girls' names, but I guess there is a lot about us on the internet now. Anyway, I think he called as a warning to me to back off."

She was certainly not going to tell Judy about the visit she'd just had.

"Are we in danger?" Judy cut to the chase of the matter, but she held back from saying 'again'.

"No. At least, I am ninety-nine percent sure you're not."

"Anything under a hundred percent is a worry."

"Yes, it is."

"Would you be happier if we moved back to our house with the girls until you are home?"

"I think maybe you should. I know it's not ideal, but I just want to be sure that they, and you guys, are okay."

"I agree. I'll tell Peter and we can do it tomorrow. I can tell the girls it's just because we want a few nights in our own beds. They'll understand. To be honest, both Peter and I are finding the hard beds here a little tough on our backs. Shouldn't you come home, though? Is it still safe out there for you?"

"I'm okay, I'm certain it's just idle threats, nothing more, and in my job, it kind of comes with the territory."

"Please be careful, Kiara. The girls need you back here, they've lost too much already, as we all have."

"No one's going to do anything, I promise," Kiara said whilst putting her free hand on the bruise around her stomach. "Can I say hi to the girls quickly?"

"Of course."

After speaking to both the girls, Kiara dialled Tyrone's number. She needed to tell him everything that had happened and hope he had a way of helping her look like she had got on the plane back home instead of taking her to the port. She also needed him to keep it a secret from his staff. She still believed one of them was involved and she couldn't risk whoever it was calling these people and telling them that she was staying.

She also knew she should call the local police and alert the hotel security to what had happened to her. But something made her hold back. The fact that those people even managed to get into the hotel and find her was a worry, and she wondered if they maybe had some connection to the hotel, or even to the local police. She hoped not, but without knowing for sure, she could not risk making those calls. And if she did, then what did she really have to tell them? Her recent experience with the police back home didn't exactly fill her with confidence that they could do anything at the moment. If she wanted the police to help her then she first had to tell them something she knew as fact, like who these people were and what they were planning on doing. Without that, there was nothing the police could do to help her. The only person she had in her corner right now was Tyrone, and she really hoped that was enough.

CHAPTER 26

Tyrone had been surprised to see a call coming in from Kiara so soon after he'd left her. He had been even more surprised when she told him everything that had happened.

His first reaction was to drive straight back to the Saxon, pick her up and take her back to his house for safety. Like most houses in Johannesburg, his own house had security gates, electric fences on top of the walls and armed security guards at the street entrance; this was pretty standard in the expensive areas of the city. Kiara had to point out to him that, despite these people getting to her, it was likely the Saxon Hotel would have far more security than he did at his home, and that if she went straight to his house then she could also be putting his sons in danger.

Up until that moment, he had not even considered any of them would be in danger, especially not his own children. He had simply thought he could refuse to pay the claim, that he would bring in an outside investigator and, ultimately, they would find the people responsible for stealing from him. His own family being in danger had not even crossed his mind until now.

Kiara being attacked and having her family threatened changed everything. Going to the police at this stage wouldn't protect them, as they still had no idea who the people were they needed protection from, and the local police were too underfunded to have enough officers available to provide round the clock help. So, it was a case of either hiring private security, or more simply keep paying the claims until the money ran out.

"I need to settle the claims," he said after a short pause, "and beef up our personal security until you go home."

"And then what? Are you going to keep insuring these shipments and risk more claims until you go out of business? Or are you going to refuse to insure them next time and risk these people making a visit to your home and insisting you do?"

"Would they do that, really?"

"You didn't get to look into their eyes like I did," she said.

"Then what the hell do you suggest?" he asked her in frustration.

"We have to find out who they are, and then we stop them. There's no other way."

"Are you really prepared to stay here and do that? Even after what's happened to you?!"

"It's because of what happened to me that I have no choice."

Tyrone had to take a second to think. She was right, he knew that, but what she was suggesting would take some serious bravery on her part. The stakes were seriously high for him as well. The business he had built from scratch into a multimillion-dollar powerhouse was being pushed to the brink of bankruptcy and yet the only way it seemed to save it was to run headfirst into a storm and hope that they managed to survive. He wasn't sure he could face either option. And he had no idea how Kiara could sound so matter of fact about the whole thing.

But he couldn't just let his business go down, he had spent his whole life building it to give him and his boys the financial stability in life that he was never given as a child. It meant too much to him to simply stand and watch it be stolen from him. But to do what Kiara was suggesting would mean he would have to be as brave as she was, and he wasn't a hundred percent sure he could do that either.

"Well?" she asked him after the pause went on a little too long.

"I need to protect my boys, from whoever these people are and also from losing their inheritance. So, I guess I have no choice, do I?"

"You always have a choice," she replied.

"I'm not sure I do."

"Can you get your boys somewhere safe, somewhere not connected with you? It's best to be prepared. I've already moved my girls away from my house to somewhere they can't be easily found, just in case these people really do have a long reach."

"I can take them in the morning to their grandparents. I doubt anyone knows where they live and if you think I'm security conscious then you've seen nothing. My ex-father-in-law looks like he's preparing for a zombie invasion."

"Okay, do that first thing and keep them off school for a few days. I'll pack my case and will check out in the morning. I'll have the hotel get me a driver to take me to the airport and I'll buy a flight back to London. I'll go through the whole thing as if I'm flying home, but I'll not actually get on the plane. I'll make up some excuse and will make my way to an exit. If they are watching me, they would see me going through security and will assume they scared me off after all. I doubt they'll have any way of checking the flight log to know if I boarded or not and I'm sure they won't be watching Heathrow to see if I landed. Will you be able to meet me at the airport? But maybe not in your white Porsche, perhaps something that doesn't stand out so much!"

"Of course. But where will we go once I've got you?"

"You need to get us to Cape Town."

"You want to go straight to the main port?" he said in shock. "But that's likely where they will be."

"Exactly."

CHAPTER 27

Caroline had arranged to meet Tony in their Cape Town office, knowing that Gavin was back in Johannesburg trying to convince the rest of the board that he needed to raise more money in the markets to make sure Platform Neptune was delivered on time, and with a fully working university and a fully tested and robust tidal generator. Tony, who was the most vocal opponent to Gavin's plans and who had already convinced the majority of the board to side with him, decided to skip the meeting and just let his brother dig his own grave.

"What have you got for me?" he asked Caroline as she walked into the small coffee shop on the Waterfront.

She handed him a small piece of paper.

Tony glanced at it and smiled, before looking back up at her.

"Is this the man who broke up our AGM?"

She nodded. "And his address," she said.

Tony looked again at the paper. "He's around the corner at Camps Bay."

Caroline got up from her chair, ready to leave.

"Where do you think you're going?" he said to her.

"I need to get back to the office."

"No, you don't. You're driving me to his house."

"Look, I said I would find his address, which is exactly what I've done. I never promised I'd do anything more than that."

"I never asked you to promise anything. I don't need to. You work for me as far as I remember. So go get your car and meet me out front. I am going to make sure that fucker stays away from my brother, especially until I take over as CEO."

Caroline hesitated for a minute, having suddenly found herself right in the middle of something that she was not equipped to handle. She knew Tony well enough to know he never made idle threats. If she took him to Amos's house, then it would not end well for the other man.

"Now, Caroline," Tony said to her as he picked up his coffee to drain the last drop.

She had no choice but to drive him there, she knew that, but she could send out a warning to Amos first.

She left the coffee shop and walked down the road to her car. Checking behind her to make sure Tony hadn't stepped out yet and was watching her, she pulled out her mobile phone and the number she had kept back. She dialled it. The phone rang three times before Amos picked it up, just in time for her to reach her car and climb inside.

"Hello?" he said down the line.

"Amos, you need to get the hell out of your house, now."

"Who is this?"

"Just get out," she said forcefully down the line.

"Not until you tell me who you are," he replied as calmly as he was able to.

"For Christ's sake," she said as she switched on the car's engine and started to pull out into the main road. "I'm from Adesco Oil. I work with the board, for Gavin and Tony."

"Oh my God, you're the lady who emailed me asking me to come in. Amazing…"

"Look, you need to get the hell out of your house, now."

"I don't understand."

"You've stirred up a right hornets' nest here. Gavin is keen to meet you, he seems to believe you can do what you are saying, but Tony won't let it happen, he'll do whatever it takes to stop his brother."

"Let me talk to him, if I show him my work, he'll understand that what I'm offering will not only help stop the damage they are causing, but will also make them a fortune, eventually even more than the oil does. What I'm offering him is…"

"You're not listening to me," she said, cutting him off mid-sentence. "We are on our way over now and Tony is going to stop you ever getting in front of his brother…"

"Caroline, open the fucking door!"

"Shit!" she said. She had been so engrossed in the call with Amos that she had driven all the way to the front of the café and pulled up outside without even realising it.

"Just get the fuck out!" she said, before cutting the call.

"Who were you talking to?" Tony said to her as she got into the car.

"It was Karly, at the Joburg office," she lied, as she pulled out of the parking space and headed off to Camps Bay. "She needed to find some financial documents for the board meeting that Gavin is in. She couldn't find them, but she knew I had a copy."

She could feel Tony looking at her. She dared not take her eyes off the road in case he saw the lies etched into her face.

CHAPTER 28

A mos put the phone down. He certainly believed Caroline when she said they were on the way to his house now. He had seen Tony in action firsthand and knew that the man was not to be messed with.

He couldn't believe what was happening to him. On the one hand he had that lunatic Hamilton threatening to come back and kill him if he didn't do what he was told, and now he had the second-in-command of Adesco Oil apparently on the way over to do what, beat him senseless? Kill him? Who knew what that man was capable of.

One part of him wanted to stay there and face Tony head on. His batteries were still attached to the pool in the basement, and he could show him exactly what they could do. And on top of that, he had also commissioned a full financial report that not only showed the cost of his project, but more importantly, showed the financial value to Adesco Oil of reselling on the fully charged batteries to the energy companies, which after only a few years would recoup all their set-up costs and then start to earn the company a small fortune. Perhaps to start with not as much as the oil did, but over a few years, it would bring the company back into profit and eventually it would even exceed the oil profits that they would lose.

But if Caroline was right and Tony was on the war path, then perhaps it would be better to retreat and fight the battle another day. The key was really to get in front of Gavin. He was the company CEO, and he clearly believed in everything that Amos believed in.

Retreat and fight another day was definitely the best option right now. He grabbed his car keys from the shelf by the door and headed out, hoping she had given him enough time to get away.

CHAPTER 29

Tony and Caroline didn't speak for the entire car journey. She pulled up into a free spot outside Amos's house. Neither she nor Tony noticed the car up the road as it turned the corner out of sight.

The moment she turned the engine off, Tony was out of the car and heading up to the front gate. Unlike other houses in the area, Amos had no armed security services monitoring his property and the gate was unlocked and easy to push open. Tony went through and headed up the stairs to the front door.

By the time Caroline had caught up with him, he was already banging on the door like a crazy man and screaming Amos's name to open up.

"Maybe he's not in," she said to him as she got to the front door.

"Amos, you fucker, let me in!"

"For Christ's sake, Tony, the whole street is going to hear you."

Tony ignored her and started kicking at the door as hard as he could.

"Tony, stop it."

"Did you tell him we were coming? Was that who you were calling back then?" He turned on her, the words coming out so fast that his spittle stuck to her face. "Did you fucking call him?!"

"I didn't," she said, suddenly frightened to be there face to face with her boss as the rage started to overtake him. "I called Karly, I told you that, she needed some numbers."

"Give me your phone, show me the number you called!" he screamed at her, pulling at her jacket to get to her phone.

"Tony, stop it!" she screamed back at him.

"Gavin's not going to fuck up my inheritance, and you and this Amos won't either!" He carried on grabbing at her jacket as he spat the words out.

"Tony…" She pulled back from him, scared that he would grab her phone and see the last number was not to the Adesco office, but she lost her footing on the top step and started to fall backwards over the small railing that looked down the side of the house ten feet to Amos's basement. Tony felt her leaving his grip, but instead of pulling her back he shoved her as hard as he could. He had lashed out in anger, knowing that she had betrayed him, but he had never intended for her to fall over the railings. In the split second it took her to leave the top step, he lunged forward to try to stop her, but he was too late.

He watched as she hit the bottom step and the blood started pouring from her head as it took the brunt of the fall. He knew there was no way she could survive a head trauma that severe.

"Shit, shit, shit!" he said to himself. "Fuck!"

He looked around and was relieved that, despite his rantings and kicking at the door, no one had stopped on the street to watch them. And because Amos's house was set up high behind gates, there were no neighbours close enough to hear or see anything. And if anyone walking by had looked up, they would not have been able to really make out his features, anyway.

He ran back down the stairs and stopped at the bottom. He knew he should carry on around to the next steps that led down to the basement to just check if Caroline was still breathing. It was not too late to save her life, if he was quick. But if he did that and then she died, he would have no way of proving it was just an argument that had gone too far. He could be done for manslaughter, or even murder. That would be the end of him replacing Gavin as CEO. And, without him there, his brother would continue with his crazy ideas and lead the family into ruin. All the work their grandfather and their father had done to build this company over the last hundred years would be for nothing, ruined by his brother chasing some childhood dream. The family name would be forgotten, or worse, be a laughing stock in the industry, something that would follow his own children around until the day they died. And he would be locked in a cell somewhere, unable to stop him.

He wouldn't let that happen, he couldn't let Caroline's death destroy his destiny. He was going to make Adesco Oil the largest and most powerful oil company in the world, even if it meant he had to murder to do it.

Without hesitation, he carried on down the drive and through the gates, pulling them closed behind him. He reached Caroline's car and pulled on the door. But, of course, it was locked. He looked back, wondering if he should go and get her keys. But he couldn't think of a single circumstance where him driving back to the office in her car, alone, with her dead body at the foot of some stairs would actually play out well for him.

He carried on walking away from the house down to the car park that led onto the beach. Near the exit was a taxi rank. He walked up to the front car and knocked on the window. The driver turned to him and signalled that he was having his lunch and not taking fares. Tony pulled out a large wad of cash from his pocket and held it up. The driver opened his window, dropped the half-eaten sandwich onto the floor and unlocked the back doors.

"Where to, sir?" he said to Tony as he climbed into the back seat.

"The Waterfront," Tony said back to him, as he slid to the far side of the bench seat, trying to stay out of the mirror that was suspended above the driver.

"Yes, sir, no problem, sir," the driver said as he pulled the car onto the main road.

CHAPTER 30

Kiara did exactly what she told Tyrone she would do. She checked out of the Saxon Hotel early and had them arrange a driver to take her to O'Tambo International Airport, but not before having them book her a one-way flight back to London. She wasn't sure if these people had a way to check all this out, but she couldn't take any chances.

Without even looking over her shoulder, she knew she was being watched as she left the hotel, she could feel it in her stomach. She had the same feeling all the way on the drive to the airport. The feeling only left her after she had checked in and headed through security into departures.

All she needed to do now was find a way of leaving the airport to meet Tyrone. That was possibly easier said than done.

Her phone rang, and she saw it was Tyrone calling.

"Are you through security?" he asked.

"Yes, a few moments ago. Where are you?"

"I've left my car in the long-term car park and I'm over at the private jet terminal. I didn't want to book us on a normal flight as it felt too chancy. Also, the private jets are a lot faster and they skip the security at both ends."

"So, how do I get to you?" she asked as she looked all around her at the hundreds of travellers heading towards the shops, the restaurants and the departure gates.

"You're in Terminal A, I guess. I'm at the Fireblade Terminal in the VIP lounge."

"Good for you!" she said sarcastically. "And I suppose I just ask someone the way and they'll let me get out of here, and give me a private buggy over to you?"

"Well, actually, there's a central atrium you can use to walk between the two."

"You're joking me?"

"I'm not. But it's a bit of a walk, a good half an hour. And you need to get a move on, our plane leaves in under an hour."

"You didn't exactly leave me a lot of time, did you?"

"You can make it. Just go back towards security and down the long ramp on the left, maybe two hundred metres and then you'll see a bank of elevators. Take them back up to the next floor and you'll see the customs tax desk at the top. From there you'll see a long walkway that takes you all the way to the end of the terminal. You'll get to another security area where you'll need to give them your name and passport. I've already added you to the VIP list, so they'll be expecting you. What did you do with your luggage?"

"I stored it in the lockers before I went to the check-in desk, then I told the check-in girl I travel light. She didn't even question me."

"Good thinking. When you get to me, we'll notify the airline you were taken unwell at one of the lounges, so you won't be travelling tonight. The fact that there is no luggage to be removed means it won't delay the flight. So, unless our friends can check-in with the airline's desk, they'll have no idea you didn't get on board. Also, I've called Mufuka and Jan at the office. I told Jan to mark the outstanding claim as agreed and told Mufuka to pay it right away."

"Wow, so you are going to pay it then, the full twenty million? Even after everything we said. I don't get it."

"I thought about trying to get hold of Gavin at Adesco again, tell him that I'm not going to pay his claim, but if you're right that someone high up there is involved in this, it could alert them to what we are doing. So I had no option, did I? But I'll get the money back when this is all over. Once we figure out what is happening, Adesco will have to refund me, they'll have no choice, or else we'll have them shut down for fraud. So, I'm just treating this as a short-term cash loan for the moment. But it does leave me pretty empty in the bank, right at the edge of the minimum cash requirements we have to maintain. So, unless we can stop them quickly, the regulators will shut me down, and then it's game over for Worldwide, I'm afraid. Hopefully, if I can keep this quiet at my office and with the cash paid over to Adesco, and you supposedly back in the UK, it'll keep everyone off our backs a little longer and give us the time we need.

"What will you tell your staff about why I left?"

"I already told them. I said I sacked you and told you to go back to England. I said you questioned me about them all personally and I didn't like it, so I took you off the job and bought you an early flight back home."

"You've been a busy boy!"

"You'd better be right about all of this, Kiara. That payment all but wipes out my reserves. I had to tell Mufuka to keep it quiet from everyone as to how tight things are now and that I was arranging to take out our reserves from the bank, which is why I am heading to Cape Town, which is not entirely untrue, by the way. I can survive a bit longer by calling on my reserves, but one more large claim like that and it could be game over for me."

"Then we'd better get them before they do it again, hadn't we?"

"And you had better get a move on, the plane goes if you are here or not."

CHAPTER 31

K arly sat in her office with the door closed and waited until her team were all back at their desks before she made the call. Whilst none of her team could hear when her door was closed, she still felt vulnerable that one of them could come in at any second and see or hear something that they shouldn't. She desperately wanted to close her blinds to give herself maximum privacy and to let them know she didn't want to be disturbed, but she was acutely aware that closed blinds drew people's attention rather than avoided it.

She put her headphones on and made the call to Zara.

The other woman frightened her, even more than Dan and Hamilton did, and making the call set her nerves on edge.

"Yes?" Zara said, answering the phone as if to a stranger.

"It's me, Karly."

"Yes, I am well aware of who you are. What do you want?"

"My contact has called me. The last claim, the one we had only received half the money on, the balance has been settled."

"In full?"

"Yes, in full. But there's more, they've also settled the other one that was on hold."

"The twenty million?!" Zara said in surprise.

"Yes."

"What's happened? There's no way they would just change their minds on something so big."

"I don't know for sure. All I do know is that the boss apparently didn't like the way the investigator was working, he took her off the contract and she's now gone back to England."

"And then he settled the claims. Just like that?"

"Apparently so."

"And has the money hit your account?"

Karly looked at her screen. It was open on the Adesco bank account and in front of her she could see two payments in from Worldwide Insurance totalling over twenty million dollars.

"Yes, I can see it now."

"Okay. Well then, transfer it over to the charity account now," Zara said before cutting the call.

"I'm doing it now," she said to the quiet phone.

She looked up to check to see if anyone was looking at her, but they were all firmly fixed on their own computers and their own work. She clicked on the payment tabs and sent both payments immediately over to Amos's charity account. Despite them being fairly large amounts, the Adesco bank was used to seeing tens of millions transferred in and out most days of the week and, as such, the transfer simply cleared from her account instantly. The final total for the day returned to the amount it was before the transfers had come in and, unless someone else took the time to read the entries, no one would be the wiser. And she knew that, within minutes, further transactions would be happening within the business, especially with the billions being spent on the new platform, that it would not be too long before those payments would be lost within all the others. It was only at the year end when their auditors might question her on the specific lines that she had to get creative, but it had worked last year and she was certain she could do it again this year.

She breathed a sigh of relief and closed the banking screen down.

CHAPTER 32

Amos sat in his car, deciding whether he should go back home, when his bank called. They told him that an unusually large amount of money had just hit his account, but they couldn't release it to him until they went through their money laundering checks first.

The fact the payment had come from a well-known company gave the bank some comfort, however, he still needed to visit the branch, sign some papers and explain what the payment was for. It was not often that over twenty million dollars was paid to a small charity like his. Also, the fact that it was paid in USD and not South African rand had set some alarm bells off at his local branch.

He agreed to go that same afternoon as he wanted this over and done with, but he had to call Rene first to arrange for Zara to meet him there, as she was the one who knew what to tell the bank."

"What do you want?" Rene said, picking up the phone to Amos in annoyance at being disturbed.

Since the power shift between them, Rene had dispensed with the niceties that he used to offer Amos and now talked to him like he talked to everyone, like they were all idiots just getting in the way of what he needed to do.

"The bank called me," Amos said, unperturbed.

"The bank?" Rene said with sudden interest.

Amos drew in a breath before he carried on.

"Spit it out, for Christ's sake."

"They said a large payment has just hit my account."

"So, Karly did it then, incredible. When will it clear your account? We need to pay Hamilton now, before he does something stupid. And we need to get Dan the rest of his cash so he can finish on his side."

"They won't clear it into my account until I go in to see them and sign some forms. Usually, I can just go online and confirm I am who I say I am, but this time the amount is so big that they are insisting I go into the branch with my photo ID. Otherwise, they'll just return the money to the place it came from."

"So, when are you going in?"

"Now, I guess, but I can't go alone. They'll know I'm lying the moment I open my mouth."

"Zara will pick you up within the hour. Are you at your house?"

"No. I had to leave." He thought for a minute about telling Rene that Caroline from Adesco had called him and that Tony was after him, but he decided there was no need to throw that in right now. They could deal with Tony separately. He was sure Rene would have a solution to that problem.

"Where are you, then?"

"I'm at Green Point Park, just behind Mouille Point."

"Stay there, and wait for Zara. And don't fuck this up, Amos. Everything now depends on this payment, for you as much as for us."

The phone went dead. Amos hadn't realised he had been holding his breath almost the entire time. He let out a huge sigh. He stepped out of his car and stood by the entrance to the park, watching the kids playing on the roundabouts and swings, being pushed back and forth by their parents.

All he wanted to do now was get back home, sit in the garden with a book and a diet cola, and forget that Rene and Zara even existed. He sometimes wished he had never even started his charity, as the stress had been taking a toll on his health. He watched as a bird flew down and landed on the one tree that still had leaves on it. The bird crept along the branch and made its way to the feeder that the park rangers kept stocked with grains. It put it in its beak and took down a mouthful. Before it flew off, he was sure it turned and looked at him with a sad smile, somehow beckoning him to follow it up into the clouds and away to nothingness.

Amos smiled to himself. Nature was incredible. The planet was incredible, he thought to himself. And it was his job to protect it, to preserve it. He reminded himself this was his sole purpose. He couldn't stop people like Rene from doing what they did, but then, why should he? They all had the same end in mind, to reverse climate change and bring the world back into its natural order of things. He might not agree with Rene's way of doing things, but he had to admit that at least the man was trying to get things done.

Amos put aside his earlier feelings and knew he was never going to stop doing what he was born to do. He needed that money as much as Rene did. He was going to get Adesco Oil first, and then, with Gavin as his partner, they would bring in all the other oil producers and ultimately transform all the oil platforms into tidal farms. Between them, they were going to save the planet.

He was suddenly, absolutely, certain of that.

He walked back to his car and waited for Zara.

CHAPTER 33

Rene had expected Dan to answer the phone. But instead, he heard the voice of Hamilton coming back to him.

"Where is my money?"

"Hamilton?" Rene asked in surprise. "Where's Dan?"

"Where is my money?" the other man repeated.

Rene knew he had dialled Dan's number, and he didn't even have Hamilton's number in his phone. So, he didn't need to check in case he had misdialled.

"Where's Dan?" Rene repeated his question, trying to sound like he was still in control of the situation, even though he certainly didn't feel like he was.

"I would be happy to pass the phone to him, Mr Rene, but just at the moment he is unable to respond."

"What have you done to him?"

"We have been very gentle, he still has all his fingers and toes, but they are perhaps just a little bruised. So, just now he is having a rest, sleeping it off, but if I have need to speak to him further like that then you will receive him back in a number of boxes, do you understand me?"

The situation was fast spiralling out of Rene's control.

"WHERE IS MY MONEY?!" Hamilton shouted down the phone again, enunciating each word so slowly as if each one held the answers to the universe.

"I told you before, the money is coming."

"I am sure Mr Dan will be very happy when we are paid, but I am certain he would like you to be faster because, every day from now, I will be passing him around our township, and at each hut they will take a little piece of him for a prize. And when there is nothing left of him to take, we will come and find you and your pretty girlfriend and start again."

"It's already done," Rene said down the line. "Half the money is being transferred to you tonight, and as we agreed, the balance will be sent when the platform is at the bottom of the ocean."

"If the money is in our account by the morning, then we will be happy to return Mr Dan in one piece. My men and I will most certainly finish our job for you. If the money is not in our account then, *we will* come for you tomorrow."

With that, Hamilton put the phone down.

Rene sat there in shock. Dan had warned him of the dangers they took employing a person like Hamilton. But Rene wouldn't listen, he wanted the job done, no matter the risk to them all. He now realised that he might have made the biggest mistake of his life.

CHAPTER 34

K iara had made it to the private terminal with just a couple of minutes to spare. Tyrone was waiting for her at the stairs at the foot of the private jet and took her small carry-on bag.

"I've arranged for you to meet my godson Aidan when we get to Cape Town. He works in cyber security and his company are employed by the Waterfront to manage all the computers and wi-fi that service every business there, which includes the port itself. So, whilst he doesn't have direct access to Adesco, he can get you into the port's server room and hopefully into their systems. I'm not sure if it'll help us, but if there is something in there, then he is our best shot at finding it."

"Does he know that what we are asking him to do is not exactly legal and if we are found out, it could not only cost him his job, but a lot more than that?"

"He knows. Don't worry, it's not his first rodeo getting me a little intel when I've needed it."

Kiara threw him a look.

"We might run a legitimate business, but it doesn't mean we don't need to bend the rules every now and then to gain a little advantage over our competitors," he said with a twinkle in his eyes.

"Are you not coming with me?" she asked, picking up on the fact that he'd said his godson would be meeting 'you' and not 'us'.

"I need to pop into my bank when we get there. I told you we

171

keep a reserve with them just in case we ever have to pay out a major claim and things get a bit tight. I've never had to call on it in all the years we've been in business, but I've also never had to pay out a twenty-million-dollar claim before without getting our re-insurers to stump up half. We keep a reserve of fifty million dollars in diamonds in their vault and I'm the only one who can access it."

"Wow, fifty million in diamonds? That's a lot of stones!"

"We've had some good years. What can I say, insurance pays well most of the time. Up until now, I never thought I'd have to dig into this reserve, it's literally all I've got for the business and, if I have any more claims this size and my re-insurers don't support me, then it'll not last long. In my business, this is really not a fortune, and using it makes me vulnerable to any big claims that follow. So, I'm relying on you finding out who's doing this before I lose the lot."

"You can be sure I'll find them. The question is what you will do about it when I do. I still think there's someone at your company who is deeply involved, and you might have to come to terms with that."

"I hope you're wrong, and I am pretty confident about that, but, if there is, then I'll deal with them, I assure you."

They spent the rest of the flight in silence, both of them contemplating what they needed to do once they landed in Cape Town.

"Are you okay?" Tyrone asked as the plane landed and they heard the engine winding down.

Kiara hadn't realised that she had been silently crying. She wiped the tears from her face and turned to face him.

"I'm fine," she said. "I've just never been to Cape Town before. It was somewhere Asher always wanted to go to. We talked about coming here for the twins' eighteenth birthdays, you know, doing a safari, climbing Table Mountain, seeing the penguin beach, all the usual touristy stuff, and now it's just a dream, something that will never happen."

"What happened to Asher?" Tyrone asked the question that he had avoided since they had met. "Nick told me he died in an accident, but not what actually happened."

"It wasn't an accident, not really. The press said so at the time, and even I thought that, but it was because of a case I was working on. If I had just stopped pushing… if I had just done what I was being told to do, he would still be alive today."

"That's crazy, you can't put that on yourself."

"I can, and I should."

"That's not fair, Kiara," Tyrone said. "If you were doing your job then you were doing the right thing. You can't blame yourself for doing your job. It's who you are, you must never apologise for that."

The aeroplane came to a complete stop and the pilot came into the main cabin to tell them that they could now disembark. Kiara took the moment to change the conversation back to business.

"When this is over, assuming we all survive, I'll tell you what happened, but for now, let's get back to your business. Where is your godson meeting me?"

"I told him I'll message him when we are in an Uber. His office is near the entrance to the V&A Waterfront, close to the port. There's a hotel there called the Cape Grace, it's where I always stay when I'm overnighting here. He's going to meet you in the lounge area; he's got your description, so he'll find you. I'm going to head straight to the bank as it'll take me a couple of hours to get the paperwork done for them and then I need to move the diamonds over to a dealer I know to arrange the sale. So, I should be able to meet you back at the Cape Grace maybe three hours later. That should give Aidan enough time to get you to the server room."

"I hope that gives me enough time. If he can get me into

Adesco's computers, I'll need to go back to see the last dozen shipments that Adesco have made, check the crew logs and all the personnel that have been involved. The logs should show the same crew who were on board, or certainly ninety-nine percent the same. However, if I cross check the shipments with the ones where there have been claims, I bet you I will all of a sudden see a new person logged on each time, someone only logged on to those trips and none of the others. If I find that name, then I find the person responsible for orchestrating the losses. The fact that no oil is actually being stolen means someone is logging on and changing the numbers, but to do that, they need to have a login, and I would guess that as they never expect anyone to be looking, they won't be changing the name each time. They will either be using their own name or one very similar. One thing all criminals do is get lazy. They all believe that they are too clever to be caught and that makes them sloppy, and that is where I come in. If I can find this one person in the port's system who logged in when all the claims occurred, then that will lead us to whoever is working at both Adesco and facilitating the claims at Worldwide. And that will lead us back to the people who attacked me."

Tyrone had to admit that she was smart.

"So, shall we?" she said, getting out of her seat and following the captain to the door.

Once they were on the tarmac, a security vehicle pulled up and they climbed in. It took them directly out of the airport and dropped them at a VIP waiting area. Tyrone had ordered the taxi whilst they were waiting to disembark, and it was already parked when they reached the holding lounge. Tyrone instructed the driver to take them directly to the Cape Grace hotel before then taking him on to his meeting at the bank.

"I'll see you in about three hours," he said to Kiara as she climbed out of the taxi.

She watched him drive away, leaving her standing outside the hotel, all alone in yet another new city. For the second time in days, she felt totally alone and totally out of her depth.

CHAPTER 35

The Cape Grace was a beautiful hotel. It had that authentic colonial look about it, exuding charm and elegance, with intricate details, such as grand columns framing the entrance doors and a white wicker plinth where the doorman stood, dressed in a beautifully manicured suit. It was like stepping into a bygone era of sophistication.

She walked into the main reception area, which, much like the outside, screamed elegance and charm, and went straight to the reception desk.

"Could you show me where your lounge area is please? I am meeting someone there."

"Certainly, madam," the lady said, looking at a book in front of her. "Mrs Fox?" the receptionist asked, looking back up at her.

Kiara was thrown off by the fact the receptionist knew her name.

"Er, yes," she replied nervously.

"Mr Aidan left your name for us and said to show you directly to the coffee lounge. Please follow me."

Kiara had no choice but to follow her, but she did so nervously, as she never expected anyone here to know her name. She was shown to a small round table by the window that looked directly onto the marina outside. Aidan sat alone at the table, a coffee and half-eaten croissant in front of him. He had all the arrogance and confidence that a handsome twenty-four-year-old boy should have; however, he managed to present it in a charming and unaggressive way.

"Kiara," he said, as if they had met before, standing up and walking around to kiss her on the cheek. "What can I get you, a coffee and something to eat?"

"No, I'm fine, thank you."

He shrugged and then walked back around to his chair as she took hers.

"Uncle Tye told me to help you anyway I can. You need to get into the server room, don't you?"

Kiara was surprised and shocked as to how open he was.

"Aidan, please keep it down," she said, looking around the empty lounge, pleased that no one was able to hear them. "This is really sensitive and what I'm asking you to do could lose you your job! And I really wish you hadn't told the receptionist my name, no one is meant to know I'm here."

"Oh, don't worry about her, she won't tell anyone. She's been working on the desk for years. I come here all the time to just have a coffee and chill in between work. She loves me, really, she does. It's never going to happen, but it's useful when I want to have the lounge to myself."

"Fine, but please don't tell anyone else. And let's keep our voices down, shall we, just in case?"

"Sure, if you think it's that important, but honestly, no one will hear us here," he said with much the same volume as he had been speaking all along.

Kiara suspected that Aidan had perhaps not been the best person to bring into their problem.

"So, what exactly do you want?" he asked her, again without adjusting his voice.

She realised she wasn't going to be able to change him, so she just pushed on. "I need to get into the port's computer systems, specifically to see the movement of Adesco Oil tankers. I have three specific dates I want to look at and then maybe two or three either side of that."

"I've logged onto their servers before, you know, when Uncle Tye needed to do some client research and stuff, and my firm provide Adesco with their cyber security, we look after almost all the companies in the Waterfront now, so actually they expect me to log on every now and then, so, it won't be a problem. What exactly are we looking for?"

Kiara explained the problem Tyrone was having and how she suspected someone had been logging in to the system and changing the numbers on the amounts of oil being moved.

"I'm sorry, but that's impossible. No one other than me has access to the back end of the servers and absolutely no one but me and my boss have the codes that would let the numbers be changed. Even the port's CEO and the head of Adesco Oil can't make changes to the numbers. Our cyber security is the best in the world, it's simply not possible to hack it. And my boss never ever logs in and I haven't changed anything."

"Well, it seems you are mistaken at how good your security software is. Someone has definitely hacked in and changed the numbers."

"Sorry, but it's just not possible," Aidan said, doubling down on his confidence, "we can't be hacked, absolutely not possible."

"And the Titanic was unsinkable, yet there she is at the bottom of the Atlantic proving everyone wrong."

Aidan had promised Tyrone he would help her, and so he would, but that didn't mean he would have to agree with her.

"I'll get you into the system, but I still don't believe you on that," he said.

"That's fine, I just need you to get me in, and I'll do the rest. And if I do find you have been hacked, then maybe you take that back to your boss and you can do a little update to your security," Kiara said, drawing a smile from Aidan.

"Sure," he said with a huge grin, "I'll even get him to pay you for finding our faults."

"Deal," Kiara said, returning his smile, before getting up. "Come on then, shall we…?"

"Can't I finish my coffee first?" he asked.

"Sorry, but we are on a tight schedule, let's go."

"Jeeze, Uncle Tye said you were bossy, but really!" Aidan said before necking his coffee in one go and leading her out of the lounge, giving the receptionist a seductive look and a wink as they left.

She returned his smile and waved.

Once Aidan and Kiara had left the building, she picked up the phone and dialled a number that no one else at the Cape Grace knew existed.

The phone was answered on the first ring.

"You told me to tell you every time the computer geek was in the hotel."

"Yes, I need to know when the server room is empty. Is he there?"

"He was."

"Was?"

"I was going to call you, but he was meeting someone else here, and I thought if it was important that maybe there would be something extra in it."

"And?" Zara asked.

"He met a lady in the lounge. I could hear everything he said, I didn't even need to leave my desk, he is such a confident cock. He's going back to the computer room now, and he's taking her with him."

"Can you describe her to me?"

"Sure. She was about five seven or eight with brownish hair to her shoulders."

"And fit looking?" Zara prompted her.

"Definitely. She had on a short T-shirt, and you could see her abs poking through. I wish I could shed some pounds and look like her."

"Did you get a name?" Zara asked.

"Yes, Kiara Fox."

Zara was expecting that, she knew Rene had been wrong, the lady was a fox indeed, popping up in the most inconvenient places.

"Is that helpful?" the receptionist asked, hoping she would earn a few rand for the weekend.

"Very. Let me know when they come back."

"Will you be in soon?"

"You'll be paid a little extra, don't worry about that," Zara said, before abruptly ending the call.

The receptionist gave herself a little smile as she thought about the money hitting her bank account and the weekend she would now be able to have.

Aidan walked next to Kiara on their way to the server room.

"Uncle Tye told me you're into triathlons," he said, as if he understood what they actually were. "I'm a mountain biker myself. I'm pretty good, to be honest."

Kiara had no doubt he was good, but probably not as good as he imagined.

"I'm training for the Cape Epic at the moment," he continued without losing a beat, "seven hundred kilometres of trails and mountains. Takes about eight or nine days, but I reckon I've got it in seven."

He glanced at Kiara to see how impressed she would be but was disappointed that she seemed more interested in the marina they were walking past than him. He took the hint and carried on the walk in silence.

"Here we are," he said a few minutes later, stopping outside a locked door. He pulled a set of keys from his pocket and opened the door without even looking around to see if anyone was watching them. Kiara was clearly not going to change him, but she really wished she could have him in a classroom for a few weeks and teach him some of the subtleties of her job.

The door led them into a large open-plan office. It was at least two thousand square feet and had fifteen workstations, most containing old computer towers under the desks and small square screens on the top. Each desk also held an old press button phone and a set of headphones. From the dust covering them, none had been touched for decades. At the far end of the room sat a bank of much more hi-tech servers, eight in total, which were encased in fire and waterproof housing.

"We don't need to open them up," he said, referring to the servers, "any of these old PCs can access them as long as you have the right passcodes. And..." he said, looking her squarely in the eyes, "... and I know the thirty-two bit cyber password that I personally change every six months."

He finished with a confident smile, just willing her to test him on it.

Kiara ignored his bravado and sat herself down at the closest desk, one which held three modern screens all linked together. Aidan, disappointed that she didn't rise to the bait, pulled up a chair next to her. She looked at the screen and was surprised to see it was already logged into the system and that the password had already been entered. She looked to Aidan, who just smiled back at her.

"No one else comes in here except me these days and without the cyber code they couldn't get in anyway," he said, feeling her eyes chastise him. "And you just happen to choose the desk I always use," he said, pulling the keyboard closer to himself and entering the thirty-two-bit cyber code, making sure she couldn't see him do it, just to make a point back to her.

Once he was logged in, he pushed the keyboard back to her.

It only took her a minute to find the home button, which then took her to a screen that was basically a huge search feature that allowed her to input the name of a company and a ship, truck or airline and also a cargo type. She input where indicated 'Adesco Oil' and the ship name 'Aframel'.

The system took her instantly to a large spreadsheet that spilled across all three screens on the desk.

"There," Aidan said, pointing to another search screen, "it's asking for specific dates. You can put in a full year or a range of years if you want to."

Kiara typed in January 2021 – December 2023.

The spreadsheet shrunk down and just filled the middle screen. He looked at her and smiled like he was a genius.

Kiara moved her mouse to the top search bar in the middle that read 'Crew'.

The spreadsheet once again spread across all three screens.

"Fuck me! There's no way we can look over all this," Aidan said, looking at his watch, "I've got to get back to the office in an hour."

"We don't need to," Kiara replied, "there's an email option. I can email it to myself."

"Okay, do that. It's better not to do it on my system, though, just in case."

She turned to him. "In case one of your team or your boss is involved?" she asked with a sly look to her face. Aidan said nothing.

Kiara emailed the spreadsheet to herself and waited until her mobile phone pinged to say an email had been received. She then logged out of the system.

They were back at the Cape Grace much earlier than she had expected. She took her small bag from the boot of Aidan's car and thanked him for all his help. She couldn't help herself telling him to be more careful in his work and she promised to tell him if she did find changed numbers so that he could deal with the poor security. Whilst he didn't bite back like he had earlier, he still didn't believe her that someone could be able to hack into his servers.

Kiara settled herself back in the hotel lounge and waited for Tyrone to join her. Meanwhile, she opened her laptop, found the email she'd sent to herself and brought up the spreadsheets.

CHAPTER 36

It was getting late when Tyrone made it back to the hotel, as his visits to both the bank and the diamond dealer had taken longer than he'd expected.

"Did you manage to get your money out?" Kiara asked him as he joined her at the table.

"Kind of. I was able to take half my diamonds out, which covers the twenty-million claim. But my diamond dealer would only take half of that. So, I've deposited that into the company, which capitalises us enough assuming we don't get another big hit in the meantime, and I've got the rest here," he said, holding up the brand-new rucksack he'd had to buy.

"You've got millions of dollars of diamonds in that thing?" Kiara said in a whisper to him.

"What could I do?" he said back, shrugging.

"Bloody hell, Tyrone. You need to get that back to your office and in the safe as soon as possible."

"I've got the jet waiting for us now. Did you get what you needed from Aidan? Good boy, isn't he?"

"He's got potential, that's for sure," she said with a wry smile, "and yes, I got the spreadsheets on my laptop. I need to go over them now. So, I don't think I should go back with you yet. My suitcase is fine at the locker in Johannesburg and I packed a few essentials into my hand luggage, so I'm okay for overnight if that's okay with you."

"I'm not sure I want to leave you here alone."

"It's fine. Cape Town is probably safer for me than Johannesburg right now. And no one but you and Aidan know I'm here. I'll feel safer staying here and getting this work done and it would be suspicious if you are not at your office tomorrow or if I'm seen coming back when everyone thinks I've flown home already."

"Okay, I guess so, but only if you're sure. Let me go to the front desk and book you in for the one night."

With that, he got back up and headed for the reception desk to book a room.

Meanwhile, Kiara went back to the spreadsheets and started reading through all the names. On her small screen, it made for extremely hard work.

Tyrone didn't hear the receptionist's call to Zara informing her Kiara had just booked in for the night, as he made his way back to the lounge.

"I need to get going if I'm to make the airport on time," Tyrone said when he got back to the table. He walked around to Kiara and gave her a kiss on the cheek, then handed over a card to her suite and told her to be careful, and to stay out of trouble. She promised she would stay at the hotel the whole night. She knew she would have to anyway, given the size of the task ahead of her. Once Tyrone had left, she closed her laptop and headed up to her room. She needed a shower and a drink if she was going to be able to concentrate enough to get this done.

The suite was only a fraction of the one she'd had at the Saxon Hotel, but it was still far too big and overly opulent for what she needed. She placed her hand luggage on the bed and plugged in her laptop on the desk by the doors that led out onto the private terrace. Looking out of the window, she saw Table Mountain staring back. It took her breath away. It rose high up into the clouds, and the top, which was just about visible, was as flat as a table, hence its name. She really wished Asher had been there with her. She thought for a moment how amazing it would have been to get up the next morning, without a care in the world, with the man she had always loved, and take a cable car to the top.

Before the thought could take hold, she pushed it away. She didn't have time for self-pity, she had a job to do.

She stripped off and jumped into the shower to wash away the day's dust. Kiara always felt messy and dirty after being on an aeroplane, even if it was a private jet like the one Tyrone had hired for them. So, a hot shower was the second perfect tonic she needed. The other tonic she needed came afterwards, from the mini bar, and was accompanied by two small bottles of mediterranean gin.

She put on the hotel's bathrobe, took her G&T over to the desk and opened the screen on her laptop. The spreadsheet was still there and ready for her to work on. She went straight to the tab that held details on Adesco Oil and then moved to the ship that was always involved in the losses that Tyrone had been paying out on, the Aframel. It had an average crew size of about twenty-five. Thankfully, it was a small enough number for her to be able to spot any names that maybe stood out as being present only on the claims dates compared to the other trips it took. She started with claim one, which was in the March, and compared its crew log to the January and February crews. She was looking to see if any names appeared in March that didn't in the months before. She then did the same with claims two and three that happened in July and August.

She began reading the names in front of her out loud, so that she could hear them herself, making it easier to remember them than just reading silently from a list. A lot of the names were native to the area and were not in her normal vocabulary, which made the task take longer and was more complicated than it really needed to be. She spent around forty-five minutes reading and re-reading the names to herself, trying to spot any changes to the crew on the claims dates.

One name stood out each time as much for being present on

the dates she wanted and none of the others, as well as for the fact that it was a name she could say without any problem. She said the name out loud again.

"Amos Bekker."

He was not listed on the ship as being on board at any time, instead he was listed as one of a handful of staff from the port itself who were attached to the ship, but worked from the port's office in Cape Town checking the online logs to ensure that the numbers being registered on the Aframel were the same numbers listed at both the starting and destination ports. In all cases, his login was only used to check the figures at the destination ports. That in itself made absolutely no sense to Kiara, as why would anyone only log on to the final delivery port? Without the other numbers, they couldn't possibly know if the delivery number was correct. Unless all they cared about was reducing the number rather than checking it, to make it look like there had been a loss. Aidan had told her that no one, not even the port's staff could actually change the numbers, all they could do was view what had been loaded up, as his security system would not allow any changes to be made to numbers once they had been input. In fact, it was clear to Kiara that the information she had in front of her included everything in one document and she could not isolate just one part of the data. So, the fact that this Amos guy was able to even log on to the destination port's servers only told her that the security system Aidan ran was so weak that it clearly could be manipulated if someone was smart enough.

Perhaps this Amos is a computer hacker rather than a member of the port staff, she thought.

She went back to the spreadsheet to double-check everything she needed. Amos's name was clearly on the March, July and August trips, but not on the ones beforehand or the ones directly afterwards. She turned to the next page and looked for the October manifest, the one that would contain the biggest claim so far, the twenty million dollars that Tyrone had just this morning authorised to be paid out.

She pulled up that tab and spotted his name right away.

"So, Amos is our man, then," she said to herself, amazed that she had found him so quickly. It occurred to her that it was perhaps far too easy to have found him and that maybe the name was made up or was planted to frame him if anyone was looking as deeply as she was into the losses.

So, assuming you are real, then who the hell are you, Amos? And how the hell did you manage to log on to Aidan's servers and change the numbers to make it look like twenty million dollars of oil had been lost?

Kiara closed the spreadsheet on Adesco and opened up the other documents she had sent herself. She flicked through them until she came to one marked Waterfront Port Staff ID. As Amos was listed as a staff member of the port rather than of the Aframel, she was certain that if his was just a fake name then there would be no record of him on this list. She was certain that would be the case.

She went straight to the 'B's and saw that Amos Becker was indeed listed and that it even had his home address on there. Number five, Victoria Drive, Camps Bay, Cape Town, SA.

This was all too easy, she thought. Sure, she had to get access to the system, which in itself was not something anyone could do, but once there, finding his name and address should have taken a lot more work.

She closed the files down and opened a Google search. She assumed that nothing would come up on him as the whole identity of Amos Bekker was clearly a fake one used by someone to conceal the fact that they had broken into the system and committed fraud to embezzle millions of dollars from the insurance company. But getting this far, she naturally had to at least check.

She literally could not believe her eyes when the search returned not only his name and address, but a website to a charity he ran: Rising Tide.

She clicked on the website link and then onto the 'who we are' section.

Her screen suddenly told her all about the man, and about his mission.

Rising Tide is a registered charity set up to save the planet from the devastation caused by the oil industry. Our mission is not to disrupt, but to partner. Rising Tide aims to work with the oil producers around the world, rather than against them, and together, by using the natural environment, move them from producing fossil fuels onto free sustainable energy. Our unique invention, the first of its kind, will allow the energy produced by the world's oceans to be stored into portable batteries and shipped around the world, offering free energy in place of fossil fuels.

At Rising Tides, we do not believe in violence as a means to reverse the damage being done to our home, we believe in collaboration, where our greatest scientific minds and our greatest business minds can one day come together in a single safe place and collaborate to save our planet.

Amos Bekker
Chairperson and Founder
Rising Tide

There he was, in full colour, on the screen in front of her. Amos Bekker. Average height, average looks, but clearly with an above average intelligence. But why would a man who was very smart, perhaps a genius even, leave his name and address on a database advertising the fact that he was taking part in a major fraud? It made no sense at all.

She needed to tell Tyrone that she had found his man, or at least taken a huge leap forward.

"Are you okay?" The worry in his voice told her that he had hated leaving her alone in Cape Town.

"I'm fine. I haven't left my room, like I promised. Are you in Johannesburg yet?"

"No, we are still flying. The wi-fi on this jet is incredible, I can hear you as if you are sitting right opposite me. I need to get me one of these toys," he said, glancing around the empty cabin.

"Maybe you can once I tell you we might have found your man, and you can get your money back," she replied.

"You're joking me," he said, his heart suddenly picking up to twice its normal beat.

"Well, yes, I am joking, kind of. To keep a long story short, I found a name that appeared on every date where there was a claim, but not on the dates before or after. He also appeared on the port's staff file as someone who on those dates had accessed the destination port's servers."

"Seriously?"

"I'm deadly serious. And listen to this: they listed his name and his address. So, I did a Google search and found him. I've just emailed you the link to a charity he runs, open it up and tell me what you think."

A minute later, Tyrone was back on the phone.

"Amos Bekker, charity founder of Rising Tides, and he wants to work with the oil companies. Is this for real? Surely it's a set-up?"

"I wondered the same. It's all very convenient, isn't it? So, it's either all an elaborate fake to hide the real person or this Amos is being set up as the fall guy."

"Or..." Tyrone cut in, "he is part of this, but his partners are hanging him out as the patsy in case they get caught."

"Yes, that was my other thought, and if that is the case, then we are one step closer to finding them."

"Fuck! You really are something," Tyrone said to Kiara.

"I told you, best in the business," Kiara replied, hiding the fact that she was as amazed as he was that this actually was coming to something real.

While Tyrone had been talking, Kiara had been doing some more searches on Amos to see if she could find out any more about the man. Google had a lot more to share. Ever since Adesco Oil had written an article about how they were developing a tidal generator to be fitted onto their newest, largest oil platform, Amos had suddenly become very prolific, posting articles and letters on various social media platforms, trying to get their attention.

He had started his charity over twenty years ago with the purpose of pulling together all the research available on tidal power, using this to develop his own tidal batteries, with the aim of partnering with the largest oil producers around the world to create enough free energy by using their oil platforms already in place. This would make the majority of oil production redundant, but still keep oil platforms in use. He understood that this was only one step in reversing the climate damage being done to the planet, but nonetheless it was a step he could take, and he would be making a difference.

And then he came across the Adesco Oil statement.

It was like the stars had suddenly aligned for him.

"You know, I think the guy might be the real deal," Kiara said, when Tyrone had finished talking. "I like his thinking, actually. He's absolutely right that trying to bring down the big oil producers will solve nothing, they are simply too big to be stopped, even though they are clearly legitimate targets. Big business verses climate warriors is a battle neither can win. Expecting profitable businesses such as in the oil and gas industry to simply stop producing in favour of free energy is wishful thinking. But then Adesco Oil steps up and announces their intention to invest in tidal power and hey presto, he has suddenly got his perfect partner, as long as he can get them to listen to him."

"So, why steal from them? How is that getting them on side? Why not just get them to invest in what he's doing?"

"What is the likelihood that a company that size will even

listen to a one-man band like Amos, let alone invest in him? So, he needs money to finish his work and to get it in front of them."

"So, you're saying he decided to steal the money from them just so he can then partner up with them? Sounds like a helluva risk to me."

"But he is not stealing from them, is he?! He is stealing from you. He, or someone he is working with, is somehow logging on to the port's computers and changing the numbers, making it look like Adesco are losing oil on their shipments. But they are not, and as such, they are still getting full value on every delivery they make. However, you, or Worldwide Insurance, are being tricked into paying out millions of dollars. But someone at Adesco must be diverting the payments over to Amos's charity without Adesco or you knowing."

"So, his little charity, which, by the look of the website, looks pretty much homemade, is sitting on tens of millions of my dollars? What the hell is he spending it on, surely not just his invention?"

"I have no idea, but we need to find out. I think a visit to Amos's office might be in order, don't you?"

"You cannot go on your own, just stay where you are. As soon as this jet lands, I'll get them to turn around and come straight back, then we can go together."

"That'll be hours yet. What am I supposed to do, just sit in my room and wait for you? Look, this guy is clearly a patsy, he's being set up by someone. I'll just go to his house and, if it looks like he's alone, I'll knock on the door, otherwise I'll just find somewhere safe and wait for you to turn up."

"I thought you were smarter than that," Tyrone said, worried that Kiara would go off on her own and do something stupid. "What if we are wrong about him? What if he actually is the bad guy in all this? These eco warriors aren't always what they seem. What if this charity is just a front for something far more sinister.

Are you sure we should go and put ourselves right in the middle of it? Shouldn't we just call the authorities?"

"You saw what they did to me, or at least the people he is probably being controlled by. You said it yourself, the police over here will likely do nothing, then that leaves you millions out of pocket and it still leaves you and me in danger. No, we can't hand this straight over to the police knowing that they will do nothing. We need to at least know who we are up against before we decide who to speak to. You said you had some security firms you deal with, so why not get them on it. I'll try to find out who this guy is working with and then your security people can protect us while we hand all this over to the authorities, all nicely packaged up."

"I'm not happy about it, but it's unlikely I can stop you. Just promise to wait for me, okay? Do not go to his house on your own."

"I won't."

"I mean it, Kiara. This is a dangerous country, and these are dangerous people. I promised Nick Taylor when I offered you this job that I would look after you. And you promised your girls you would be careful, so let me look after you, okay? Just wait."

"I said I would wait, so I will wait, I promise."

Kiara had no intention of keeping that promise. As soon as the call ended, she closed the laptop and started to get dressed.

CHAPTER 37

The meeting at the bank went pretty much as Zara had told him it would. After they had checked Amos's ID against the mandates they held in their system, they asked him to explain where the money was coming from and why. At this point, it was Zara who took over. She explained that the money was coming from Adesco Oil, a well-respected company, who were known for their philanthropy, especially within the area of sustainability, such as the area Amos's charity worked in. She explained also that Rising Tide was a regulated charity under the charity commission and was able to receive donations of any size from any regulated company. The bank tried to push back further as they were not convinced the payment was legitimate due to its size, but Zara said that they were incorrect and this was simply a donation, certainly a large one, but nonetheless a donation to a long-running charity.

Finally, after much toing and froing, Zara ended the meeting by being utterly patronising to the bank manager and making it clear that if he did not allow a donation from a reputable company to go through immediately then the authorities and the media would be alerted the moment they left his building. With no legal reason to actually stop the money clearing into Amos's account, the manager had to hit the button. The whole meeting took no more than thirty minutes and Amos had said no more than ten words during the entire time.

Once the funds were cleared, Amos then needed to transfer

the majority of it over to the account that Hamilton had given them. Once again, this was something that Zara needed to handle. She explained to the bank manager that their charity was funding a project in the African townships to bring them electricity, water, food and, more importantly, education. She pulled from her briefcase a brochure that explained exactly how they were going to help the people of the township, which included a picture of a fantastic school that she knew was never going to be built.

She had only put the brochure together the day before and Rene had thought it was a stroke of genius when she showed him. Amos's own bank had themselves selected a local charity to deliver education to the townships, which of course Zara already knew, so when they saw the reason she wanted to release the funds immediately to the largest township in Cape Town, they were suddenly delighted to help.

Amos was stunned at how easily Zara had manipulated them into believing what she was saying.

For her, it was just another hustle that she had perfected and used many times before.

"Do nothing," Zara said when they left the bank and were back in her car. "The money will take a couple of hours to leave your account. When you see it happen, you need to call Rene and tell him it's gone."

"Are you not waiting with me?" he asked her.

"I'm needed at Rene's," she said.

"What about my money?" Amos said. "Rene said that I would be keeping some for my project."

"Grow up, Amos. You'll be left some slush money, a couple of million rand, if you're lucky. But we have big plans, and the money we've got now is only the start, there is a much bigger game at play here."

Amos was ready to argue his point further, but Zara had already pulled up outside his house and he could see that there was absolutely no point trying to reason with her.

He went up to his front door and into the house. He then walked down to his office, completely missing Caroline's dead body that was at the bottom of the outside stairs to the side. He turned his computer on, logged into the bank and saw the money still sitting there. He also saw in the pending payments the full amount due to leave his account at any moment. Without even a second's hesitation, he hit the cancel payment button. The authorisation vanished from his screen.

He took in a deep breath, knowing that what he had just done was possibly going to mean his death.

Fuck them all, he thought to himself. He wouldn't let them commit murder using him and his charity to justify it.

Despite what Rene and the others thought, he was not the idiot that they took him for. He always knew that there was a risk of them not helping him, so he had a plan of his own ready if that ever happened.

He shut his laptop and added it to the suitcase that he had hidden under his desk. The suitcase already contained nearly everything he would need for the next part of his escape plan. He just needed to go and pack up all his plans and notes on the batteries, which littered his house and were stuck to almost every wall, and then destroy the only working model he had to ensure no one else would steal his designs. What he did need to do, which was now more urgent than anything, was to get hold of Caroline and make sure that he was given access to Gavin Adriaanse. He had to get his designs to Adesco, but meanwhile get to somewhere safe, where Rene and Hamilton couldn't get to him. Adesco's office in Johannesburg seemed the obvious way to kill two birds with one stone.

He still had Caroline's number from when she called him. He dialled it.

Almost instantly, he noticed a phone ringing close by. He

looked around his office, wondering where the sound was coming from, but he couldn't trace it. He only had one phone himself, and he was using it now. He cut off the call, and the ringing phone stopped.

"Is someone here?" he called out into the empty room.

The room stayed silent.

He slowly walked around and checked behind his pool area where his battery still sat. His heart was racing as he waited for one of them, Hamilton, Rene or Zara, to jump out and accuse him of stealing their money. But no one jumped out, the room was empty.

He slowly redialled Caroline's number. The same ringtone rang again. He closed his eyes and tried to block everything else out, just concentrating on the ringing. He followed the sound until it led him to the side door. He turned the key, knowing he had no choice but to open the door, expecting someone to burst in and grab him. He had to push hard, as something was blocking the door. He managed to get it partway open and was relieved no one was standing there ready to jump him. He then looked down and saw what was stopping the door from fully opening. Caroline's body was there, sprawled across the bottom step, and her blood had seeped into the small area outside his door, turning it a shade of red. He stepped back involuntarily into his office, falling over the case he had left behind him and fell to the floor. He managed to roll to the other side of his case before throwing up.

CHAPTER 38

When Zara arrived at the small office Rene had rented, she was surprised to find only him and Karly waiting. "Where's Dan?" she asked. "I thought this was going to be one of the last meetings together before we moved to the final stage."

"Hamilton's got him," Karly said, still angry that Rene had sent him there alone.

"The moment the ten million hits Hamilton's account, he'll bring Dan here. On that matter, how did it go at the bank, is it done?"

"It went as expected," Zara said.

"I need more than that," Rene said, frustrated by her lack of information.

"Amos stood there like a fool, and I did all the work. They moved the money to his account and then I used the charity ruse to get them to send the money onto Hamilton's account, just as you told me to do."

"And you stayed there until it was all done, like I said?"

"… of course."

Rene didn't like the way Zara's reply had the smallest pause. He stared hard at her in silence, forcing a further confirmation.

"I saw the money hit his account with my own eyes. And then we saw the bank transfer it to Hamilton's account. It was all set up and about to go by the time I left. There's always a delay of an hour or so before money actually moves, but it was authorised and pending."

"So, you didn't physically see it leave his account, is that what you are saying?"

"What was the point of me waiting for what could have been hours when it was set up to just go through? There was nothing more for Me or Amos to do. So I told him to just wait for your call. I left him outside his office and came straight here."

"Are you worried about him?" Karly asked Rene, picking up on the sudden change in his voice.

"Trust me, Amos doesn't have the balls to do anything stupid, he's too scared of us," Zara said.

"You underestimate him," Karly said to her. "You underestimate everyone, you always do. He's no one's fool, he's designed a tidal energy system that could change the world and built it in his garage, the man's a friggin' genius."

"He's built something that we have no idea even works," Zara cut in.

"If he says it works, then it works"

"You're too trusting" Zara replied.

"He cares about our planet as much as we all do. He's spent his entire life, every hour he's had, and all his family's money to invent something that will give the world free energy. He's asked for nothing for himself. Everything he does is to help the planet. And you treat him like he's nothing, like he's completely unimportant."

"He is unimportant," Zara shot back. "Whilst he sits and tinkles with his toys, the world is going to shit. What we are doing will have the biggest impact on the oil industry ever, and it will happen now, right away, not in another ten years like Amos will take."

"Oh, sure, like you give a shit about any of this, it's just another bit of fun for you to get off on."

Zara stood in her place until Karly had finished and then just looked at her in silence for a minute. Before she burst into laughter. "I like her, I really do," she said, turning to Rene.

Karly breathed out the air she had been holding in, before turning to Rene, hoping he could say something that would make sense of his girlfriend. Even he was lost for words and had nothing to say to that response.

"Anyway…" Zara carried on, as if the whole episode hadn't even happened. "Maybe she's right. Maybe I did underestimate Amos. I'll go back there, and make sure he did it, if that makes you happy."

"If he has screwed us then I need to know right away, and we need to correct it."

"You should call Hamilton first. Maybe the money has already got to him, and we are worried about nothing," Karly said.

Rene agreed. He pulled out his phone and called Dan's number again, knowing Hamilton would answer it. He put it on speaker. It rang five times before cutting off. He looked at both women, the worry etched on his face.

The room stayed silent a few seconds more before they heard the outer door to the office open. The release of tension from them all was palpable.

"It's Dan," Zara said, "Hamilton got the money. It's all fine, see, like I said, Amos doesn't have the balls to screw with us."

As she spoke, the inner door to their room flung open and Dan was pushed in, falling onto his knees in front of them, bloodstains covering his face and his shirt, and his left hand held together by a crude bandage, which showed the loss of two of his fingers.

He was followed in by Hamilton and two of his men, all three of them huge, muscled and menacing.

"Where's my money?!" Hamilton shouted into the room.

"It's been sent, I assure you…" Rene said, the words in his voice shaking as he looked down at his friend on the floor in front of him.

"He's right, I had the claim paid and it was sent to Amos. He's now sent it on to you…"

200

Karly never finished the sentence.

Hamilton had pulled a gun from the inside of his coat at the exact second Karly began to speak and, without a word or a glance towards her, he pulled the trigger, placing a bullet square into the top of her head, spraying blood, brain and pieces of her skull all over Zara and Rene. Dan barely looked up. Rene stumbled backwards into the wall and slid to the floor, Karly's blood running down his face and onto his lips. He gagged and then threw up as some of her blood slipped into his mouth.

Zara just stood there, motionless, seemingly more annoyed than fazed. She fixed her eyes on Hamilton. She pulled the back of her right hand across her face, smudging the blood, but clearing her face of the pieces of broken skull and brain.

"Where's my money?" Hamilton said softly, this time focusing on Zara, the only person seemingly able to hold herself together.

"As my friend said, before you blew her brains across the room, we sent it to you!" Zara replied curtly to the man in front of her. "Now, of course, you've made it all a little more difficult for us and for you, as she was the link that brought in the money, and I have no idea how we will get any more from the insurance company or the oil company with her gone. So, that was a dumb thing to have done, wasn't it?"

Hamilton didn't know how to react. People always did what Rene did, threw up, lost their breath, became instantly compliant. This was the first time anyone had just stood there and admonished him. He always knew he would one day meet his match, but he never expected it to be a young girl. He looked hard at Zara, trying to work her out. He guessed she was younger than him, he didn't know for sure; he was in his late twenties, maybe she was a few years younger, it was hard to tell. She was impressive looking, though, someone who caught your attention, slim, in good physical shape. *Like a dancer, or a gymnast*, he thought. He stared at her properly for the first time. Her bleached hair with pink strands hung beyond her shoulders, and she had tattoos all up her arms and some even from her neck to the edge of her face. He tried to make out the colour of her eyes, but they seemed to change as he looked into them, one second blue and the next grey. She was nothing like any woman he had ever been with, but he recognised beauty when he saw it. He also recognised a sociopath when he saw one, for it was just like looking into a mirror.

"Well?" she continued. "Are you going to shoot us all, or do you want me to find you your money?" she asked, her hands going to her hips as her stare challenged him to take the next step.

Hamilton just stood there, his two soldiers by his side, and said nothing.

"Dan, can you stand up?" Zara said to the man still on his knees.

"Dan," she said again, more forcibly when he didn't at first respond. He reacted by standing up and moving over to the window, where Rene was.

"Good," she said, looking to them both. "You two clear up this mess, somehow, get rid of her." She looked down at what was left of Karly. "Then stay put until I call you. And you…" she said to Hamilton as she walked straight up to him, "… come with me. We need to pay a little visit to Amos, I think."

CHAPTER 39

K iara stood outside Amos's house as the driver from the Cape Grace pulled away, having given her his number so she could call him to come and pick her up when she was ready.

She gazed up at the house. It was tired and in need of some TLC, but she was sure it once would have been breathtaking, especially with its surroundings. In front of it, directly behind where she now stood, was a beautiful sandy bay that led straight into the Atlantic Ocean. She turned around and gazed out to sea. Just a few hundred metres from the shore was a little island. She had read about it when she was waiting to board the plane back in Heathrow. It was called Seal Island and was home to a huge number of Cape fur seals – over sixty thousand of them. The whole island was only about five acres and was lush and green. Kiara longed to strip off, dive into the sea and swim all the way around the little island, stretching her muscles and forgetting about the madness she had once again found herself in. She breathed out a sigh and turned back to face the house. Her eyes were drawn upwards to Table Mountain in the distance, which, even though it was miles away, still seemed to frame the area. She could just about make out a diagonal trail up the side of the mountain and was able to see some very small movement that looked like hikers, or perhaps mountain bikers by the speed they were moving. Again, her mind tried to take her up there, on her own mountain bike, riding the trails and heading up into the clouds. *Maybe when this is all over,*

Tyrone will lend me one of his bikes and he and I can do that, head off into the hills and ride into the clouds, she thought to herself.

In just a few days, Kiara's life seemed to have changed so much. She had gone from looking over a few claim files in the safety and comfort of her lovely peaceful house in Hurstpierpoint, to flying to the other end of the world, being assaulted outside her hotel, having her family threatened, being chased out of the country, sneaking out of an airport, breaking into a secure port, and now, here she was, about to confront a climate activist who may or may not be trying to kill her.

She needed to take a minute to think this through. She still had a way out of this if she wanted.

She could easily just turn around and head back home to her girls. That would keep her and her family safe from any further threats.

It would mean she would let Tyrone down and, of course, she could not then take any fees from him, but she could live without that payday; she still had clients back home and could earn enough money to cover all the bills. But could she really let Tyrone down? That would be hard, as it was in her nature to finish a job and see it through to the end.

Overriding all that was the fact that someone was committing fraud, and Kiara hated that.

"I really am fucked up, aren't I, Ash?" she said out loud to her husband, as she looked up into the heavens.

She stepped forward and walked up to the gates, pushing them open before walking up to the front door. She gave it a knock and waited. She couldn't hear a sound. She put her ear to the door, but nothing, total silence. She really had hoped he was in, even though she knew it carried a risk to her. She was about to knock again when she noticed an old-fashioned doorbell pulley in the top corner. So, she tried that, hearing the bell ring within the house, and she waited. Still nothing. Looking around, she saw a set of stairs to the left that led back down, this time to the side of the house. She walked over to a small balcony and looked over. It was hard to see to the bottom, as it was dark down there. She thought she could see a shadow that looked like a person, but it was too dark to really be sure.

"Mr Bekker, is that you?" she called down. "Amos? My name is Kiara Fox, I work with an insurance company. I just wanted to have a chat about a client of theirs. Amos, are you there?"

As she called out, she watched carefully, knowing that if he was there, she would pick up a change in the shadows or the sound of some movement. But there was no one. She did notice a faint smell, something stale and unpleasant. She figured he must leave his rubbish bins down there. She knew it was foolish to go any further and she should wait for Tyrone to come, but she was here, this was her chance to get some answers, and Amos's profile on the website gave her no reason to think he was a violent man. So, against her own better judgement and knowing it was a foolish thing to do, she found herself checking around the back of the house just in case he was in the garden and hadn't heard the bell.

Around the back, she came to a small garden area that overlooked the kitchen.

"Hello?" she shouted through the window.

Again, there wasn't a sound. She tried the handle out of natural instinct and was surprised when it actually turned, allowing her to push the door open. She paused for a moment, looked back at the garden and then back into the kitchen. Entering someone's house without permission was a serious crime in England and she suspected that the same could be said of South Africa, but she had come too far to just walk away now.

So, as quietly as she was able, she pulled the door open and stepped inside. Amos clearly wasn't security conscious, she thought, as she walked into the house. She went through the kitchen and saw another room directly to her left, which also looked back out

205

onto the garden. This room was more like a conservatory, mostly glass with another door that led outside, probably also unlocked, she thought. Straight ahead from the kitchen was a hallway that had the weirdest wallpaper she had even seen and was littered with all sorts of odds and sods. It all felt so chaotic, like a crazy professor's mind laid out in front of her. The hallway was long, and off it were several doors. There was also a spiral staircase that seemed to fall straight into the floor as if it led into the pits of hell. It made her shiver inside, especially since she knew she would not be able to resist heading down it like the stupid kids always do in cheaply made horror movies. *What the hell am I doing here?* she thought to herself for what seemed like the hundredth time.

She tentatively walked forward out of the kitchen towards the dark hole in the floor. As she walked, small lights appeared in the ceiling above, which stopped her in her tracks. They were not too bright, just pinpricks that enabled her to see where she was going. It was a strange thing to have automatic lights inside a house and it made her consider the man she was looking for, someone who on the one hand lived in a state of chaos, yet also needed to shine light on it.

The pinpricks also shone on the wallpaper, which she now could see was not wallpaper at all. She stepped closer to them and could see that they were drawings, in various stages, of what appeared to be designs for the tidal batteries that she had read about on his website. Looking around, she could see that the walls were covered with his scribbles or drawings. There seemed to be gaps all over the place where he must have taken some of them off, but nevertheless she started to form a picture of Amos in her head, and it was not of a person she should be scared of, but more of someone whose passion to save the planet had led him to dedicate his whole life to the problem, even to the point of maybe driving him crazy. It seemed equal parts chaotic and planned. Without having met him, she instantly felt the need to protect him, as if he were another one of her children. It was her instincts kicking in once again. And she therefore knew it to be true, for her instincts rarely lied to her. She had to find him, and she had to keep him safe from the men who had attacked her.

To find him, she first needed to know more about what he was doing and how it tied into Tyrone's business. She stepped closer to the walls. The detail was extraordinary. Following the drawings down the hall, she was able to see how he planned to not only build his batteries but then to attach them to the underside of an oil platform in the middle of the ocean. *The man is clearly either a genius or a complete lunatic,* she thought to herself.

One of the papers, near the top of the stairs, caught her eye. It contained a logo she had seen so many times since she had landed in South Africa. Adesco Oil PLC. She stopped and took a closer look. It showed a full printout of Adesco's latest and biggest oil platform, Neptune. It was huge. Basically, a semi-submersible platform that reached hundreds of thousands of feet down to the seabed, where it would float rather than be fixed, and then it reached out of the ocean and up two thousand five hundred feet into the air. That made it the tallest and largest of its kind ever to be built. It was an immense structure, and it needed to be, as it had to not only hold all the drilling equipment needed to bring oil out of the seabed, as well as refine and store it, but it also had to accommodate the large crew numbers that were there to operate it twenty-four hours a day, seven days a week. That included bedrooms, canteens, hospital facilities and numerous offices and leisure facilities. Really, it was a floating village in the middle of the wildest oceans on the planet.

The next drawing along looked at the platform from below the waves. Amos had amended the drawings to show tidal generators attached to the bottom, , and then pictures of his own batteries were fixed to those. The generators themselves were huge, over three hundred feet in width. They looked to have been specifically designed to take up the entire underside of the platform. And his batteries then covered them. Even without having a brain for engineering, Kiara could see the beauty in his plans.

The next drawing would take her down the staircase under the house. Now that the automatic lights were switching on, she no longer felt scared of the hidden dangers below. The lights seemed to draw her down, beckoning her onwards to hidden treasure. She took the first steps and continued looking at the drawings as she went. The next set showed the partial removal of the oil drilling equipment, taking it down to just ten percent of its original size, and being replaced with energy storage tanks, which he described on the page as being able to hold and retain the energy created by the sea, input into his specially designed batteries and then load onto undersea vessels, also powered by the free energy, which would transport these batteries around the world. This explanation of how it would all work seemed more like a sales pitch from Amos to Adesco Oil, explaining how the smaller drilling rig would let them continue extracting small amounts of oil for uses other than energy, but how their generator and his batteries would eventually replace their lost income and perhaps even grow it.

In effect, he was showing Adesco that, by adopting his changes, they could reduce the fossil fuel extraction that was ultimately destroying the planet and replace it with green unlimited energy that would not only provide the population with all its energy needs but would still maintain Adesco's profits.

Kiara was amazed that in this small house in the suburbs of Cape Town, a single man had been able to not only devise a solution to the problem of providing free unlimited energy, but at the same time he had been smart enough to understand that it would only work if he fed the beast that was big business. Keep your friends close and your enemies closer.

Seeing everything he had done, she understood that Amos was more than smart, the man was a bloody genius and should be awarded the Nobel prize.

Instead of heading back down the stairs, she walked to the top and took out her phone. She now understood everything and needed to tell Tyrone right away. She knew how Worldwide Insurance was tied into this, and she was starting to understand the dynamics between all the players.

She took out her mobile and called him. He answered on the first ring.

"Where the hell are you?" he spoke before she could say anything. "I've been calling you ever since I landed back in Joburg, but your phone keeps going to voicemail. So, I called the Cape Grace and they said you had taken one of their cars, but they didn't know where to. You told me you'd stay in the hotel and would wait until I came back. You're at his house, aren't you? You went on your own, even though you promised me you wouldn't!"

He was seriously angry at her.

She looked at her phone, and it was on silent. She quickly switched the ring back on.

"I'm sorry," she said. "And I promise you I'll not do that again, but for the moment, just listen to me. I think I understand it all now. How Worldwide, Adesco Oil and Amos are all linked. I don't know who all the players are yet, but I do understand the game that's going on."

She could hear Tyrone take a breath. She knew he was desperate to hear what she had to say, but he was also angry that she had ignored him and gone to the house on her own.

"Can you get out of the house please? Get back to the hotel and wait for me there. The plane is ready to go, but I am waiting for Bea, Mufuka and Jan. I wanted them to be with us when we told them we had found this guy Amos. If you're right and one of them is really involved, then this is the way to draw whoever it is out into the open. They are almost here, so we should be in Cape Town in a couple of hours. But I can't do this if I think you're in danger. So please, just this time, do as I ask and get back to the hotel before he comes home."

"I will, I promise, but just let me tell you what I have found first, okay? It's important you know the link, especially if you are coming back with your team."

"For Christ's sake, Kiara, you're killing me here. Go on then, but make it quick, please."

She jumped straight in and told him about the house, and the wallpaper of plans and drawings. "… if you stop for a second and think about it, it's genius. And if, as I suspect, he has already built working models, then he would have definitely needed millions to do it."

"My millions," Tyrone said in frustration.

"Yes, your millions."

"You sound like you admire him, even though he's been stealing from me."

"I'm sorry, but well, I kind of do, I guess. I mean, it's incredible, if you think about it. He can change the world with this."

"With my bloody money, though! Let's not forget that, shall we. How the hell did he come up with the idea to steal my money to do it?!"

"I've been thinking about that, about what links you and him. And the answer is Adesco Oil. They are your largest client. And they are also the only oil company who are exploring the use of tidal energy; in fact, not only exploring it, but building it right now and setting up universities on their oil platforms to study it. It's all here, stuck on his walls. I have no idea what his links are to your company or to Adesco, but my best guess is that there is someone at both companies connected to him who are also working for those people who attacked me, and it is them who are committing the fraud, and then passing the money to Amos for his invention. They are making it look like oil is being lost on the ships, then claiming that from you and somehow diverting it to Amos's charity, all without Adesco even knowing that any claims are being made to you. Because no oil is actually missing, Adesco are still selling the amount they expected to sell and therefore are not investigating anything themselves.

"So, there has to be someone senior at Adesco who is putting these claims in and then hiding it from the owners, and maybe destroying any evidence it ever happened. With their accounts not showing any losses, I guess the directors have no reason to even look for anything out of the ordinary," Tyrone said.

"And then someone at Worldwide is allowing the claims to be paid without you knowing, until now, of course," Kiara agreed. "But they went too big too quickly and you spotted it. So, again, this would indicate a senior person is involved, this time in your company."

Tyrone had gone quiet on the other end of the phone, taking it all in.

"You still there?" she asked him.

"So, someone at my office has been doing this, after all, you were right from the get-go."

"I'm sorry," she said, meaning it.

"And who do we think are those goons who attacked you?"

"I've no idea. Either they work with Amos and are doing what he tells them to do or, more likely, they are controlling him and he's just doing what they are making him do."

"Which is it? Who should we be afraid of?"

"I'd say whoever is in charge. Perhaps Amos brought them in to help him, but he has got himself in a mess with the wrong people. If you could see what I can see, you'd know that he is in it to save people, not to hurt them. Someone who sets up a charity and tries to save the planet would not be sending goons out to beat up a lady."

"You need to get out of there," Tyrone said suddenly very seriously. "Either way, you are in danger being there on your own. Get back to the hotel right now and wait for me. I'm calling my security people to meet you there and then I'm calling the port authorities and the police. I'm also going to visit Gavin at their offices. I should have made him meet me months ago when the claims first came to my attention, rather than letting Bea handle it all. But it's gone too far now, he needs to know someone at his company has been defrauding me, using his business to do it, and that is a conversation only I can have with him."

Before she had a chance to answer, she heard something from the front of the house, a car pulling up.

"Shit!"

"What's wrong?"

"I think someone might be here."

"You need to get out, now."

"If it's Amos, I think I'll be safe, I honestly don't think he'll hurt me."

"You don't know that. And what if it's not him? You need to get out, Kiara."

"Shit, someone is at the door." She cut the call and switched off the sound again, in case Tyrone rang straight back and gave her position away. She stepped down a few of the stairs, out of sight of the front door and held her breath, trying to be as quiet as she could.

CHAPTER 40

The drive to Amos's house had been done in complete silence. Zara drove, with Hamilton next to her and one of his men in the rear. The other had stayed with Dan and Rene to help clear up the office and dispose of Karly's body.

Zara parked the car on the street and led the men through the gate, which had been left partially open, and up to the main front door. Hamilton pushed her to the side and charged shoulder first into the door. Being a solid mass of muscles, if he wanted to get in somewhere, then nine out of ten times his shoulders were all that he needed.

At the exact instant he smashed the door open, Kiara moved into action with lightning fast speed. Her years of triathlon racing meant she was always ready to move from one thing to another, from swim to bike, from bike to run and now from standing still at the top of the stairs to instant movement down. She jumped the last few steps, landing almost with no sound. She was pleased that Amos was as security lax down there as he was with his back door. She pulled the door towards her and stepped into the darkness of his workroom. The pinprick lights in the ceiling came on automatically, lighting up a huge pool in the middle of the room, showing her the massive battery hanging from a pulley system above it.

Upstairs, the front door hung from it hinges as the two men walked into the hallway, with Zara coming in behind them.

"Very subtle," she said, looking at the smashed door. "Nothing like creating the element of surprise."

"Where are you?!" Hamilton boomed into the house, as he walked down the hallway towards the kitchen and the conservatory, passing the staircase as he went.

"You have my money!" he continued shouting.

"I'm not sure that's the way to entice him out of hiding," Zara said.

Hamilton ignored her and ordered his man to search the house. He walked into the conservatory and over to the desk in the middle, dragging the chair from under it, pulling it back out of the room into the hallway and sat down.

"You will help my man find this rat," he said to Zara.

"And you will be doing what in the meantime?" Zara said to him. "I thought killing Karly in cold blood was dumb enough, as now we have no one in the insurance company to pay the claims." Zara walked up to him, clearly unafraid. "But then bursting in here like a raging rhinoceros and screaming the place down, letting Amos know we are after him is a complete other level of stupid!"

Hamilton jumped up from his chair and moved at a speed that Zara would have considered impossible for a man of his size. He lifted her into the air, constricting her throat and looked her in the eyes as the oxygen started to drain out of her. He spoke so slowly that she couldn't help but understand him.

"Your friend, Karly," he said her name as if she were merely just a piece of furniture, "was lucky I chose to put a single bullet in her brain. If I had chosen to, I could have made her suffer a thousand times over for talking to me when it was not invited. I suggest you remember that the next time you decide to open that mouth of yours."

With that, he opened his hand and let her drop to the floor. She rubbed her throat where he had squeezed it and got herself back to her feet, trying to decide if she had it in her to respond to his threat.

Hamilton returned to his chair at the same instant as his man made his way down the stairs and back into the hallway.

"The house is empty," his man said.

"Where would he go?" Hamilton got up from the chair and turned to Zara.

Down in the basement, Kiara had been standing looking at the pool, fascinated by what she was seeing. Amos had managed to finish his model, and it was beautiful to see. She also noticed another battery plugged into what must have been a large generator and the lights indicated it was full of power.

"Wow, it's amazing," she said quietly to herself in awe.

The noise at the top of the stairs brought her back to the moment. She knew she had to get out of there before they saw the stairs and followed her down.

Her eyes caught a door in the corner that she assumed led to the bottom of the stairwell that she had looked down on from the front door. It was a risk going that way, she knew, as it meant going back upstairs to the front door, but it was probably less of a risk than just waiting down there for them to come and find her.

She turned the handle and, once again, found herself amazed that this genius of a man would not have the common sense to lock this door. She silently thanked him for his lack of sense.

She pushed the door, and it partially opened. But there was something on the other side stopping it. She pushed as hard as she could, but it wouldn't budge.

Upstairs, Zara heard the noise. She turned to the stairs.

"He's down there," she said excitedly.

Hamilton rushed to the steps, followed by Zara and then his man. Hamilton, once again, thrust his shoulders in the door and smashed it open.

"There was a handle, you know," Zara said, standing and watching him stumble into the room.

Kiara heard the door crash open and pushed as hard as she could into her door, but it still wouldn't budge. Hamilton didn't see her at first, as his eyes took in the workroom.

Kiara took that extra second to breathe out all the air in her body, making herself as thin as she could and squeezed herself through the small gap, just about managing to get outside.

Zara saw the door in the corner move slightly.

"Over there," she said to Hamilton.

The huge man crossed the room in just a few strides and slammed his shoulders into the door, as was his way. This time, though, it didn't crash open. Something on the other side had stopped it in its tracks.

Kiara found herself stepping onto Caroline's dead body.

"Oh shit!" she said out loud. For a split second, she looked down on the lady's face, trying to decide who to call first, the police, Tyrone, even Asher sprung to mind, which made her grimace at the thought that he could never help her again.

Then the door was thrust forward, stopped only by Caroline's body. It was enough to bring Kiara back to her senses.

She stepped over the body and ran back up the stairs, two at a time, towards the front door.

"Get out of my way, you fucking ox!" Zara said to Hamilton. "I can get through there."

The big man had no choice but to stand back and let her through. Being even slighter in frame than Kiara, she squeezed through the gap without any problem. She looked up and just caught sight of her as she reached the top step. Zara knew that by the time she would make it to the top, Kiara would already be long gone. There were plenty of places Kiara could go, least not down to the beach to those crazy sea swimmers or to one of the many cafés that lined the area. She turned back to the door and, for the first time, saw what had been stopping it opening.

"Well, I never expected that," she said aloud.

"Have you got him?!" Hamilton screamed through the door.

"It wasn't him," Zara replied. "It was the insurance lady, she clearly didn't take your warning to leave after all. And who are you?" she said, kneeling down to look more closely at Caroline. "Amos, I really didn't think you had this in you." She laughed out loud to herself. "You really are one to watch, aren't you?"

"Who are you talking to?" Hamilton's voice blasted through the door.

Zara squeezed back in and stood face to face with him, although it really was more her face to his chest.

"I want my money!" Hamilton said again like a broken record.

"You'll get your money," Zara said at him. "I never expected Amos would have the balls to cancel the payment, or to be so clever as to run away. He is clearly braver than I took him for," she said, glancing back at the door to where she knew the dead body would be waiting. She turned back around to Hamilton, and walked around him before he could grab her by the throat again and choke her to death in his rage.

"He'll be back, we just need to give him a little time, that's all."

Hamilton pulled out his phone and made a call. "Our money is not here," he said to his second-in-command whom he had left at the office guarding Rene and Dan. "Kill them both," he said without a second's thought.

"Wait!" Zara screamed at him. "We need them. *You* need them. Dan is the only one who knows where all the explosives are stored and Rene is the one who will have a plan to get the rest of the money. Without them, it's all over, you'll get nothing, not a dollar."

Hamilton stalked forward until he was so close that Zara could smell the rotting biltong staining his teeth.

Hamilton said nothing, he just stood and stared at her.

"Tell your man to let them live," she said. "Now!" she said far more forcibly.

Hamilton raised the phone to his mouth. Zara couldn't tell for sure which way this was going to go.

"Let them live," he said into the phone, not taking his eyes off her. "It seems no matter what I want, I am dealing with you now, but, if you double cross me…" He didn't have to finish the sentence.

Hamilton picked up the chair and sat down again. "Put the door back on," he said to his man. "We will wait for him to come back."

CHAPTER 41

Tony reached the office by the Waterfront at almost the same time as Gavin. He was not expecting his brother to be there, he thought he had been in the Johannesburg office trying to bring the board back around to his side.

"What the hell are you doing here?" Tony said to him as they walked into the building together.

"Where's Caroline?" Gavin barked at him.

Tony went white and stopped walking as soon as the secretary's name was mentioned. Gavin noticed the change in his brother and turned to him, walking up as close to him as he could.

"Where is she, Tony?" he whispered into his brother's ear, knowing that something had happened.

His brother went paler. He looked at him, barely able to speak.

"There was an accident. I didn't mean it to happen…"

"Not here," Gavin said, taking his brother by the arm.

"Is the board room free?" Gavin asked the receptionist.

"Yes, sir. Shall I have coffee sent up?"

"No!" Gavin barked at her. "I don't want anyone to disturb us."

"Yes, sir," she said, before opening up the calendar on the computer in front of her and marking the board room as engaged.

Once Gavin was sure they were alone, and the boardroom door was locked, he turned to his brother.

"What did you do?" he asked Tony in the most controlled way he could. He had never seen his brother in a state of shock before and he strangely found himself wanting to protect Tony, just like he did when they were little children, and their father was taking the belt to them having had one too many whiskeys before coming home from the oil fields. "What happened?" Gavin said calmly as he sat Tony on a chair and brought him over a glass of water.

"I killed her," Tony said, looking up to his older brother. "I didn't mean to, I swear, it was an accident. We went to that man's house, the guy who broke into our meeting. I wanted to stop him talking to you. Caroline was with me, she was scared I was going to do something silly, and we had a fight, I lost my temper, and she fell…" Tony put his face in his hands.

Gavin was shocked by what his brother had told him. At the end of the day, they were brothers and, despite being at odds over the company, he still felt a paternal need to protect him.

"Okay," Gavin said, pulling up the chair next to him and going into his classic CEO mode. "I can sort this out. Where is she?"

"I left her at the bottom of the stairs."

"I can get someone to the house, and we can get rid of her body and somehow cover this up, make it look like she had taken some leave from work or something, I don't know, but we can make it work. She wasn't married and there are no kids, so it's a mess, but a fixable one. I've got a security team we can trust, and they can be at Camps Bay within the hour."

Tony looked to his brother and gave him a nod, not realising that Gavin hadn't even needed to ask for Amos's address.

"There is something else you need to know. Something important, about the company," Gavin said.

Tony wiped his eyes and looked at his brother. The company was everything to him, to both of them, and he had to pull himself together now.

Gavin told him about the call he had just received from their insurance broker, Tyrone. He explained that Amos had been working with others to defraud them both, Worldwide Insurance and Adesco Oil. That someone in their company had been making millions of dollars of claims and then feeding them back to Amos for his project.

"So, that fucking lunatic has been using our company to defraud the insurers and to build something to then sell back to us? Well, he's got more brass than I expected him to have, that's for sure."

"Tyrone said he thinks there's more to this, though. He's worried that there are other people involved who may be out to harm us as well, and not just steal from us. We need to know who's involved. And we need to stop them."

"What do you suggest?" Tony asked.

"The first thing is to find out who in our firm has been doing this to us. It has to be someone in our accounts department, as only they would be able to make payments without me getting suspicious. I told Tyrone we would find whoever it is and let him know. He's going to do the same at his company. So, for the moment, that's our main job. I'll call the head of our security and send him to Amos's house. Then I'll get our head of accounts in and see what I can find out."

Gavin was pretty sure he had convinced Tony that everything he was saying was true, he certainly could not at this point risk Tony or anyone else, knowing that he had been secretly funding Amos all along. If that came out then his position as CEO would definitely be over. But as soon as everything was in place and Adesco was recognised by the world as the one true innovator in the energy space then he would show his hand and take all the glory himself, maybe even winning himself a Nobel prize along the way.

But until then no one could know his part in this.

"What do you need me to do?" Tony asked, seemingly having brought into Gavins version of events.

"At the moment, do nothing. Go home, clean yourself up, and wait for my call."

CHAPTER 42

Kiara had worked her way down to the taxi rank at the top of the beach, the same one Tony had gone to a few hours before. There was already an Uber waiting.

It took her straight to the Cape Grace Hotel on the Waterfront, where she knew Tyrone would be coming to meet her.

She looked at her watch; she had about an hour before he would get there. She was suddenly ravenous. She had been going nonstop and hadn't even thought about eating anything. She called room service and ordered up a club sandwich and side salad, along with a bottle of fizzy water. She would have died for a whisky sour right about then, but it was too important for her to keep a clear head now.

Whilst she waited for the food, she called her mother-in-law.

"Kiara, dear, we have been so worried about you. You said you would phone first thing, but the whole day's gone. Are you okay?"

The sound of her mother-in-law's voice brought a tear to her eye. She realised she needed to get home right away. She needed to be with her girls, Mia and Jasmin, and she needed to be back in her own small house in the middle of the Sussex Countryside and not in this crazy country. She held back the tears and tried to steady her voice.

"I'm fine, Judy. I won't lie, it's been a tough trip, but I'm almost done now. I've just one more meeting shortly and then I'll be on the next flight home."

"Oh good, I'm pleased. We've all missed you so much. I think going away so soon was maybe not such a good idea for you, or the girls. Then that call we took, it really scared us."

"I know, and I'm sorry, I really am. I thought I was ready to dive back into work, and a change of scenery seemed like it would be a good idea. But what's done is done. And the people who called are dealt with now, they won't be bothering you or any of us again. Tell the girls I'll be home tomorrow some time."

"Mia is here, actually, I can get her for you. Jasmin is at a friend's, but maybe you can call her back later?"

"Yes, that would be amazing. And I think it's okay for you all to go home now, back to my house."

"Actually, we didn't move out in the end. Nick Taylor, as usual, came to the rescue. He called Bruce, his friend from the police, and they stationed a car outside the house the whole time. They are going to leave it here until you get back. And Nick has hardly left our sides since you went away."

"I'm so sorry, I have caused you all so much trouble."

"It wasn't your fault, darling. Just come home now."

"Please tell Nick that everything's okay, and thank him for me. And tell him I'm meeting Tyrone shortly, so all will be dealt with by this evening, I'm positive of that."

"Of course I'll tell him. Let me go and get Mia for you now. Just come home safely, darling, that's all we want."

Kiara didn't know what she would have done without her in-laws, or Nick Taylor.

Mia came to the phone, full of stories about college and her latest hockey match. She had recently joined Brighton and Hove hockey club and had just played her first match.

"Oh, my darling girl, I can't believe I missed your first match," Kiara said.

"Mum, I'm seventeen, I'm not a kid anymore. You don't need to be there for all my games."

"I know, I just feel bad, I really wanted to go. How was it?"

"We won two to one, and I scored the winner. I got girl of the game, as well."

"Amazing!"

After Mia had caught her up on everything that her and Jasmin had been up to, she made Kiara promise to come straight home.

After the call ended, Kiara packed her small case and waited for Tyrone to turn up. For her, the job was almost done. Tyrone would no longer have to pay out any more fraudulent claims and the fact that he had helped Adesco Oil by telling them that they were also being scammed, and were possibly in danger, meant he had done enough by his client to hopefully keep their business going forward. As to where Amos was, or who the dead lady at the bottom of his stairs was, she had no idea. Even the identity of the people who attacked her was still a mystery. But it was time to get back home and much as it pained her to leave any loose ends behind, she had to now let Tyrone and his people bring everyone else to justice. She would make sure he knew that she was still able to help him remotely, but that was pretty much all she had left to offer.

She logged on to the British Airways app on her phone and booked herself onto the late flight home. All that was left to do was wait for him and his staff, find out which one of them was working for Amos, then head to the airport and go home. Tyrone could get her suitcase from the locker in the Johannesburg airport and courier it on to her in a day or two.

Ninety minutes later, she was woken from the sleep she had fallen into by a knocking on her door.

It was Tyrone, along with Bea, Mufuka and Jan.

"Are you okay?" he asked, taking her into his arms. "I was so worried when you messaged me from your Uber."

She told him everything that had happened back at the house, as well as updating him and the other three on everything she had learned.

"Did you call the police?" she asked him.

"Yes, but, as expected, without any proof, they were not able to commit to doing anything to help us. I told them to get to Amos's house right away and said there was a dead body waiting for them, but it was still a battle getting them to take me seriously on that. When this is all over, they are going to get a visit from me and my lawyers, I can tell you. I did get hold of my security firm, and they were heading right there, but when you sent me the message to meet you here I called them off for the moment. I've asked them to try and trace Amos, to maybe keep an eye on his house in case he returns there. I also called Gavin at Adesco. He knows everything now. Him and his brother are going to find out who at their company is working with Amos. I told him that we should share info when this is over to make sure it can't ever happen again."

He then turned to the other three.

"So, which one of you is it?" he said as calmly as he possible could.

"Excuse me?" Bea said, the anger in her voice clear for them all to hear.

"This is not the time to raise your voice to me, Bea. One of you three, or all of you, are in on this. You heard everything Kiara has told us; if you don't tell me now, then you can tell the police. Don't forget that this is now a murder investigation as well."

Kiara pulled up a chair and sat down with them.

"I'm sorry, I really am, two of you may be innocent and this has to be hard to take, but this is not a joke. This is now a double murder. So, this is more than just a matter of insurance fraud. If you don't come forward right now, then you might be arrested for being part of that."

"Double murder?" Bea said, her voice now a shadow of what it was just a moment ago.

"Who was killed?" Mufuka asked.

"Someone called Karly was killed, I didn't get a surname, but I believe she worked at Adesco. I heard the people who had attacked me talking about her when I was at the house. And then there was also a dead body I almost tripped over when I got out. I don't know who that lady is either. I heard the woman say something about the claims not being paid without Karly. Tyrone has never mentioned that name before, or another lady missing from your team, so I assumed Karly must work at Adesco Oil and that she was a link between my attackers and one of you?"

"I don't know a Karly," Tyrone said.

"Me either," said Mufuka.

"Nor me," said Bea.

All of them looked at Jan, expecting him to say the same, but he didn't; he had turned pale and seemed frozen to his chair.

"Jan," Tyrone said, "mate, don't tell me it's you. You've been with me from the start, since I set up Worldwide. Surely you can't be involved in this?"

Jan looked from Tyrone to Kiara, seemingly not able to decide to whom he should be confessing.

"You fucker!" Bea screamed at him, lunging forward and slapping him across the face. "How could you do this?!"

The slap startled him so much that he slid into the back of the chair so hard that the entire chair moved back and only stopped when it reached the wall a few inches behind it.

"Bea, please," Kiara said, standing up, taking the other woman by the shoulder and forcing her back down into her chair. She then turned to Jan.

"Who is Karly?" she asked him.

Jan cleared his voice.

"I knew her from university, we studied finance together. We both ended up working for an insurance company, and stayed there for a few years, before she wanted a change of company and moved to a job in the accounts department at Adesco Oil. I was also looking for something else to do when Tye offered me the job heading up the claims department. You were just starting Worldwide…" he said, looking at Tyrone. "It was still working in finance, to a degree, but just seemed so much more interesting, so I joined you. I had lost touch with Karly for a few years, and then you managed to pick up Adesco's insurance policies and we found ourselves in each other's lives once again."

"And she became your girlfriend, I presume?" Bea cut in.

"Actually, no, she didn't," Jan shot back at her, "but I did want her to be. I was in love with her, back from university days. I told her that when we went to work for the insurance company, but she said it just wouldn't work, being together all day and then again after work. I said I'd leave and get another job, but she wouldn't have that. When she eventually left to work at Adesco, I thought maybe that was the time, but we seemed to just lose touch. But I never stopped loving her. Then suddenly, from nowhere, she was back in my life again."

"So, she recruited you into this, then?" Kiara asked him.

"She said she needed help. She didn't tell me exactly what this was about, but she said it was to do with climate change; the fact that she was now working in the oil industry, it made some sense that she wanted to take a stand against what they were doing. She was always into that, even back in the university days. You know, saving the planet and everything. So, I agreed to help her."

"And you decided you could rob me to do it then?" Tyrone said to him, the anger in his voice rising at being betrayed by his friend. "It was that fucking easy for you, was it?"

"It wasn't like that," Jan said back to him.

"What was it like then?! Go on, explain it, help me understand how you could do that to me."

Jan looked down, knowing that even as he explained it that it would not sound like it did when he had first justified it to himself.

"I didn't think you would lose much. I figured you would just claim most of it back from our re-insurers, and Karly said it would only be a few really small claims. She said it was to just help this scientist guy who was working on some climate project that she was involved in. She said the money would be going to a good cause, to help save the planet. I mean, it was only meant to be small amounts, and I figured you wouldn't even notice…"

"Fuck me!" Tyrone said, looking at Kiara and back to Jan. Kiara sat there happy to let Jan talk, although she really wanted to comfort Tyrone, as it was clearly tearing him apart.

"You think because I can afford it that you could give my money to your girlfriend? I'm honestly lost for words."

"That came out badly, I didn't mean it to sound like that. I just thought Adesco would end up paying. You know, we would put their premiums up and they would have to pay a higher claims excess? I don't know, I just thought they would end up paying rather than you. And they should pay, shouldn't' they? I mean, look at the damage they are causing to the planet, and look at all the money they earn…"

"Listen to yourself, Jan, trying to justify it, but you can't, can you? Not really. And now your girlfriend is dead, and that's on you, as well. And don't give me that crap about the planet, you couldn't care less about climate change, you were just doing it to try to get your girlfriend back…"

"Tye," Kiara said, holding his shoulder. "What's done is done. You now know it was Jan and why he did it. Let's just let the police do the rest. Call them again, please."

"Mufuka, can you?" he said, turning to his CFO, all the fight now running out of him.

"I got it," she said, giving Jan a look before she left the room and headed down to reception to make the call.

"And who are those other people involved?" Kiara asked Jan. "The ones who attacked me?"

228

"I don't know," he said, trying his best not to burst into tears at the thought that Karly had gone.

"Come on, Jan, they have killed someone now, maybe even multiple people. This is serious, you have to give us something," she pressed him harder.

"All I know is that some very bad people were involved, people I didn't even know existed at the start. The main guy is called Rene Bester, he was the one in charge. But there were others, some really bad people, and they threatened her. They made her increase the claims, and she had to do it because she was scared for her life. She was frightened they would make her tell them about me as well, but I know she never would have. But I was scared for her as well, so I had to just go along with it, to protect her. Surely you understand that?" he said to Tyrone.

"Some good it did you both," Tyrone said, "they killed her anyway and nearly bankrupted me in the process."

"So, who are the others this Rene has with him?" Kiara asked.

"One of them is Rene's girlfriend. I don't know her name, but Karly was really scared of her, and there was Rene's best friend, Dan something, he was ex-army, and she said something about him buying bombs."

"Oh, for fuck's sake," Tyrone said.

Kiara gave him a look to keep him quiet.

"Is that all?" Kiara asked.

"No, there was the big guy as well. She didn't tell me his name. She just said he was someone that Dan had found to set the bombs."

"What are they going to do?"

"I don't know, honestly, I don't. She refused to tell me. She knew I would have to tell someone if I knew. I couldn't just let people die, could I?"

"But you didn't tell anyone, did you?" Tyrone cut in once again. "You might not have known what they were going to do, but you knew that they had bombs, which meant people could die, and still you said nothing."

"I loved her," he said, unable to make eye contact again.

Tyrone looked at Kiara and just shook his head, lost for words.

Mufuka came back into the room; Kiara looked at her.

"Are the police coming?" she asked the other lady.

"I called the police from reception and put the hotel manager on to them. I told him what I could, including that someone had been murdered and that we had the suspect in your room. I'd imagine the manager of the Cape Grace holds more sway than any of us do with the authorities, so the police took him seriously and should be here soon, I hope."

"Good," Kiara said to Tyrone. "And, as soon as they are here, I am going to the airport, if you don't mind."

CHAPTER 43

Z ara was nowhere near as patient as Hamilton was. She marvelled at the fact that this man could be a monster one minute and as quiet as a mouse the next. She studied him for quite some time.

I could actually learn a trick or two from him, she thought.

"Shouldn't we call Rene and see how the clearing up is going?" she asked, breaking the silence.

Hamilton didn't even bat an eyelid. He just sat staring at the front door.

A few seconds later, they heard a noise as someone was putting a key into the lock. The door swung forward on its broken hinges and crashed flat into the hallway. Amos just stood there, a look of surprise on his face.

"Amos, you little pickle, I think you've been hiding things from us, haven't you?" Zara said, walking towards him.

Amos was too slow to react when the huge man sprung from his chair and moved forward at a speed that someone a quarter of his size would not have been able to do. He struck Amos in the face with such force that it not only sent him flying backwards and almost over the balcony to the bottom of the steps where Caroline was lying, but it also left his nose shattered and spread across his face.

Zara walked outside and stood directly over Amos, her legs on either side of him, and looked down as if she were studying a dead animal lying on the pavement.

It took Amos a few seconds to come back to consciousness. He felt woozy and was unable to pull himself to standing.

"Would you mind helping our friend up?" Zara asked Hamilton's man, who was now standing next to her. "Maybe take him into the conservatory, where no one can see us." She looked down the drive to make sure the road was still empty, which it was.

Hamilton's man dragged Amos inside, over to the desk at the end of the conservatory and plopped him down into the chair.

Amos's laptop sat on the desk, still switched on. Zara caught sight of it for the first time and shook her head.

"Oh my God, your laptop was here all the time. I assumed you'd taken it with you." She turned to Hamilton. "See, if you hadn't been all crazy and ogre-like with me, I might had taken the time to look around the room properly myself." She shook her head, scolding him.

Hamilton and his man just looked at each other, both perplexed by the fact Zara still acted as if she were in charge of the situation.

"Oh well, as you are here..." she said to Amos, giving him a little slap on the back "... it saves me time hacking into your bank, doesn't it? Go on, then," Zara said to him, "tell us why you did it."

"Did what?" he replied weakly, wiping the blood from his eyes and wincing at the pain caused by his smashed nose.

"Really? You honestly want to do it this way?" she asked him incredulously. "Have you not seen the size of that man?"

"You don't need to blow up Adesco's platform," he said to her through clenched lips. "Yes, I know that is your plan."

Amos knew that if he was going to survive these next few minutes that he would somehow have to try to get her onside.

"I knew from the first day Rene approached me that he would gladly die for his cause. And I respect him for that, I really do. I'm the same. Climate change has weighed down on me since I can remember. And I will give my life for the cause in a heartbeat. But we can't take someone else's life for it, we just can't do that. With companies like Adesco, we can stop them, but we don't need to blow them all apart to do it. We can work with them, we can use their own money to show them a better way…"

Zara interrupted him mid-flow "This is all extremely fascinating, Amos, but as you have brought up the subject of money, please can we have ours back?" she said with a smile.

Amos ignored her question and carried on talking, hoping she would give him enough time to convert her and Hamilton to his plans.

"And now the head of Adesco Oil knows I can do it. I've shown him my plans, haven't I? And he has now invited me to visit him. His secretary was meant to be meeting me here to talk about it, but I got scared and went out. She might even still be coming…"

Zara laughed, now understanding who was outside the doorway downstairs.

"Oh my God, she's the secretary. The dead girl down in your basement works at Adesco. That is so precious…"

Before Amos could reply, Hamilton walked forward menacingly..

"Enough," he said, grabbing Amos roughly by the neck. "Where is my money?"

Zara tried to get him off Amos, but he simply pushed her away sending her backwards, into a coffee table, briefly stunning her.

"I need our money!" Hamilton said again as he lifted Amos out of the chair with ease, looking into the man's eyes. "You live in this, this palace, whilst my family died living in the slums. You get to eat fresh food whilst we fight for scraps. We have nothing, whilst you, and her…" he said, referring to Zara, "… have everything. And you think I need to worry about saving the planet?! I worry about where I will next eat, and whether I will even wake up in the morning. I worry about saving my township, not about stopping the world falling apart. That money will get me and mine out of there. Without it, we may as well never wake up again. Now give it to me, before I tear you apart to find it," he said, gripping Amos so tightly around the throat that the other man could not take a breath.

"He was coming to that bit, you idiot!" Zara shouted, getting her breath back. "He's about to tell us where it is. Just put him down, you fucking idiot, before you kill him!" she shouted, jumping up.

She could see Amos was about to pass out again. If she didn't stop him, then they would never know where the money had gone. She swung at him as hard as she was able to, but once again made no impact. Hamilton just swatted her away, knocking one of her front teeth clean out and sending her back onto the floor by the coffee table.

He dropped Amos back down onto the chair, before hitting him again with enough force to break his jaw and permanently close one of his eyes.

Zara pulled herself up yet again, her head cloudy from the force of his blow.

"Give us back our money!" he shouted at Amos, his hand raised again, ready to take another shot at him, possibly ending Amos's life before he was able to tell them where the money was.

Zara felt a knife lying next to her. It was an old tribal knife that had, until a few moments ago, sat on a small wooden display easel in the centre of the table before it was knocked over as she flew past.

Before Hamilton could deliver his fatal blow, Zara jumped up and rushed forward. Hamilton's man jumped between him and his boss as Zara thrusted the blade forward. It was razor sharp, despite being over a hundred years old, and it plunged through the man's chest, deep into his heart. He fell to the floor dead in an instant.

"Look what you have done to me!" she said to Hamilton with a lisp, hardly even glancing at the dead man now at her feet. "I'm going to have to get a new tooth now, and that's really a pain to do. They are so expensive." She looked down at Amos, who was covered in blood, one eye completely closed, and his jaw broken in two places, still trying to get a breath. "Mind you, I think I fared rather well in comparison to your friend," she said, looking over at Hamilton's man with a smirk. "Oops, sorry about that. Now let him breathe," she said, referring to Amos. "And let him tell us where the money is."

Hamilton, who was hardly ever shocked, automatically did as he was told and took a step back.

"Good boy," Zara said to him, before turning back to Amos.

"Ouch. It hurts to smile as well," she said to Hamilton as he stared at his man, now dead at their feet. "You really didn't need to do that to me, we were actually on the same side, you idiot."

Amos opened his one good eye and tried to speak. His jaw could only just move, so the words were muted and almost unintelligible. Zara leant in as close as she could to hear him.

"My batteries work," he said through the pain. "They really work. I just had to give Adesco the money we stole so they can build them into their platform."

"You sent the money back to Adesco?" she said in shock. "You sent them back the money we stole from them? All of it?! Over twenty million dollars?"

"I had to," he whispered back. "I needed to make them see I was serious about working with them."

"How do we get it back from them?" she said, before pushing him away from the desk, letting him fall from the chair onto the floor next to the dead man.

She clicked onto his laptop, bringing it alive. She saw the bank icon on the main screen and clicked onto it. The app opened up right away. It needed a password.

"What's the password?" she said.

"It's too late," he whispered.

"Give me the password! I'll hack in if I have to. You know I can do it. So, stop us hurting you even more and give me the password, you freak!"

"Starfish1," he said, as quickly as he was able.

"Starfish1," Zara repeated as she typed it into the box.

The app opened, revealing the charity's bank account. It showed a balance of only one thousand dollars. She clicked on the tab that said recent transactions. It showed a payment to Adesco Oil for twenty-two million, one hundred thousand, twenty-two dollars and fifteen cents. She couldn't believe her eyes. He really had sent almost everything he had back to them, not just the recent payment, but most of what he had left. He had only kept a thousand dollars back, the rest had all gone to Adesco's bank.

When he had said it was too late, he had not been lying. The money had gone. And, because of Hamilton, Karly was also gone. So, there was no way they could get it back again.

She looked down at Amos with utter contempt.

"My batteries work," he said again.

"Amos, you silly little fool," she said to him, now with pity rather than contempt. "The oil companies would never have worked with you. They will drill for their oil, until it's all been drained away, and then they'll start digging up the coal again, and then start drilling for more gas. They'll not stop until the planet is drained. It's just what they do."

"Please…" he whispered, the pain in his face almost unbearable.

"The only way to save our planet is to stop them all, every single oil company, every single gas company, every single one of them. At least that's what Rene keeps telling me, not that I actually give a toss, if I am being totally honest with you. I was only in it for the money, which now it seems you've taken away from me anyway."

Amos looked up at her, no longer able to speak.

"You are a silly little man," she said. She spat out each word and accompanied each one with a direct stamp onto his face. "Silly, naïve, little man," she continued, as the heels from her shoes split open his face and covered her feet in his blood. "Annoying, spoilt, little bug."

It was only her phone ringing that stopped her from caving in his entire head. She took the phone from her pocket.

"And look at the mess you have made of my shoes," she said to Amos's dead body.

"Yes, darling?" she said into the phone to Rene as if it were just another ordinary day.

"Did you find him? Did he tell you where the money is?" Rene said sharply into her ear.

"The little prick gave it back to Adesco Oil."

"What?!" Rene screamed at her.

"He sent the entire amount back to Adesco, so that they could build his stupid machine. I told him they would never have built it anyway."

"Can you get it back?"

"How the hell can I do that?"

"You're the fucking computer genius! Find a fucking way!"

"There isn't a way. I can't just dial into their bank and steal it out. It's not possible."

"Hamilton is going to kill us all as soon as he finds out."

"He already knows," she said, smiling at Hamilton as he stared straight at her

"Can't you get Amos to call his bank and get the money returned?"

She looked down at the mess on the floor.

"I think we are a little beyond that now," she said, realising that she had gone and done exactly what she had told Hamilton not to do.

"What's happened?" Rene asked, knowing from her tone that what she was about to tell him was going to be painful to hear.

"Let's just say that once I severed his spinal cord, the life ran out of him."

"What the fuck did you do that for?!"

"I don't know, it just seemed to happen."

"For fuck's sake, Zara."

Rene was almost lost for words.

"That's it, then. We are screwed. It's all over. Everything I've planned, everything I have sacrificed to get here was all for nothing. And the oil companies will just continue fucking our planet up, well done, well fucking done."

"Maybe not. There is actually something else, something I saw before Amos got back that could still make this happen."

"Go on," Rene said, almost at the point where he was ready to just sit down and take his own life.

"The Kiara Fox lady is still here. She was at this house when we arrived. And I bet she's gone back to the Waterfront, to the Cape Grace. I doubt she can get the money back from Adesco, but maybe she can get the insurance man to make us out a big fuck-off payment, a proper payout covering everything we need. Hamilton can have his money, and we can still complete our plan."

Rene thought about that for a second.

Maybe there is a way to finish this after all, he thought.

"And why would she get him to do that?" Rene asked, knowing that Zara would have a plan already.

"If she's at Cape Grace then Hamilton and I can head over there now. I can get our receptionist friend to tell us which room she's in and Hamilton can take her. I'd imagine after a few minutes with us she'll agree to call him and convince him to pay up, don't you?" She looked over at Hamilton and saw a small smile creep across his face.

"Do it," Rene said wearily. "We will meet you there shortly."

Zara ended the call.

Zara found Amos's bathroom and cleaned herself up. There

was no way she could go back to the Cape Grace looking like she did. She got all the blood off her shoes and face, but her lips were already swelling up where her tooth had been knocked out. "For fuck's sake," she said to the mirror. "Fucking Rene and his fucking climate shit," she said, as she walked back down to the lounge. "Come on, big boy," she said to Hamilton, "it's time to go hunt us a fox."

CHAPTER 44

Rene knew it was over the moment Zara told him that Amos had returned the money. Up until then, he'd genuinely thought that he could pull this off, that he could not only destroy Adesco's new oil platform, but that it would then be the catalyst for bringing down the entire oil industry. He had let his obsession with climate change completely cloud his judgement. If he had been honest with himself, he would have known that one man could never bring an entire industry to its knees. They could disrupt it for sure, but to think he could destroy it was pure folly.

He looked around the small office. Between the three of them, they had managed to move Karly's body into the storage cupboard and clean up most of the mess, but it would not be long before someone, a cleaner or the office maintenance guy, would find her. And they had not been able to completely clean up the blood that had splattered the floor where her body had fallen or make any sort of repairs to the wall behind where the bullet had ended up after exiting her head.

He signalled for Dan to come and join him, giving them enough privacy to talk freely whilst Hamilton's man stood guarding the door.

"It's all gone to shit," he said when Dan was next to him and they were facing away from the door, looking out of the window. "Hamilton has completely lost the plot now, all he wants is his money and he's going to kill us all to get it, and Zara is becoming unhinged. She's killed Amos, and he was the only hope of us

240

getting the money we need to finish this. And when Karly's body is found, it won't be long until we are arrested and banged up for life."

Dan looked at his friend. "So, what do you want to do then? I can take Hamilton's man out, but then what, where will we go?"

"Even if we get out of here, we can't run forever, and even if we can't stop the oil companies from fucking up the planet, we can still hurt them, but I can't do this on my own."

"I was always with you until the end, you know that. What do you want to do?"

"We can still bring Adesco down." He turned to Dan and looked him squarely in the eyes, whilst keeping his voice so low that it didn't carry to the door where Hamilton's man continued to stand guard. "Your bombs are still on site, aren't they?"

"Yes. But not enough to bring it completely down."

"But enough to cause a delay in them drilling?"

"If we can get the bombs into position and all set off together, we can probably set them back a number of years."

"We might be screwed, but let's finish this, then."

"What about Hamilton and his men? They won't just let us get away afterwards, especially if we don't pay them."

"Even if we can get the money, we aren't going to pay him anything, not after he killed Karly, and almost killed you. If we can get them onto the platform as the bombs go off, then we can get rid of them all at the same time."

"And Zara?"

"I know what she's like, I always have, but I still love her, and you. You are as close to family as I've ever had. I'll find a way that both of you can get away."

"We are in this together, we always have been," Dan replied, not willing to let Rene take the fall all on his own.

"No, this one is down to me. And I want you out there long after I'm gone to carry on the fight. We might have lost this battle, but the war goes on, and you can still make the change I haven't been able to do. I need to call this Tyrone and get our money. But just promise me that somehow you'll get Zara off the platform before it's too late."

"You know I will."

"I need to make a call," Rene said, turning to Hamilton's man.

"We need to go," the man replied from the door.

"We're coming, but I have a call to make first," Rene replied.

"Now," the other man said sternly.

"If you want your money, then I need to do this."

The man wasn't sure what to do. Reluctantly, he nodded.

Rene took out his phone and dialled a number he had stored many months before but as yet had never had to use.

CHAPTER 45

"So now what?" Tyrone asked Kiara after the police had come and taken Jan away in cuffs, along with Mufuka and Bea, who had both agreed to tell the officers everything that they had heard him admit to. Tyrone had agreed to follow on once he had helped Kiara leave. The police had wanted her to go as well, but once she explained that she needed to get the next flight out for her own safety, they had agreed to let her go, as long as she made a statement as soon as she got home.

"Jan will be charged with fraud, at the very least," Kiara said. "The police have tried to call Karly, but there's no reply, and her flat is empty. They'll keep looking for her, but she is probably dead, as we suspect. Once you have finished at the police station, you should go and see Adesco and bring them up to speed. Hopefully they can help you get your money back, as they did end up making fraudulent claims, even if they didn't know about it."

"I just hope we can keep their business after all this," Tyrone said, "their account might be the only thing that keeps me afloat right now."

"You've still got those diamonds you took from the bank," she said.

"My backup money. I still hope I don't have to use them. As I said, they are my very last port in a storm."

"Well, I think my job's definitely done now, don't you?" Kiara said.

"It certainly looks that way. I don't know how to thank you,"

Tyrone said. "I am sure that the police will track this Rene and the others down pretty quickly. Maybe you can stay a bit longer? The police will protect you now and it would be good for you to see them all arrested, I'd imagine. And then I can treat you to a few days back at the Saxon Hotel, to get some rest and catch up on a little sun. They are also known to have the best spa in the area. I'd really like to say thank you properly for everything you've done."

"As much as a couple of days lying by the pool sounds nice, I really need to get home, to be honest. My girls need me, and I think getting home and sitting in my own garden in my own little house would be much more relaxing at the moment."

"I understand," he said, disappointed, but silently agreeing with her. "And I should get going to the police station, Bea and Mufuka will need me there to add in my bits to the story. I want to see them take that prick Jan away and lock him up."

"If I don't go soon, I'll miss my flight," Kiara said. "Do you think you could collect my suitcase from the airport in Joburg if I message you the locker number and combination? You would just need to courier it on to me."

"Of course, no problem at all. I'll transfer your fee over before the day ends, you certainly earned it."

"I most definitely have earned it!" Kiara agreed.

"Okay, let me call the police and tell them I'm on the way now and I'll ask them to send a car to escort you to the airport."

"There's no need for that, I'll get the hotel to take me in one of their cars."

"I'd prefer having the police take you."

Tyrone called the police. They said it would take them an hour or so, but they would send someone over. Before he left, Tyrone made Kiara promise to stay in touch and come back one day soon with her girls for a family holiday with him and his boys to his favourite safari lodge.

Kiara didn't tell him, but she doubted she would ever be up to coming back again after everything she had been through.

Once he was gone, she waited just over an hour before asking the hotel to check if the police car was coming. She needed to get to the airport before check-in closed and time was running out.

"I'm sorry, Mrs Fox, they said they cannot give you an exact time, but they will be here as soon as they can."

Kiara looked at her watch for what must have been the hundredth time and decided she needed to get going. The sooner she was at the airport, the sooner she would feel safe again, and the sooner she could start the journey home.

"Do you have a driver available at the moment?" she asked.

"Let me check," the receptionist said. She made a few calls and organised Kiara a driver.

As soon as Kiara had climbed into the car, the receptionist picked up her phone and made another call.

CHAPTER 46

Z ara finished the call and looked at Hamilton. This time he was driving, and she sat next to him. The back seat was, of course, no longer occupied.

"That was my person at the Cape Grace," she said. "They have just put her in a car, a silver Mercedes, registration CA 542-654. They only just left, so if you step on it, we should be able to catch them before they reach the airport turnoff."

CHAPTER 47

The hotel car with Kiara in the back seat was heading to the airport when a van painted with yellow stripes pulled up behind them and started furiously flashing its headlights.

"It must be the police," Kiara said to the driver, "I was meant to wait for them. I did ask the girl at the reception to tell them I didn't need them any more."

"I think we should continue to the airport, ma'am," the driver said without looking back at her.

"They are flashing at us, maybe they need something else."

"It is unusual. I don't think we should stop. They can catch us at the airport."

Kiara sat back in her chair, suddenly feeling unnerved. Surely Tyrone, or the police, would call her if they needed her, they had her number. She turned back and saw the van getting dangerously close; there was no way the police would be driving like that.

"I don't think it's the police, let's just get to the airport as quickly as we can."

The driver put his foot down and sped up. Kiara pulled out her phone to call Tyrone, but before she could dial the number, there was a huge bang as the van drove into the rear of the Mercedes, causing it to spin wildly. Somehow it missed the other cars around it on the motorway as it spun from the middle lane into the inside lane and then into the barrier. The car came to a sudden stop.

The driver's head had banged into the steering wheel, causing him to lose consciousness. Kiara's phone had left her hand and flew into the back of the seat in front of her, followed instantly by her. She was held back by the seat belt, but the speed at which the car had hit the barrier caused the belt to pull so tightly around her that she felt one of her ribs snap in half.

The van pulled up next to them and, in a split second, both her door and the driver's door were pulled open.

Hamilton leant in and unbuckled Kiara, before grabbing her and dragging her into the van. Zara, calmly and without any hesitation, put a bullet into the driver's head. The driver had still been unconscious when his door was pulled open, so he was not a threat to them, but that hadn't saved his life.

The van pulled back onto the motorway and sped off in the same direction as the airport.

Kiara came to and looked at the people who had grabbed her. She recognised them both from the attack at the Saxon Hotel and Amos's house.

"We warned you to go back home, didn't we? You should have taken our advice," Hamilton said, looking at Kiara huddled onto the floor of the van clutching her damaged ribs, whilst Zara kept the gun pointing at her.

"Take me home," he barked to his driver.

CHAPTER 48

Tyrone picked up his phone at the same second that the chief of police did. Both men listened to their respective callers, before moving to different sides of the room, so that each could talk in private without the other hearing.

When the calls were over, they looked at each other and tried to decide if they should share what they had both been told.

"Go on, you first," the police chief said.

"No. You first," Tyrone replied, still unsure whether he should tell them about the demand he had just been given.

"My officers went to the house in Camps Bay. They found three bodies. One fits the description of the owner, the man you called Amos. The other two are not yet known to us, one is a white female, aged about thirty and the other was a black man, suspected to have come from the Khayelitsha township."

"They killed Amos," Tyrone said in dismay.

"There is more. There was a carjacking just before the trunk road to the airport. A van drove a car off the road, forcing it into the central reservation. A woman was seen being dragged into the van before it then sped off. The driver was shot at point blank into the head. This wasn't some random carjacking, was it? This was tied into everything here. The woman was Kiara Fox, wasn't it?"

Tyrone nodded in agreement.

"It must be," he said.

"And that call you just took, that was them, I assume?"

"Yes."

"Are you going to tell me what they said?"

"He told me not to say anything to you. He said if I get the police involved, he'll kill her. And I believe him."

"We are already involved. Tell me everything he said to you."

"He'll kill her if I tell you."

The chief of police walked over to him. "And they'll kill her if you don't."

"Agreed," Tyrone said, after a second. "He wanted ten million dollars, today."

"Do you have that amount available?"

"Not in cash I don't, but I can get it," he said, looking down at the bag of diamonds that had not left his side since he had taken them out of the bank.

"Where are they taking her?"

"He didn't say. He just said they will call me within the hour and if I don't answer Kiara is dead."

CHAPTER 49

The van pulled up outside the township.

As soon as it was clear that Hamilton was the driver, a pathway was cleared that enabled him to drive the van in. Due to the density of the shacks that made up the housing, he could not drive in more than a few feet before he had to pull over. As soon as he was in, the pathway was closed, and the van was covered, giving the impression that it had never been there in the first place.

Hamilton climbed out and was met by two dozen men from the various gangs, all there awaiting his return. Zara climbed out, inviting Kiara to join her. With a gun still pointing at her, Kiara put up no resistance.

"Bring them," Hamilton said to his men as he headed off into the dense township.

"What do you mean 'them'?" Zara called out to him. "Hey!" she shouted at one of the men as he yanked the gun from her hand whilst two more grabbed her by the arms. Another two had grabbed Kiara and were marching after Hamilton.

"Looks like we are both in trouble now, doesn't it?" Zara said to Kiara, giving her a wink and a smirk.

"What are you going to do with me?" Kiara asked the other woman.

"I'm not going to do anything with you. Does it look like I'm in charge now? But Hamilton may have some ideas for a pretty lady like you."

"Hamilton," Kiara repeated to herself.

"Oh, of course, you don't know who we are, do you? You knew Amos, though, didn't you? That was clever, finding him, but I did leave a few clues, just in case someone needed to take the blame."

Kiara picked up on what Zara had just said. "What do you mean *knew* him?"

"After you ran away, we waited for him to come back and sadly he had a little accident under my heels. These things happen," Zara replied.

"No more talking," one of the men said to them both.

Zara just shrugged and let the two men pull her forwards, following Hamilton ever deeper into the maze of shacks. Kiara said nothing more, doing her best to block out the pain from her broken rib whilst at the same time trying to memorise which way they were being taken.

The walk seemed to take forever, and the stench of the place reached all the way into her stomach. The degradation all around made Kiara question how on earth she had ended up there, and how these people called this living.

The township housed over a million people and was considered one of the top five largest slums in the world. As the township had grown, the local government had tried to instal sanitation and electricity, but the facilities could simply not cope with the number of people flooding in, leaving over half of them with little or no way of providing heating or clean water to their small metal homes. If they needed to use the toilet, they either had to find a small area to create their own, or they had to walk right to the edge of the township, which in some cases could take over an hour to get to. Due to the dense growing population, the local municipality could not get deep into the township to service or empty the toilets, so instead they had placed them all around the outside, creating a ring of toilets like a moat around a castle.

Coming from part of the world where living space was abundant and comparatively cheap, Kiara felt the walls closing in on her, claustrophobic at being forced into an area packed so tightly with people. It oddly reminded her of the crazy swim start in a triathlon where everyone was fighting just to get enough space to move forward whilst being kicked in the head and forced under the water.

The smell of all those toilets was so intense that she had to fight back the urge to gag. But no matter how frightened she was, she knew that to show fear would be the worst thing she could do at that moment. Equally, if she were to have any chance of getting away, she would have to be left alone somewhere, and they would only do that if they thought she was too scared to run.

She needed to tread a fine line between fear and bravery if she was going to survive this.

After about forty minutes of marching, they broke out into an open space. It was a large area, around two acres, much the same size as her garden back at home in Hurstpierpoint. It felt like a sudden oasis in the middle of a dry desert compared to what they had just been dragged through. It was not quite at the centre of the township, but it was far enough from the edges to enable Hamilton to feel safe from the authorities who constantly hunted for him. His own home was not like the other shacks they had walked past, all made of corrugated steel and held together by wire and old ropes. His was built of brick, with glass windows and a solid front door. It reminded Kiara of the scout hut that serviced the local kids back in the park near her house. The homes surrounding it were also better built than the corrugated shacks, although not as grand as Hamilton's was. They were all small, round huts, made mostly from wood, and could have come straight out of a high-end glamping magazine. None of them butted onto the other, each one standing slightly detached from its neighbour, and each had electricity running to it, serviced by a communal water pump in the middle.

Hamilton was waiting for them by the water pump when they arrived a minute after him.

The men forced Zara and Kiara onto the ground in front of him and then took their places, creating a circle from which the ladies had no chance of escape.

Kiara stayed on the ground where she had been left, but Zara stood straight up. She brushed herself down, removing the dirt and dust from her clothes and walked towards him. The two men who had been holding her shot forward, but Hamilton put his hands out wide to stop them.

"Phone Rene," he said, holding out his phone to her.

She walked right up to him and took the phone out of his hand.

"My gun please," she said, turning to the man who had taken it.

"You will get that back when I say you can have it," Hamilton said to her.

"You really are a grouch," she replied to him, shaking her head. She dialled Rene.

"Hello, darling," she said, as calmly as she always did when she called him.

"Zara, where are you?"

"We are in the township, and I've got the girl," she said, giving Kiara a glance. "Now can you please tell your man here that you have a plan to get him his money?"

She passed the phone back to Hamilton.

"If you hurt her…" Rene started.

"I want my money," Hamilton said down the phone in reply. It had quickly become his mantra.

"Your money is being dealt with."

"When you have it, bring it here to me and then we can talk about finishing your job."

"Not a chance. If you think Dan and I are going to come to you there, especially after what you did to him…"

"Then where?"

"I told Tyrone to bring our money to Neptune. He has his own helicopter, and he's coming alone. It's almost impossible for the authorities to organise themselves quickly enough to follow him out into the middle of nowhere, so we'll be safe there. I want to finish this once and for all. Take the woman to the airfield where Dan has stored our own helicopter. We will meet you there tomorrow at five am. Once I know Zara is safe and your men have put the bombs in place, you can have your money, and we can all get off the platform in one piece. But, if you hurt Zara in any way before then…"

Hamilton had already handed her the phone back and walked off into his hut.

"Oh, darling, you do care, that is so sweet," Zara said to him.

"Are you okay?" he asked, ignoring her sarcastic comment.

"Don't worry your sweet head about me, I can handle him. Have you sorted the payment out?"

"Kind of. He's said he's got ten million in diamonds. It's enough for you and Dan to get away from this, go somewhere safe and wait until it all dies down."

"What do you mean Dan and me?" she whispered into the phone. "Where will you go?"

"I'm not getting out of this one. But you two don't need to go down with me."

"Rene!" she said, shocked.

"Just listen to me, okay. Keep the girl safe. Tyrone is going to bring the money to us, and I'll get you and Dan away somehow. I need to do this."

She knew better than to argue with him.

"And you believe he's got that much cash lying around?"

"Not in cash. But he has diamonds. And he's bringing them with him to the platform. I want us all to be there when he arrives."

"Diamonds? Are you sure he wasn't just making that up? It sounds a bit farfetched."

"That's what he told me. He said he had taken it out of the bank to cover his losses; he sounded genuine to me."

"How are you going to pay Hamilton in diamonds and not cash?" she whispered, making sure no one could hear her.

"Hamilton will never see a cent. Just make sure he doesn't hurt the girl, okay? The only way Tyrone will hand the diamonds over is if he knows she's still alive."

"I'll make sure she's okay."

"Meet me at the airfield, first thing tomorrow. It's almost over, we just need to get onto Neptune. Don't let me down."

"Never," she said, meaning it.

She cut off the call to Rene and walked into Hamilton's house. She handed him back his phone.

"It's set. We are meeting Rene and Dan first thing tomorrow, at the airfield, and you need to bring your men. There's enough room on the flight for us three, the Fox lady and then you and twelve of your men. You'll need to deal with the few security staff already living there, set the bombs and then we can all get safely off. Your cash will be delivered once the bombs are set. At that point, you can do what you want with the Fox lady. As long as the bombs are set, and we all fly out of there in time, I don't much care what happens to her."

"You just have the money ready, and we will do the rest. Darka…" he called out to one of his men.

"Yes, boss?" the man said, coming straight into the house.

"Take the other woman into your hut and keep her there until the morning."

"Yes, boss," Darka said, rushing back out to grab Kiara.

"And what shall *we* do for the rest of the night?" Zara said to Hamilton with a smirk.

"Do not tempt me," Hamilton sneered back at her.

CHAPTER 50

Kiara was grabbed by her legs and dragged to the hut opposite Hamilton's, where she was then pulled up and thrown inside. Apart from the throbbing of a broken rib, she also had scratches all down her back from the rough ground she had been dragged across, which had started to bleed into the thin top she was wearing. Darka, who was almost the same size as Hamilton and equally as brutal, didn't said a word to her. He knew that his physical size and deep-set eyes would be enough to put the fear of God into anybody, not least a weak white woman like her.

"You want us to stand guard?" one of the other men said to him as he walked outside pulling the hut's door closed.

"Get some food first and then come back and sit by the fire. She'll not go anywhere, she's too scared."

"Yes, boss," the man said.

"Do what you must with her, but keep her alive, you hear me?"

"Yes, boss," the man said, getting up and heading off to the food tent, a huge smile on his face as he realised Kiara was going be his dessert.

"The rest of you, come with me," Darka said to the remaining men before leading them all back into Hamilton's house to discuss what was going to be done the next day on Platform Neptune.

Kiara had wasted no time. As soon as the man had gone, she got herself up and over to the entrance. She listened to the discussion outside through the thin walls and realised she had to do this immediately or else it would be too late for her. As she tried to pull herself together, the fear started to hit her. Not only was her back bleeding, but her right-hand side, where the seat belt had broken her rib, burnt like fire. Added to that, she was in the middle of one of the largest townships in the world. She would be a target to anyone who saw her. The only things in her favour were that it was already dark, the township was basically circular, meaning anywhere she ran would eventually lead her to the edge, and, of course, she was a triathlete, someone used to running in all sorts of terrain and at speed.

Okay Fox, it's now or it really is never, she said to herself.

Without a pause, she gritted her teeth, turning all the pain she was feeling into lightning bolts, and sprinted through the door, in a straight line past Hamilton's home, past the fire and the food hut and back into the dense population of the township.

What the fuck? Zara thought as she sat outside Hamilton's place waiting for the men to finish their planning.

Wow, that Fox can really run, she thought.

"Hey Hamilton, I think we might have a little problem."

She waited for a reply, but none was forthcoming.

"Hamilton!" she screamed louder.

One of his men came out of the house.

"What you want, little lady?" the man said, looking down on her.

She looked up at him, not moving a muscle as she spoke.

"Tell your boss that his prize has just run away."

Hamilton had already walked outside to see what Zara wanted and heard her tell his man the news.

"Darka!" Hamilton shouted.

The other man joined him outside.

"You said the girl was being guarded."

Darka looked around and saw his man walking back to the fire.

"Where's the girl?!" he screamed at his man.

"In your hut, boss."

"Check on her."

The man ran into Darka's hut. He stopped at the door and turned back. "She's gone, boss."

"You fool!" Darka said to his man.

Before Darka could get his own men moving, Hamilton grabbed him by the head and twisted it so violently that his neck snapped in two. He dropped Darka's dead body onto the ground and turned to the other man.

"Find her, or you will die too," he said, before storming back into the house and ordering his men to join in the hunt for Kiara.

Zara sat on the step, as all the men, including Hamilton, ran back into the density of the township. "Men!" she said to no one, shaking her head.

Kiara ran without fear clogging her mind and without feeling any of the pain she should have felt. She was an athlete, used to long distance running, and she was fast and strong. The moment she had sprinted out of Darka's hut, her natural instincts had taken over. She suddenly embodied a unique beauty that went well beyond any physical appearance. Her movement became graceful and rhythmic, and she quickly fell into the steady pace that only an endurance athlete could maintain. Her face no longer showed the fear and pain she had felt only a few moments before. Now it was filled with determination and resilience as she pushed through the fatigue and reached a state of flow where her mind and body worked in perfect harmony.

She never faltered and never missed a step. The shacks themselves were so tightly packed together that any normal person would have had to stop and take their bearings, trying to find a way through, but Kiara was like a chess player, planning all her moves one step ahead of each other, turning at split seconds without missing a step, jumping over small fires and discarded sheets of metal. All the people around her could do nothing, as she danced amongst them and left them with nothing but a shadow.

Close behind her, gaining ground by the second, came Hamilton and his men. They had neither the grace or the stamina of Kiara, but they did have the muscle and the force, and they knew the terrain like the backs of their hands. Where she had danced gracefully through the shacks, they in turn ploughed through them, causing mayhem and destruction. As they went through, the people jumped out of the way as fast as they could, watching as their fragile homes turned to nothing but piles of waste.

Kiara ran at a steady pace of six minutes a mile and reached the edge of the township in under thirty minutes, almost running straight into the wall of portable toilets. She had no idea where the actual entrances to the township were, so she had to stop running and squeeze in between the Portaloos, and then trudge through the dirt and mess until she came to a twenty-foot ringed fence that kept everyone inside – or perhaps it was there to keep everyone outside. She knew she had no choice but to climb over. She looked up and could see a ring of barbed wire running the whole way around. All she had with her were the bloodied shirt on her back and the tracksuit bottoms she had chosen for the long flight home, which were definitely not fit anymore for a business-class trip on a British Airways international flight. She pulled off her shirt and tied it around her waist, and in nothing but her mud-splattered tracksuit and her sports bra, set about climbing the fence. She got to the top just as Hamilton and his men toppled one of the toilets over and came to stand directly below her. They looked up in unison.

"There!" shouted one of the men.

"Get her!" shouted Hamilton, forcing three of his men to start the climb upwards.

Kiara held onto the fence with one hand, whilst untying her

shirt with the other before throwing it over the barbed wire and then rolling herself over it. The shirt mostly protected her, but a couple of the spikes managed to tear through the fabric and rip into her skin. She shouted out in pain, causing Hamilton to smile as he kept his eye on her. He watched her closely, expecting her to just wait there until his men were able to get to the top. But to his surprise, she arched her back out, forcing the two spikes to slip out of her stomach and then she rolled forward, off the fence, and fell twenty feet to the ground. He watched in surprise and awe as she managed to make a forward roll as she landed, not as gracefully as a gymnast could, but enough that she was able to pull herself to standing once again and sprint off down the road with nothing but a slight limp.

These women are crazier than me and my men, he thought to himself, considering both Kiara and Zara.

"Follow me to the opening," he said to the men around him. "You go over the top and follow her!" he shouted to the three who were almost at the top of the fence.

CHAPTER 51

Kiara followed the road as it curved away from Khayelitsha and wound its way back towards Cape Town. She tried to flag down every car that drove past her in both directions, but none stopped. She knew she must have looked a sight, running down the side of the road in the middle of the night in nothing but her sports bra and tracksuit bottoms, covered in mud, with blood dripping from the cuts on her back and the two holes in her stomach. She liked to think that she would have pulled over and offered help if she had been driving by and seen someone like that, but in all honesty, she wasn't convinced that even she would do that in this area of the city.

She ran for what seemed like hours, but in truth was only about twenty-five minutes, until she came to a road sign that pointed to Cape Town City, just thirty kilometres away. In her state, and with the blood loss she was experiencing, she knew that there was no way she could run that far. She looked up at the sign again and saw a smaller arrow pointing directly over the road to another township, called Langa. She could see it was much smaller than Khayelitsha and that it had no utility toilets surrounding it. She figured that maybe this was one of the legal townships in the area rather than the illegal one she had just come from. She had no idea if that meant it would be safer for her or if she could find refuge there or not, but a thirty-kilometre run was out of the question, so she had no choice in the matter; it was Langa or certain capture.

She limped across the quiet road and crossed the entrance.

This township looked in many ways similar to what she would have expected any township to, but the lack of security fences and barbed wire came as a massive relief.

As she walked, she was amazed at the fact that there were streetlights illuminating the roads. In fact, she was surprised that there were any lights at all, considering the one she had just escaped from was only lit up by open fires.

The area was not as bright as the villages back in the United Kingdom, but nevertheless, the lights gave a feeling of warmth and normality that lifted her spirits enough to push away the pain that had started to slow her down. As she walked down the dirt tracks that tried to resemble roads, she went past small brick houses rather than corrugated metal shacks. Most of them had been painted in a mix of vibrant rich colours. Some of them were even adorned with murals and street art that reflected what she imagined was the community's spirit and creativity. It was obvious that Langa still had the challenges that many of the poor deprived areas had, but that it had captured the essence of the real South Africa township life that she had read about on the plane journey over from London just a few days before.

She continued down the main street until she came to a junction. On the corner, across the road, she heard the most beautiful melodic music she had ever heard in her whole life. She watched as a group of brightly dressed families danced outside a building, which she assumed was a community church. She walked across the street, trying to hide the pain that was now travelling down from her ribs to her legs, and stopped next to a small group of women who seemed to be trying to herd the dancing folk back into the building.

The women all stopped what they were doing as she approached them.

"Do you speak English?" Kiara asked them, hoping that they understood her.

"Of course we do, my child," one of the ladies said, stepping closer to Kiara and looking her over. "We are not savages, you know."

"Sorry, I just wasn't sure… I'm sorry."

"Don't be, child." She turned to the other ladies. "Get the rest of them in and please finish the service."

"Yes, Mother," three of the women replied to her in unison, and quickly left.

Kiara noticed that they were all of a similar age to the woman who ordered them, perhaps sixty-something, or older, it was hard to tell in that light. So 'Mother' must have been a term of respect for someone in authority.

"What has happened to you?" the woman asked, as the four remaining women got busy fetching warm water, bandages and some fresh clothes for her. "Come, sit," the woman in charge said, leading Kiara to a table and chairs near the entrance to their church.

The music in the building started to die down and was replaced with a strong male voice reading from the scriptures, *or perhaps preaching to his flock,* Kiara thought randomly.

The other ladies started to clean Kiara up and bandage her cuts, whilst the one in charge helped her remove her torn tracksuit bottoms and put on a traditional South African wrapper dress made of Ankara and covered in colourful rich patterns. Kiara looked down at the dress as the women tied it at the waist.

"It's beautiful, isn't it?" Mother said. "The pattern comes from here in Langa, it was drawn by our local children and represents the community, how we are a single family, looking out for each other."

"It's very beautiful," Kiara replied.

Mother smiled at her, waiting to hear how Kiara came to be there late on a Sunday evening, and in such a terrible state. Kiara picked up on the fact that all five women were now patiently waiting for her to talk.

"I am sorry to have come here like this," she started "I was taken to a large township a few miles down that road. I have been working here, in Cape Town, for a company, and was on my way to the airport, when my car was stopped and I was dragged out."

"And these people who did that, did they know you?"

"Does that make a difference?" Kiara asked, perhaps a little too aggressively.

"Of course not," Mother said with a smile in her voice, trying to calm Kiara's nerves.

"I'm sorry," Kiara said.

"You are in shock, my child, it is fine. I only ask because it is not usual, even for those men from Khayelitsha, to force women from cars. Usually, they stay within their own communities and avoid bringing themselves to the attention of the authorities. They do not want attention from anyone. Here in Langa we welcome people to visit us, we want them to see how we live, we want to show them that life here can thrive and that we are good God-loving people. So, for them to harm you and take you into Khayelitsha is most unusual."

"I did know them… well, one of them," she confessed. "I only know his first name, though, they call him Hamilton."

All the women drew the cross of the church over themselves and said a silent prayer.

"Yes, him we all know," Mother said. "He is unlike men we have here in Langa. He controls the gangs in Khayelitsha. He is not someone we would welcome here."

"I am sorry," Kiara said, standing up, "I don't want to bring you any trouble. I just had nowhere else to go. If you can help me find a way to get back to the Waterfront in Cape Town…"

"Oh no, my child, I was not suggesting you have to leave. We need to keep you safe. You are fortunate, tonight we are holding an evening service. Come inside, we can keep you safely hidden until the morning. They will not come to take you from here. And in the morning, when our entire community starts gathering, we will have one of our church elders drive you back to the main city, to the police station, perhaps."

Kiara felt the tiredness of the last few hours set in as the relief set over her. She let the women take her into the church and felt even safer when they closed the door behind them. They led her to a room near the back and settled her onto a bed whilst they went back into the main hall to join in their evening prayers. Kiara felt her eyes start to close as the drumming from hundreds of feet on the floor and clapping hands in the air created a rhythmic beat around the building.

She had no idea how long she had been asleep for, maybe minutes or maybe hours, but when she awoke, it was to complete silence. It took her a few seconds to remember where she was. It seemed strange that they would have closed the church and just left her alone. She started to climb from the bed when a gunshot rang out from the other side of the door. Instinctively, without any thought for her own safety, she rushed forward, pulling the door open.

What she saw shocked her.

Hamilton stood in the middle of the church, gun drawn, and Mother lying on the floor in front of him, blood pouring from her chest. He turned and saw Kiara standing there.

"This is a house of God!" the preacher said, stepping forward.

Hamilton raised the gun again and pointed it at him. The rest of the congregation, who had been sitting in complete silence as Hamilton's men stood around them, collectively held their breath.

"Don't do it!" Kiara screamed at Hamilton as she raced forward and fell onto her knees next to Mother. "One of you help me, she's still alive!" Kiara shouted to the women who had helped her only thirty minutes before, but who all now sat in fear at the men surrounding them. "Let them help her, you animal!" Kiara screamed up at Hamilton.

"Take her," Hamilton said to his men as he ignored her pleas and walked to the exit.

Kiara managed to look back and see the other women rush forward towards Mother with water and bandages. Seconds later, her vision blurred and eventually faded as Hamilton placed a needle into her neck, sending her into a deep sleep.

CHAPTER 52

Tyrone turned to the chief of police the moment he put the phone down from the call he had just taken from Rene. "They are taking her to the new Adesco Oil platform."

"It is not yet open. Why take her there?" he said in surprise.

"All I know is that they told me to bring the diamonds to them there, and then I can take Kiara away. And they said that if they see any other helicopters coming, they will kill her on the spot."

"You do know that we can't protect you, or her, if you do this alone," the chief of police said to Tyrone.

"What choice do I have? I can't just leave her, can I?"

"I can have armed responses in the air and at the platform before you and I even get to the airport. They'll have her safe and in custody before we even take off."

"I told you what that man said to me. If I don't go alone, if they see even one more helicopter, then she'll be dead before your men even land. He told me he knows I only have a four-seater, so they will spot your troop carrier the moment it gets near."

"And you think they'll let her, and you, go when they have the money?!"

"We'll be gone before they have a chance to do anything."

"And how do you see that happening?"

"I have no idea. All I know is that I'll not be handing over the case to them before Kiara is given to me and then she'll think of something to save us. She's far more resourceful than you and me combined, I promise you."

"And that's it, is it? You think she will come up with a plan to save you both. That's the best you have got, is it?" the chief said incredulously.

"I never said it was a good idea, did I, but yes, it's all I've got. What I do know is that if they see a load of police helicopters flying in then it's all over. And I believe that they meant that."

"Well, I don't approve. It's your money, and it's your life. But I can't sit by and do nothing. We can still follow you, stealthily by sea, and we can stay close by. And once I see you land, we are coming straight in."

"Good, I hope you do. Come get the bastards. Just let us get away to safety first, okay?"

He wasn't happy, but he knew Tyrone was right. If they went in all gung-ho, then Kiara would be one of the first to die, he was certain of that. And his priority had to be her safety, over everything else.

"I'll have my men meet us at the port, by the helipad. They'll have your 'copter fuelled and waiting by the time we get there and then we'll follow a few minutes later by boat. But I'm only giving you twenty minutes to land and take off and then we are coming in. You got that? Twenty minutes, and if you're still there, then so be it."

"Understood," Tyrone said, giving him a nervous look. "Shouldn't we warn Adesco that we are about to land on their new billion-dollar oil platform, possibly with guns blazing?"

"Don't worry about them. We have their CEO in custody, answering questions. When my men went to the house in Camps Bay and were clearing up the mess, who should show up there but the CEO himself?"

"Gavin was at Amos's house?" Tyrone said in surprise.

"Yes, along with two armed men at his side. It seems the other body we found outside, the lady, was his personal assistant. He told us that she went there to speak to Amos, something about

269

setting up a meeting to discuss a project they were working jointly on. He said he had no idea who her killer was, or even that she was dead. And he thought we would just believe him. We brought them all straight back to the station and they have been answering our questions ever since. They are telling us nothing, but I have a feeling that he is involved in all this, somehow. I'm not sure how much longer we can hold him, though, as to be honest we have no proof he has done anything other than be at the wrong place at the wrong time. But before I let him go, I can fill him in on what's happening, and I assure you, if he knows what's good for him, he will give us the permission we need to land there."

CHAPTER 53

The helicopter carrying Kiara hovered over the oil platform and waited until the men below signalled them that it was safe to touch down. Rene and Dan, along with Hamilton's man, had met the others at the airport as agreed, ready for the final act. As the helicopter started to descend, he looked out of the window at the behemoth below them.

It stood within the vast ocean, surrounded by nothing but the endless blue horizon. It emerged from the depths like a colossal metal giant. Its towering structure seemed to pierce the sky. From his small window in the helicopter, Rene couldn't help but marvel at what the Adesco engineers had achieved. Even hovering above, he could make out the hum of activity, as Hamilton's men scurried about making sure the landing platform was set for them whilst herding the small troupe of Adesco employees downstairs to the lower floors.

From down below, deep within the oil rig's belly, he could hear the machinery roar to life as the rest of the Adesco engineers tested their beast, unaware that the men directly above them were about to bring it all crashing down into the sea. As the helicopter started to bank around to find its landing position, he fixed his gaze on the ocean directly beneath them, where the waves crashed against the sturdy legs that ran deep to the floating bags below. He closed his eyes and tried to imagine a time, not far from now, when there would be nothing left here apart from the ocean itself.

This had been his dream, his only focus, ever since he had first heard about Adesco's plan to build the largest ever oil platform in the middle of the ocean. He could remember word for word the interview he had watched when the CEO shared his plans with the world.

"Adesco's latest platform, Neptune, is the new face of oil exploration. This platform will be a gateway to the hidden riches buried deep beneath the seabed. It will be a symbol of mankind's relentless pursuit of energy, the power and ingenuity of human innovation. Neptune will not only release the hidden oil reserves within the deepest parts of the ocean, but at the same time will be a floating university to study and understand the earth's own ability to create free, clean and sustainable energy. Our planet has for millennia provided us with the black gold underneath its carpet to enable us to produce the energy we need to live in the modern world we have created, but we know that not only is there a finite amount of oil left, but that with all the good it does for us as human beings, it also causes damage to our planet. Unlike other oil producers, who refuse to accept that our industry plays a huge part in the climate crisis, we at Adesco Oil want to be the ones who lead the new clean energy revolution. We can't simply turn off oil production, to do so would set the world back hundreds of years, but what we can do, what we must do, is look to the future, discover new energy sources that are around us and learn to harness their power, much the same as we did at the start of the Industrial Revolution. Our university, located on Platform Neptune, will do just that. We will study the oceans we are sitting on and understand the tides in ways that no human has ever done before us. We will find a way to harness tidal energy, and when we do, we will give it to the world as our gift. Adesco will one day be the largest supplier of green energy in the world."

Rene opened his eyes and stared down at Neptune. *What if Amos was right?* he thought. *What if Adesco are not the enemy I think they are? What if they really are doing everything they can to find the solution that Amos was offering them? After all this, could I really have been that wrong? Am I attacking the one company who is prepared to change?*

"What is it?" Zara turned to him, seeing the confusion etched on his face.

Rene just kept looking out of the window.

"For a moment, I thought that maybe I had it all wrong. What if Amos's tidal batteries actually worked? What if he was right and Adesco are not the enemy after all?"

"Amos was a dreamer. And Adesco are never going to change. You told me yourself, it was all just a line they were spinning, a hustle to the press. You said that they only talked about saving the world to get the planning permission to build this here. You said they'd never stop drilling for oil until we stopped them. You remember that speech."

"I know what I said."

"So, why the doubt now?"

He looked her in the eyes and his resolve returned.

"There's no doubt, we are doing this," he said firmly. "What's taking so long? Why are we not landing?" He turned aggressively to Hamilton. The other man ignored him and carried on directing his men below via the headphones he was wearing.

"We're landing," Zara said to him, drawing his attention back to the window where Platform Neptune was rushing up to meet them.

The helicopter landed at the corner of the top platform. Hamilton was the first to climb out, followed closely by his men. Kiara, still unconscious, was dragged out between them. Rene, Hamilton, Dan and Zara climbed out after them. The air was filled with the scent of saltwater and machinery, creating a unique atmosphere that blended the raw power of nature with the ingenuity of human innovation.

"This way," Hamilton shouted to Rene above the noise of the helicopter as it started to power down. Rene followed Zara and Hamilton towards the metal staircase that led down to the platform below.

Dan left them, walking over to the side, and climbed into a metal-caged lift that would take him down to the lowest platform, where Hamilton's men were rounding up the last of the engineers.

CHAPTER 54

The metal cage ran down the outside of Neptune and stopped at the lowest platform. Dan climbed out. Looking down through the criss-crossed flooring, he could see the Atlantic Ocean in all its glory just a few metres below him. But he had no time to stand and enjoy the power of the waves that sent spray all the way up and over his feet, he had a job to finish.

"Are all the security team loaded onto the boats?" he called to Hamilton's head man.

"All the security from the upper platforms have been loaded on and we are just moving the engineers in now."

"And they are all secured? And the GPS is set to start sending a signal within the hour?" he asked.

"Yes," the man replied.

Rene had been clear to Hamilton. The plan was to bring Neptune down, pure and simple. To send it to the bottom of the ocean forever. To show the world that drilling into the seabed was no longer an option. He wanted to make Adesco and its shareholders pay the price for the damage they were causing. And he did not believe for one minute that Gavin and Tony would ever give up their oil profits. He was absolutely certain that, once open, Neptune would be the biggest oil producer in their fleet. He would never let that happen, he would bring this platform down, even if it was the last thing he ever did. But he was not prepared to send the innocent men and women, who were just doing their jobs, to their death. He knew that some innocent people would get hurt, that was inevitable, and maybe some even might die in the fighting, he was also prepared to die to stop climate change ravaging the earth. But he wanted no part in the mass murder of the innocent workforce that were there just doing their jobs.

"As soon as you hear from us on the radio, you send their boats out and away from here. Is your own escape boat ready to clear you and your men when I give the signal?"

"Yes, boss," Hamilton's man replied.

"As soon as you see our helicopter take us away, I'll signal you, so you and your men can get on that boat and get the hell out of here. You'll have no more than twenty minutes to get far enough away to avoid the explosions."

The man just nodded in agreement. Him and his men would be ready, they had no intention of being anywhere near this place when the fireworks started.

"Okay then, let's get to work," Dan said.

Hamilton's man signalled to his gang of twenty. In pairs, they headed over to a row of diesel barrels that had been delivered a few weeks back and started to prise open all the ones that had been marked with a cross. These were the ones that Dan had loaded with their bombs and secretly stored at Adesco's warehouse to be delivered along with the real oil barrels. There had been a risk that someone would open them up either before or after delivery, but as the diesel barrels were simply for backup use, he had felt it was unlikely the engineers or security guards onsite would look, and that by the time the platform was due to go online, it would all be over anyway. The risk had paid off, as most of the barrels had been there for nearly a month and not even one had been moved into the storage areas yet.

Once the ten teams had collected their bombs, they stood on the centre of the bottom platform and waited for Dan to give them their instructions. He stepped forward.

"You four pairs stay here with me, the rest of you head to the upper platforms. You have already been told exactly where to place them; you will see a mark I have already set up for you. All you need to do is set them down, attach them to the holding points we made and then turn them on like this." He demonstrated by walking over to one of the four pairs he was holding back and pressed a large red button at the top of the bomb. The screen on the side of the bomb lit up and thirty minutes flashed. He carried on with the instruction.

"Then turn the red button anticlockwise one place and press it again, like this." The screen stopped flashing and the thirty minutes stayed fixed.

"Finally, turn the button one more step anticlockwise and press it again," he said, but this time he didn't complete the sequence.

"Do not do this final step until you receive my order." He handed each team a small digital screen that he had been keeping in his jacket pocket and pressed start on them all. "This means that in half an hour, you will hear from me, you will arm the bombs, and then you have another half an hour to get back down to the floor directly under us now, climb onto that boat…" He pointed to the boat moored next to the one the workers had been piled into to, "… and head out of here. Hamilton, the rest of your men and my team will leave here on the helicopter at the same time. If any of you are still here by the time we take off, then you will still be in the blast zone, so if I were you, I would watch that countdown as if your life depended on it."

He gave them a few seconds to familiarise themselves with the equipment they all now held.

"Go on, then, the clocks are ticking," he said.

Six pairs of men skuttled off as quickly as they could, some into the lift and others up the stairs. Dan turned to the four teams that had stayed with him. He walked over to each pair and handed them each their own timers and pressed start. These ones were set for two minutes more.

"Once the bombs go off on the top decks, ours will be set to each of the four legs and will go off two minutes later. These ones, as you can see, are almost three times the size, which is why you need to work together to move them. And they are ten times as powerful. They have enough energy in them to fracture each of the four main legs. When these go off, we all need to have left, you do not want to be on here when that happens. Are you two listening to me...?" he said, turning to one of the pairs who seemed to be more interested in staring down into the ocean at the escape boats.

The two men quickly looked up.

"Yes, boss," they said in unison.

"This is not a fucking game!" he shouted at the four pairs. "If you get this wrong, we all die. Do you understand me?"

All the men just stared at him in silence. From nowhere, he felt his stomach knot with fear.

He pushed that feeling away and gave them their instructions on detonating their bombs.

"... You all understand that, yes?" he said, looking each pair in the eyes. "Anticlockwise, not clockwise. If you go clockwise, you set the timer to energy and have thirty seconds until detonation. You do that and we all die. You understand?" The men all just looked at him, not a word was muttered.

He sent them all off to finish their jobs. As they moved, he followed the two men he had spoken to earlier. As he did so, he pulled his phone out of his pocket and dialled Rene's number.

"Are you all set?" Rene asked him.

"Yes. The men are setting them now. We have one hour until this is done. If we are not out of here by then..."

"We'll be long gone by then. Tyrone will be here in the next ten minutes. We'll take the cash, and we will take his helicopter."

"What about Hamilton and the girl?"

"They know too much about us."

278

"Does the girl really have to die?"

"When this one goes down, we'll have to move quickly. The authorities, and Adesco, will all be looking for us. We can't risk her telling them who we are."

"I don't care about Hamilton, or his men, they are savages. But to leave her and Tyrone to die like that is just not right."

"They are just more victims of the cause, my friend, and they'll never see it happen. We've got her in a room, she's going nowhere. When he lands, we'll take him down to her and Zara will kill them both. She'll do it quickly, unlike that lunatic. They'll not feel a thing. It's the only way, Dan."

"I guess."

Rene heard the pain in his friend's voice.

"I get it. I don't want to see innocent people die, either, but we warned her off, didn't we, we warned them both off, but they've left us no choice now. This is bigger than them. It's bigger than us, you know that."

"I know," he reluctantly agreed.

Before Dan put the phone down, he realised the two men were already at the corner setting their bomb. He watched as they screwed it into place in the foot plates he had preset weeks earlier.

And then the crippling fear in his stomach returned.

"Noooo!" he screamed at the man.

"What is it?!" Rene shouted down the phone.

Dan never heard his friend. He had already dropped the phone and was running towards the two men. "The other way, turn it the other way!" he was screaming at them. But it was too late. The screen on the bomb was already counting down. Dan reached it with fifteen seconds to spare. Nowhere near enough time to disarm it.

CHAPTER 55

U pstairs in the small room, one floor below the top platform, Kiara was just waking up from the sedative that Hamilton had given her. Her surroundings came slowly into focus. Her whole body hurt, and she had a hell of a headache starting to form. She could see she was in a small room, and she felt her hands tied behind her. She was sitting in a chair in the middle of the room. In front of her stood Rene and Zara, deep in conversation. Around the room stood half a dozen of Hamilton's men, none of them armed, but all of them clearly capable of tearing her in half with their bare hands if they chose to.

"Let me do it now," Zara said to Rene, "we are just wasting time keeping her here. As soon as he lands, we can take the money and kill him as well, he doesn't need to even come to this room."

"You know the plan," he replied curtly to her, before leaning in to whisper to stop the men around the room hearing him. "I don't want Hamilton to see us do it. We bring him down here and you can then take care of them both. Hamilton will come down here soon after, and as he comes in that door, You and I leave by the other door, where Dan will be waiting for us. We'll have the keys to both 'copters by then. Dan will fly us out on Tyrone's and Hamilton will have no way to escape."

"If I do it now, or then, I don't see why it matters," she replied.

"Just do it my way, okay?" he said, finishing the conversation. Zara shrugged and turned around to see Kiara waking up.

"Morning, sleeping beauty."

"Where are we?" Kiara asked hoarsely through the pain in her ribs.

"We are all out at sea," Zara said with a lisp, walking over to her, sweeping the hair away from Kiara's face. "That's better," she said, before walking back to Rene.

Rene's phone rang. He turned away from Zara and walked to the corner. As Rene talked on the phone, Zara stood staring at Kiara.

"You don't have to do this," Kiara said to the other woman.

"You were told to go home, weren't you," Zara said.

"I'll go. I promise you," Kiara begged.

Behind her, Zara could hear something happening. *'Noooo!'* Dans voice rang out of Rene's phone.

"What is it?!" Rene shouted down the phone to him.

Zara rushed over to where he was standing.

"What's happening? What did he say…?"

Before Rene had a chance to answer her, the whole platform shook violently. Kiara's chair crashed over, leaving her on her side, whilst Rene, Zara and Hamilton's men found themselves thrown violently into the walls.

"What the fuck?!" Zara screamed.

"One of the bombs must have gone off early. We need to get out of here now!" Rene screamed.

"What about her, and the money?"

"It's too late. If we don't get off now, we're going to die."

He ran from the room, Zara hot on his tail. Hamilton's men, seeing them run away, also started to run as well. They dashed out of the door, straight into the smoke-filled corridors, crashing into each other in their panic to escape.

By the time the second explosion came, Kiara was all alone in the room.

She flexed her shoulders and managed to pull the binding apart, letting her slip free of the chair. Zara had used the oldest ropes she could find when tying Kiara up. She had not bargained on her being much stronger than she looked.

The first explosion, whilst utterly shocking and disorientating, was just the stroke of luck Kiara had needed to stop Zara killing her there and then. The second explosion gave her a chance to break the rope. She had no idea what the third explosion would mean, and she didn't want to wait around to find out.

Having pulled herself free from the chair, and with the smoke starting to drift into the room, she could see that in their panic to leave, the guards had left the door open. Without considering what she might face on the other side, Kiara sprinted from the room and took the stairs up three at a time.

She crouched down at the top as the flames from below started to climb and lick the deck. The smoke was becoming so thick that the only way she could breathe without choking was to stay as low to the ground as she possibly could.

She had worked out where she was the moment she had reached the top. It was Platform Neptune, Adesco's new oil rig, the same one to which Amos had wanted to attach his energy batteries.

She assumed that the structure would be able to withstand mighty forces, it had to being in the middle of the ocean. But she had no idea how long it could last under massive explosions or with this intensity of heat. The platform seemed to move under her feet, as if the ocean were now shaking the entire rig back and forth like a fairground ride. She could imagine the sea waiting impatiently, its hunger building, desperate for that final moment when it could swallow them all up and drag them hundreds of metres down into its depths.

And then there was Rene and Zara, and Hamilton, of course. She had to get moving before they caught her again, but the smoke was making her eyes water so much that she could hardly see which way to go. She shook her head, trying to clear her ears, but the last explosion had been so close that her eardrums had taken a battering and the noises around her made everything feel like she was swimming in a fishbowl. She wiped her eyes once more to clear the tears and forced herself to look through the thick haze. She could just about make out shapes darting around. She couldn't see any faces, but clearly they were Hamilton's men, trying to find a way down to the lower levels and the escape boats.

Every fibre of her wanted to follow them, even if it meant being caught again.

That is still a better option than staying free to then being roasted alive up here, she thought.

She assumed that everyone had the same reasoning, that being in the sea would protect them from the raging fires above. Her brain was going into natural fight or flight mode: there was fire and there was water, so head for the water.

But something was holding her back and making her wait. Despite her brain screaming at her to get up and run back down the stairs to the ocean, her instincts were telling her to stay put and come up with a better plan.

She shook her head again to try to clear her mind.

Think, Kiara, think, she said to her herself as the lack of oxygen was making her mind drift away into different corners.

There had to be a way of surviving this by staying up top, she just didn't know what the hell it could be.

Another explosion rocked the platform, pinning Kiara to the spot and sending a burning oil barrel high into the sky and over the edge, propelling it a hundred metres out into the sea, leaving a trail of black smoke in its wake.

It was all happening so quickly.

This time, she was knocked off her feet and sent tumbling past the helicopter that brought her there, crashing into the railings right at the back. The helicopter broke free of its holdings and was sliding towards the edge. She watched in horror as two of

Hamilton's men pulled the doors open and tried to jump in just as it plunged over the edge heading down towards the sea below taking them with it.

The railings stopped her just before she followed the helicopter down. The smoke from the burning oil was suffocating and the heat from the fires, which were now springing up everywhere, had already seared the hair on her arms. She stayed down as low as she could to try to grab some breathable oxygen and give herself a few extra seconds to make a plan.

Through her blurred vision, she could see another helicopter. It was hovering just a few feet above her, trying to find a place to land. *Bloody fool!* she thought. *There's no way you can make it safely down here.*

But she was wrong. It landed almost perfectly on the painted X that marked a landing spot. The blades continued turning, and she could just make out the pilot fighting with the controls to keep it from sliding down the deck. She had no idea why the pilot had taken the decision to land, considering the flames that were now spurting up randomly from below and could set his bird alight at any given moment. But she knew that, if she could make it over there, it was going to be her only chance of getting off alive.

She reached behind her, grabbed the railing and yanked herself to standing, trying as hard as she could not to take in a lungful of acrid smoke. She pulled her hand away with a scream as the metal railing had already heated up to such an extent that the skin on her fingers instantly blistered up.

Looking around, through the billowing clouds of smoke, she tried to see a safe path to the landing pad. By now, the platform was awash with burning oil and the scarred bodies of Hamilton's men who had been caught out by the last explosion and flung into the fiery puddles. Their screams, mixed with the noise of the dying rig added to the chaos around her.

"Boss, she's not there."

Kiara stopped moving and held her breath. Despite her ears still making everything sound dull, she recognised the voices that were seemingly close to her.

"What did you say, boy?"

"I went back down to kill her as you told me to, but the room was empty."

Kiara could hear them close by, but because of the smoke, she didn't know how close. If she made a run for it, she might just go straight into them. She tried to stay still, despite the movement of the rig beneath her.

"I'm telling you, she was gone, boss."

"Then find her, before I rip your face off!" he screamed back at his man.

"But boss, where will she go? She's probably already dead. We need to get off this thing now, before we all die."

"Just get her!" the bigger man screamed back. "She must have run down to the lower platforms where the escape boats are. Get down there, and do not let her board any of them, or the fires will be the least of your problems, you understand?!"

The voices of her captors were so clear that it meant they had to be standing very close to her, even though she couldn't see them. She moved slightly to her right and caught sight of the tall black man with the long dreadlocks talking to his two juniors. Even though they were clearly scared of dying in this place, they were more scared of him to disobey. They immediately sprang into action.

Standing so close to him, she felt like a small child next to a giant. She couldn't let him see her; if she did, she knew that would be the end. She crept further to the left, to move away from him, hoping that the billowing smoke would keep her hidden.

She waited until she saw the two men rush off back to the stairs she had just come up, before reaching down and picking up a large copper pipe that had found its way to where she had been crouching. Stepping out, she raised the pipe over her head and took a swing at him, just as he turned to face her. He raised his hand and grabbed the pipe from midair before she could hit him with it, sending her flying backwards once again. She screamed as the railing burnt through her top and scorched her back.

Hamilton lunged forward, swinging the pipe so violently it looked as if he hoped to take her head off in one go. In the same second he was swinging the pipe, the platform reared upwards from yet another explosion down below, throwing them both off balance, Kiara onto her knees and Hamilton onto his back, stunning him as his head hit the metal floor. Before he had a chance to recover, Kiara was up once again and had jumped over him. She sprinted towards the helicopter that had somehow survived the last explosion intact. She could sense Hamilton getting up and moving once again towards her at the same instant that she watched the helicopter, now ready to fly, lift up from the X it had been sitting on. Her heart sank, as her only means of escape looked as if it would carry on rising into the clouds. But instead of carrying on upwards, it came gently back down and landed on the same spot.

She sprang forward, reaching it just as the rotors once again started to lift it up. A voice from inside screamed at her to jump on before it was too late. She threw herself through the open door, pulling it shut behind her as the skids rose from the ground and the helicopter started to finally climb.

Hamilton had managed to reach the helicopter's door at the same moment that she had pulled it shut.

"Hang on!" the pilot screamed as he pulled the stick towards himself and shot the helicopter straight upwards.

Hamilton grabbed hold of one of the skids and he took off into the air with them, hanging on by just one hand. He was strong, very strong. But not enough to withstand the force of their sudden flight upwards. Kiara looked out of the glass doors and watched as his grip gave way and he fell down into the fiery oil pit below.

The final explosion came seconds later, but it was too late to kill him, as he was already dead by the time the burning oil found him.

"That was a hell of an escape, Mrs Fox."

Despite her ears still ringing from the damage they had taken, she knew the voice cutting through to her.

"Tyrone!" she said in a surprised whisper, seeing him in the pilot's seat.

She had never expected that he had been the crazy man flying the helicopter.

"Surprise!" he said, as he pointed the stick forwards, taking them towards land.

Epilogue

Kiara sat at her desk, the laptop open to Teams, awaiting the connection to start. Tyrone's face appeared on the screen a few seconds later.

"It's good to see you. How are all the injuries doing?" he asked her.

It had been three weeks since she had arrived back home to the UK and her family in Hurstpierpoint.

After Tyrone had rescued her from the oil platform, he had flown straight back to the main hospital in Cape Town, where she had spent two weeks in recovery. Incredibly, none of her injuries were too bad; a broken rib that had to be left to heal on its own, some stitches down her back from the cuts sustained during her short time in Hamilton's township and light burns to her hands, arm and back from the railings on the platform. All in all, she had escaped the whole ordeal physically in pretty good shape. The same could not have been said about her mental state. She had spent the first three nights at the hospital unable to get the picture of the fires out of her head, and she could still smell the burning oil, even now. But Kiara was strong, and she knew that over time it would start to fade.

"I'm feeling okay, actually," she said. "I'm back swimming in the sea already, not for too long, just enough to give me that mental boost it always does and to help my injuries heal quicker. And I'm planning on doing my first run this afternoon."

"That's great, but don't push yourself too hard too soon."

"Coming from you, that's rich."

"Do as I say, not as I do," he said with a smile. "And how's the head? Have you been able to get any sleep yet?"

"Actually, I'm doing well on that as well. The first few weeks were hard, trying not to relive everything, but it's all kind of settling. It doesn't even feel like it was me there now, it's more like it was someone else and I watched it on TV."

"Oh, it was definitely you. You're like a superhero to everyone over here."

"Stop it!" she replied, not comfortable with that level of praise.

"I mean it. You didn't just save my business, but because we could get the police and port authorities there so quickly, they were able to save all Adesco's staff before their boats got caught up in the fires and, by some miracle, they got the fires under control enough to stop the whole platform ending up at the bottom of the Atlantic. Because of you, fifty-three people are alive and well, and Adesco have been saved hundreds of millions of dollars. There is still a massive amount of work to do to save their platform, but they are already starting to rebuild it."

"Will they be using Amos's tide batteries when they finish? He would have liked that."

"Whilst we were escaping the platform, someone else was burning down his house, along with all his drawings, his plans, everything. Whoever it was also took hammers to the working model you saw, there was literally nothing left."

"Do you know who did that?!" she asked in despair.

"Well, the police arrested Gavin soon after. They have charged him with the fire and for the murder of his secretary."

"Was it her body I saw at the house?"

"Yes. They still have no idea how or why he would have killed her, and I'm not sure they have anything yet to tie him to it, but his brother Tony is the star witness in their case against him and apparently has proof that his brother did it."

"Wow, I never saw that coming!"

"I don't think Gavin did either. And why would he destroy all Amos's work? It makes no sense. So, I'm not sure he was the one who did it. I've known him for years and I'm not convinced he had it in him to kill anyone. I can't say the same about Tony, to be honest, but you just never know with people, do you?"

"So, Gavin's plans to develop tidal energy to replace oil is over then?"

"I'd say so, certainly for now, at least. He's been removed as CEO, and his board have given the job to Tony. I think Tony will not only rebuild Neptune, but he will even ramp up their oil production to cover all the extra costs."

"All Amos's plans, his whole life, was for nothing, then."

"And Gavin's plans to move their industry to a more sustainable future is now on hold, perhaps over for good," Tyrone agreed.

Kiara was sad at hearing this. She knew that Amos had got involved with some very bad people and, by default, was involved in the deaths of innocent people, but everything he was doing was for the good of the planet. And Gavin, for all his faults, was a true visionary who saw that the future had to be free clean energy if they were ever going to reverse climate change.

"Did they ever find the others, Rene and Zara, and the other one, Dan, wasn't it?"

"Not the girl. No one knows if she died on Neptune or if she somehow escaped. But they are pretty sure Dan died in the first explosion, as he was seen by the engineers setting the bombs when the first one went off. And Rene was spotted by the police helicopter leaving in a speed boat. When they started to follow him, he turned the boat around and went straight back to the platform. The police think it was suicide, as he had no way to survive that."

"And what about Worldwide Insurance? Will you survive all this?"

"Well, actually, we are in pretty good shape, to be honest. Before Jan was sent down for fraud, he told us about all the fake claims we paid out and Tony made sure that Adesco repaid all the losses to us, which he didn't have to do, as he had not even known about them. I had to sign an NDA and agree not to go to the press about any of this, of course. He has agreed to leave all their business with me, even the new oil platform when it's rebuilt. I was even able to return the diamonds back to the bank."

"So, it all worked out for you in the end, then?"

"For me it did. Only thanks to you. I've paid over your fee now, by the way."

"Yes, I saw that. Thank you."

"You certainly earned it."

"Yes, I think I did. But it all feels a bit wrong still, that I have been paid and yet all those people were killed, Amos, Karly, and so many others, and that Adesco are now going to start drilling for oil again…"

"But you saved so many lives, and you saved me and my business. So, you have absolutely nothing to feel guilty about. You earned every cent, you should be proud of what you did."

"Thanks," she said.

"So, will I ever be able to tempt you and your girls to come over for that holiday I promised you? No expenses spared, you will be treated like royalty, I promise you."

"I'm not sure the girls will let me go back there for a while, but let's never say never."

"I understand. Please don't be a stranger, Kiara Fox. I have a feeling life for me will be slightly duller without you in it."

"Good!" she said with a smile. "I think we can all do with a little dull right now."

They ended the call promising each other to catch up in a few weeks, and Kiara expected that they really would.

She looked up at the clock. It was already nine o'clock. She had been up since six thirty catching up on all the work emails that had built up since she had been away. Most of them had been from people wishing her better. Whilst a lot of information about what had happened had not made the news, the largest oil platform in the world catching fire was newsworthy, even back in the UK, and her name had been listed as one of the people caught up in it. The stories never expanded on her role, but just being there in the middle of it had done her reputation no harm, and the good wishes had flooded in, as well as the job offers.

She wasn't sure she was ready to get back to work yet, and in truth, most of the job offers she'd received were once again uninspiring to her. Apart from one. It was from a major health insurance firm who suspected that there was a man in Turkey posing as a surgeon, completing surgery on women and leaving a lot of damage in his wake. The file was still open on her laptop when Nick Taylor walked into her office.

"I thought you were told to stay away from work," he said, having walked up to her desk and peered over her shoulder.

She pushed the lid of her laptop down to stop him reading.

"I'm just catching up on my emails. You know you don't have to keep such a close eye on me. I'm doing okay."

"Are you, though?"

"I am, honestly."

"Mia and Jasmin called me yesterday. They said you all need a holiday."

"Did they? Cheeky monkeys! What I need is some time at home, not going away again so soon. I think that call was more about what they want, not what is good for me."

"Of course. Friends of mine have an amazing holiday home in the west country and they have offered it to us for a few days. How about you and the girls join us for a few days? Some lovely clean air, fresh fish for supper, no work…!"

"That's kind. Maybe we will. Let me speak with the girls."

"And tell me, what was that on your computer? Did I see the words surgeon and Turkey? Please tell me you're not…?"

"What, getting something enhanced?" she laughed. "Absolutely not!"

"What was it then?"

"Nothing much, just a little contract I'm looking at."

"I thought we agreed no more work for a while?"

"I can't do nothing, Nick, I'll go mad just sitting here looking out of my window."

"Kiara…"

"Nothing dangerous, I promise. It'll be just office based from now on, I promise."

"You promise," he repeated, not believing her one iota.

"Well, maybe promise is too strong a word," she said, smiling at him.

Acknowledgements

There are a few people I want to thank here, who either helped me bring this second Kiara Fox novel out into the open or who let me drop them into the story by name – very brave of them, considering how many people seem to die uncomfortable deaths.

Whilst the story itself was all from my imagination, I seem to have a tendency in my writing to use the characteristics (and often the names) of people I know. But please let me say that, just because I paint them a certain way, does not mean that is how they really are – it is called artistic licence and I use it to the extreme. So, if you find yourself appearing in the pages, please accept my apologies if you ended up doing something you wouldn't normally do – like killing people, stealing things or just being downright moody. All of that is made up by me and no reflection on you, but I have to say, it was rather good fun for me to do that!

To my South African brother from another mother, Tyrone Waterstone. You are actually way cooler than the Tyrone in my story – less handsome, perhaps, but more resourceful and a true diamond in every way. And your boys, Troy and Matty are little mini you's and I love them dearly.

Worldwide Marine Insurance is actually 'Worldwide Advisory', and it's the best insurance business in the whole of Africa. And I can say that with absolute certainty. Thanks to all the Worldwide employees I also squeezed in.

Rene Bester, my other South African brother (the older,

poorer one). I have no idea why I made you the villain of the piece, but somehow it seems to fit. But then I also made you the eco warrior, so at least you were trying to save the world whilst causing mayhem and destruction. Not a bad legacy, my friend!

Jan Hendrik Hollenbach, thanks, my friend, for letting me use you, and sorry to make you a slave to love; I guess no change there then!

Nick Taylor, the best lawyer in the world (or so you keep telling me). At least with you I kept as close to the truth as I could with anyone. I have to be very careful what I say about you, don't I?

My two editors, Scott Izzard and Jen Parker, without you two I have nothing but some words. You helped me turn this into a story; you are both heroes to me.

Everyone at MIDAS PR, Stephen, Maddie and Henrietta, thanks for holding my hand and doing the jobs that I still find perplexing. Without you guys, Kiara Fox would be languishing somewhere in a drawer rather than out there bringing the bad guys to justice.

Lizzie Gardiner for yet another fantastic book cover.

All my Starrs, my wife Sharon and my littler Starrs Asher, Mia and Jesse. You all shine so bright for me, thank you.

And finally, to Robert Starr MBE, yes me, myself. I mean, I wrote it after all ☺

Kiara Fox will return soon in *Wild Blackberries*.

www.rob-starr.com